Canvas Bound

CAPTIVE ART

BOOK 1

LAURA M. KOLAR

Canvas Bound
Captive Art™ Series
A Red Adept Publishing Book

Red Adept Publishing, LLC
104 Bugenfield Court
Garner, NC 27529
http://RedAdeptPublishing.com/

First Print Edition: June 2013
ISBN-10: 1-940215-15-3
ISBN-13: 978-1-940215-15-0
Library of Congress Control Number: 2013940805

Cover and Formatting: Streetlight Graphics

To Matthew
Because you captivate me with your love every day.

Chapter One

I PACED MY STUDIO FLOOR AS evening descended on the field in my painting. The sparse oak trees cast lengthening shadows on the acorn-littered ground, where the grass was more golden brown than green. The sunny sky became a star-filled night, and the field turned murky as the shadows faded into the black oblivion… just like my mystery boy.

He'd vanished.

Again.

So did the rush of him appearing in my finished work, my joy squelched by the expression on his face. Usually he wore a smile—a sad one, but still a smile. That night, he'd just looked miserable.

I stopped pacing and stared at the canvas, reaching out to the spot where I'd last seen him. Maybe if I could touch him or knew where he went when he disappeared, I wouldn't feel so hollow from his absence.

An icy trail ran down my arm a moment before my fingers grazed the wet paint. I pulled away, checking to make sure I hadn't smeared the field. It was the first time he'd appeared since I'd arrived at Aldridge, and I didn't want to ruin whatever connection I had to him. My hands shook as I picked at my nails, which were coated in splatters of color from painting all day. A glimpse of him, sad or not, had been enough to keep me working, hoping to see him again. I'd picked my fingers mostly clean when a knock came from the door to the adjoining room.

Please go away.

The knock came again, more urgent.

If you're here, he won't come back.

He wouldn't anyway, though. He never came to the same painting twice.

"Libby, if you don't open this door, I'm going to break it down." Travis sounded more concerned than angry.

I sighed heavily as I dragged myself across my studio and into my bedroom, kicking a path through my discarded clothes to open the door. "This is solid walnut and has a steel lock. You'd only hurt yourself trying to break it down."

"Hmm... good point." His eyebrows knitted as he gave me a once-over. "Did you forget, or are you wearing *that* to dinner?"

I glanced down at my paint-covered T-shirt and jeans. "This is what I always wear to dinner."

"Right. Surprise, surprise. Olivia Tanner forgot." He breezed past me, patting my shoulder on his way to my bathroom where my closet and dresser were located. "You're lucky you have me as your social director," he said, ducking behind the door.

He wasn't joking. If not for Travis, I'd probably never leave my private suite. We'd met two weeks ago, on my first day at Aldridge Art Academy. He'd enrolled several months before me and was assigned as my student liaison, a job he took very seriously. We were both from the States and had clicked right away—probably because he was the only person I'd ever met who liked Humphrey Bogart and Lauren Bacall movies as much as I did.

Travis emerged from my bathroom, holding up my red dress. "You're also lucky you have me as a fashion consultant."

I hadn't been paying attention to what he was wearing, but as he stood waving the gossamer fabric between us, I noticed his white shirt, black coat, slacks, and tie. His usually tousled blond hair was combed neatly, and he wasn't covered in bits of clay from sculpting all day.

"Oh, crap. I forgot."

"Yep, we've established that." He thrust the dress at me. "I know you'd rather stay locked in your room like an old maid and sniff paint fumes all night, but trust me, you do not want to miss this."

I grabbed the dress and glared at him. "I don't sniff the fumes. My studio is well ventilated. And if you're telling me I don't want to miss a fluffy dinner where a bunch of teenage girls ogle over a bunch of teenage boys, *sorry*. Not for me."

"See, *that* is something an old maid would say, and *you* are a teenage girl." He shook his finger at me. "Or did you *lie* about being sixteen?"

"No, I didn't lie. I'm sixteen going on seven*teen*, not seven*ty*."

"Anyway..." He waved me off. "I hear there's a fresh batch of cute guys, and you haven't met any of the performing arts students yet. Most of them are great people."

"*Most* of them?" I put one hand on my hip, the other still clutching my dress.

"Well, I don't know *all* of them. Yet." He waggled his eyebrows. "But the point is, you have to come out of your studio, and this dinner is mandatory."

Huffing at him, I flung the dress over my shoulder and stomped into the bathroom. After an impressively fast shower, I pulled my chestnut hair into a bun and fastened it with bobby pins, allowing a few curls to fall around my neck. I stepped into my dress, glad I'd shaved recently, and tugged at the hem. The style reminded me of the famous Marilyn Monroe image, the one with her skirt billowing up around her. Mine had the same plunging neckline and gathered waist.

I'd thought I brought a simple black dress, the one I always wore to gallery showings. But sometime after I'd packed my garment bag, my mom swapped it for this one, with a note that read, "Saw this and thought of you. For a girl who sees the world in such vivid colors, you should dress that way, too. Wish I could see you in it. You always look beautiful in red. Love, Mom." I sucked in a deep breath, willing away my thoughts of home as I tugged at the hem again.

"You almost done?" Travis called from the other room. "We're going to be late."

"I still can't believe they make us do this." I applied some foundation, wishing I were painting a canvas instead of my face.

"You mean independent study and no one *enforcing* a ridiculous curfew isn't enough freedom for you? Wait. Don't answer that. If your parents had any idea how loose they *actually* are with the rules around here, they would yank you out so fast it would make *my* head spin. Oh, the scandal! Teenagers sneaking in and out of each other's rooms under the cover of night. Anyway, think of it like an assembly, England's Emily Aldridge Academy of Arts' special brand of torture."

I laughed at his horrible attempt at a British accent as he uttered our prep school's original name. "I thought you said no cell phones and blocked social media sites were their own special brand of torture?"

"Yes, well, they want us to be *free-spirited,* just not over the Internet." He sighed. "At least tonight is better than one of my parents' stupid dinner parties. I have to pretend to be someone I'm not at those."

"I'll let you be whomever you want if you let me skip tonight." I dabbed my lips with a tissue then picked up my jewelry from the counter. "I'm going to lose several hours of painting time, and I'll probably be out of the mood when dinner is over."

"Even you don't believe that. You're never out of the mood to paint. But sure, I'll let you skip tonight. You can skip out the door, down the hall, and all the way to the dining room. Though if your goal is to *not* draw attention to yourself, I'd suggest walking."

I didn't respond as I fumbled with my necklace. The delicate silver chain held a single teardrop-shaped topaz, my birthstone. Eventually, I gave up trying to get it on and opened the bathroom door.

"Whoa!" His sky-blue eyes grew to the size of saucers.

I glanced down at myself. "Too much?"

He stood up from my desk chair and circled around me. "No, but I'm seriously questioning my sexuality right now."

I rolled my eyes and dangled the necklace in front of him. "I need help with this."

"I'm serious, Libby. You're..." He took the chain and fastened the clasp with ease before his gaze wandered down to my plunging neckline.

"Eyes up here," I said.

His lips spread in a wide Cheshire cat grin. "Sorry, even *I* can appreciate a nice rack."

"Well, don't get used to it." I smoothed down my skirt.

"I won't. But this"—he waved his hand at me—"is not the way to avoid attention."

"That's it." I gritted my teeth, realizing my *rack* would soon be on display for the whole student body. "I'm chang—"

"Oh no, you don't." He grabbed my hand. "We're late, and besides, in my opinion, not even your cleavage beats a well-defined six-pack on Mr. Tall, Dark, and Handsome."

"You win." I pulled my hand from his grasp. "Let's go." I slipped on my black heels and made my way to the door. "You coming?"

"Yep, just enjoying the view." He shut the door to my suite behind us. "Committing it to memory actually. It may never happen again."

I glanced over my shoulder, almost wishing I'd let him try to break down the door. I didn't want him to get hurt, but I would've had more time to paint.

Halfway down the hall, my legs wobbled. Travis looped his arm through mine to keep me from slipping on the cloud-white marble floor. Everywhere I looked, the walls were filled to capacity with paintings running the gamut in style and color. One in particular caught my eye with its abstract figures in solid sapphire that seemed to be dancing, reminding me of the bold shapes and colors of Matisse.

Travis held me tight as we descended the wide staircase leading to the central area of the school. He laughed when I sighed in relief at reaching the bottom without falling. "You'd have an easier time if you'd pay attention to where you were going instead of gawking at the walls."

"Is the performing arts side of the school like this too?"

"I think the east wing still has a few bare inches, but yes, mostly."

My legs wobbled again, and I had to force myself to pay attention to where I stepped. We reached the edge of the fine arts' wing—home to painters like me and sculptors like him—and entered the main concourse.

"As I was trying to say earlier,"—Travis nudged my shoulder as we passed darkened corridors leading to the theater, gymnasium, ballroom, and administrative offices—"we have to endure dinner so we can go to the after-party."

I groaned. "In other words, my reward for going to dinner is a party?"

"Oh, stop. You're going... at least to show off this." He waved his hand in front of my chest.

I smacked his hand away, and my cheeks warmed to what felt like a full blush. A moment later, we entered the dining hall as he hummed the melody of what I feared would become my theme song: "Lady in Red."

Crystal chandeliers and gold sconces cast an ethereal glow on each of the floor-to-ceiling murals. Together, the murals created a single medieval scene reminiscent of the pilgrimage in Chaucer's *Canterbury Tales*. A caravan of horseback riders dressed in Renaissance attire traveled down a dirt road along a winding hillside that circled the entire room. Printed above the largest painting were the words, "This world nys but a thurghfare ful of wo, And we been pilgrymes, passynge to and fro; Deeth is an ende of every worldly soore."

Ivory linens on the tables complemented the rich wood trim and carved moldings. Even the chairs were dressed for the evening, draped in matching linen monogrammed with the school's initials in elegant script and accented with satin bows.

We found two seats together at one of the large round tables off to the side. Maggie Bates sat across from us, gawking at me before turning to the girl next to her and whispering something. I wondered how many people she'd gossip with before dinner was served, and how much of it would be about me.

Maggie's room was a few doors down from mine, and she never passed up an opportunity to point out how rarely I left my suite. According to her, I thought I was better than the rest of them. That was laughable since everyone at the school was uniquely talented.

Even Maggie, I supposed. I eased into my chair and placed my napkin neatly in my lap. Travis stood nearby, doling out hugs to some of his other friends and discussing the new faces since the last mandatory school gathering.

Planning my escape, I looked toward the closest door, but my attention was caught by something else. A perfectly poised Asian girl stood with a blank expression, like a porcelain doll, but the boy standing next to her was who caught my eye. He was the spitting image of young Marlon Brando in *A Streetcar Named Desire*, before time and his obsession with junk food got to him.

The boy's tuxedo jacket hung open over his tall frame, revealing a crisp, white shirt flat against his chest. I squirmed in my seat as he lowered his head and rubbed his hand against the side of his leg before slipping it into his pants pocket. He turned in my direction, and his gaze locked with mine. The fierceness of his expression took my breath away.

I could never paint eyes like that—deep indigo, almost black, and piercing to the core. But I'd love to try.

When he tilted his face and the corner of his mouth twitched up, I realized I was staring. Heat washed over me as if I'd stepped into a furnace, and I snapped my head in the opposite direction, reminding myself to breathe.

"First the cleavage and now *you're* ogling." Travis feigned a pout as he sat down next to me. "It's like I don't even know you anymore."

"I wasn't ogling." I straightened my silverware and took a sip of water.

"Well, *I* was. The gorgeous one is Dean James. He's in the performing arts school. Rumor has it, he requested special permission to attend Aldridge even though he's older. Nineteen, I think. The ice princess on his right is his girlfriend, Neely. They're not big on PDA, but the two of them are almost never apart. The guy they're talking to—the one who looks like a bridal magazine model—is Brent Henderson. He's also in the performing arts school, but not currently attached. See what you find out when you leave your room? You meet the most interesting people on the other side of your door."

"I'm not—" I started, but a light hand on my back prevented me from responding further.

"Hello, Mr. Weston, Olivia," Madam Harris said. "Don't you both look lovely?" The Mary Poppins accent of the school's headmistress drifted over me like the melody of a song. She let her hand fall, her soft green eyes sparkling as she gazed down at us. "I'm pleased we finally coaxed you from your studio, Olivia."

I wanted to tell her to call me Libby, but she was always so formal, I didn't think I should. "Thank you," I said. "You look lovely as well."

Her long black gown accented her thin figure, and the modern cut of her short brown hair made her appear younger than she probably was. So young, in fact, she could almost blend in as a student.

"Thank you, dear. I hope you enjoy your evening." She gave my shoulder a gentle squeeze then walked away.

"That was weird," Travis said when she was gone.

I glanced at him then watched as she mingled through the room. She walked toward the three students we'd just been discussing, and as if on cue, Brent turned on his heel and left the group, a smirk on his face.

"What was weird?" I asked Travis.

"She's been a recluse lately, *and* she called you by your first name then *dear*. And don't even get me started on the shoulder squeeze. That's practically a hug from her these days. I heard she used to be more involved in the students' activities and even helped with painting sets and stuff, but in the last few months, she's been really distant and hiding out in her office a lot."

I shook my head. "Well, maybe she's busy. She does have an entire academy to run." I shrugged, wishing I'd had the chance to talk more with her. "Besides, she was being polite since I gave her a compliment."

A tuxedoed waiter placed a salad in front of me. I picked up my fork and stabbed it into the gold-rimmed bowl full of mixed greens and assorted tidbits.

"Anyway, about our conversation earlier..." Travis popped a crouton in his mouth and crunched with abandon.

"Which one? The one where you try to convince me to go to the dance or the one where you accuse me of ogling?"

"The dance is a closed subject. You're going."

"Great." I took a sip of water to wash down the tangy vinaigrette dressing. "I was *admiring*."

"Call it what you like." He lowered his voice and leaned toward me. "But you could totally give Neely a run for her money."

"Enough." I dropped my hand to the table. "Dean seems familiar to me, okay? Like if I walked up to him, he'd know exactly who I was." I lied, sort of. He did seem a little familiar, but I was *not* going to mention how unbelievably good looking I thought he was. That would be like giving Travis full consent to meddle in my love life.

"Lots of people know who you are, Libby." Travis sat back. "It's not a secret, especially not here."

"That's not what I meant."

The waiter appeared, picked up my salad, and placed my dinner in front of me. A mosaic of beef, potatoes, and carrots filled the delicate China plate.

Once he left, I looked at Travis. "Now will you please let me eat my meal in peace?"

"Well, maybe you knew him in a past life or something." He focused his eyes on his own dinner, and we finished our meals in silence.

Shortly after we were done eating, he excused himself from the table, leaving me to fend for myself. Not interested in mingling, I got up and headed for the door, thinking I might sneak back to my room. I'd almost made it to the exit when I heard someone say my name.

"Libby, where are you running off to so early?"

I stopped and turned to see Maggie peering at me with dull gray eyes over a full glass of red punch. "To change." I inched away.

"Oh?" Maggie took a few steps closer, invading my personal space with her body and her overly sweet, heavily applied raspberry perfume. "I'm sure you'd be more comfortable in your painter's smock."

At that moment, some guy bumped Maggie from behind. Her arm jerked forward, and I gasped as her entire glass of crime-scene-crimson punch spilled down the front of my dress.

"Oh, bugger! I mean, I'm sorry. I wasn't paying attention." The boy's silver-tongued accent was more fluid, but less sugary, than the liquid soaking my front.

I grabbed a napkin from a nearby table and swiped at the wetness on my dress. I hadn't noticed who the guy was, but at the fourth or fifth apology, I raised my eyes to meet the hazel ones of bridal-magazine-model Brent Henderson.

"I'm sorry," he said again, stepping between Maggie and me. "That was bloody brilliant. Let me walk you to your room, and I'll take care of the dress."

"Spilling a drink on me does not earn you a free trip to my room to watch me undress." I dabbed at my chest some more, though the linen napkin did little to soak up the punch.

He took a step away and held up his hand. Something flashed in his eyes but disappeared an instant later. "What? Oh! No, that wasn't... I meant I'll get the dress cleaned for you."

Behind him, Maggie giggled. "At least the color matches your dress." She set her empty glass on a nearby table and walked away.

I headed out of the dining hall and into the main concourse, then stopped and looked over my shoulder. "You're welcome to come with me, but you're *still* not coming into my room."

He was cute, with his lean frame and golden brown hair, but it was hard to concentrate on anything other than the sticky beverage leaking into my cleavage.

Why did I wear this stupid dress?

He caught up and walked beside me. "I'm Brent Henderson, by the way."

"Libby Tanner."

"Yes, I know, but I didn't know you preferred to be called *Libby*."

Apparently, my plan to disappear amongst other artists wasn't working out for me. "I'm not famous." I glanced at him.

His tuxedo jacket had tails, and he wore a matching black vest and ascot. He walked with his shoulders straight and hands clasped behind him, more formal, overall, than the other male students.

"No, not Hollywood famous," he said. "But you're more talented than any other painter here. That's probably why Maggie's jealous of you. That and you're as pretty as any movie star I've seen."

My cheeks flared, probably turning the same color as the punch. "Thanks, but we're all talented… and you must not watch many movies." I kept my eyes forward, doing my best to step quickly and steadily in my heels.

"Maybe you're right. Are you going to the party later?"

What's with this party, and why does everyone care if I go?

"I don't know," I said as we approached the stairs.

I stopped, leaned against the railing, and slipped off my heels to relieve my aching feet. It didn't matter what I looked like anymore, and I didn't want to embarrass myself further by tripping while climbing the steps. The cool stone sent goose bumps up my bare legs, adding to the chill I already had from my wet dress, and I shivered.

"Would you like my jacket?" He made a move to take it off.

"No."

We ascended the steps and rounded the corner toward my suite. When we reached my door, I punched in the numeric code and listened for the click before turning the handle.

"You can wait here." I slipped inside and tossed my shoes in a corner. Gingerly peeling off the sodden dress, I allowed it to puddle on the floor and went into the bathroom to wash the sugary punch from my skin. Once clean, I rummaged through my dresser and pulled out a lemony yellow T-shirt and a pair of jeans. I was debating switching them out for pajamas when I heard someone knocking. *He must be in a hurry to get to this party.*

I threw on the clothes then flung open the door to find Travis standing on the other side.

"This guy bothering you?" He shot his thumb at Brent, who peered around at me.

"Aside from the punch he spilled on me, no." I scooped the icky, sticky dress off the floor. "He did offer to pay for the dry cleaning, though." I reached around Travis and handed the dress to Brent. "No rush returning that to me. I don't plan on wearing it again soon."

"That's a shame." Brent laid the red fabric neatly over his arm. "I'll see you later then?" He smiled at me, ignoring Travis.

"Maybe." I shrugged, then grabbed Travis's arm, pulling him into my room. "Bye." I shut the door.

"What was that all about?" Travis plunked down on my unmade bed then stood up again to straighten my deep purple velvet comforter.

"I told you," I said, yanking the bobby pins from my hair. "He spilled punch on me. It's not like I let him in while I changed."

"Yeah, probably best not to invite guys you don't know into your room." Then he grinned and settled onto my bed, kicking off his shoes. "For him, though, I wouldn't blame you."

I rolled my eyes and sat down next to him. "I'll be sure to tell him that the next time he feels like spilling punch on someone." I rubbed my hand over one of the teal embroidered flowers that decorated my bedspread then nudged his shoulder. "Why are you so good to me? You don't come to the rescue of anyone else here at school."

"Ha. You *need* me. Plus, you remind me of my little sister. You're both stubborn and clumsy." He nudged me back. "Sooo... are you going to accidentally bump into *him* at the party?" He raised an eyebrow.

"Um..." I glanced toward my studio. Even as charming as Brent seemed to be, the draw of starting another painting was overwhelming.

"I saw that." Travis sat upright. "And no, you are not bailing on me, especially since *I* met someone."

"What?" I snapped my eyes in his direction. "Who? When?"

"I was going to introduce you downstairs, but you left so fast, I guess you'll have to meet him at the party."

"That's not fair. I left because I smelled like a fruit salad—unintentionally, unlike Maggie and her perfume."

"Don't tell me you weren't already headed for the door." He winked at me then got off the bed and grabbed his shoes. "I'm going to change. Meet me in ten."

As soon as he was gone, I went into my studio. The painting on my easel was still a starry night, and my mystery boy was nowhere to be seen. A wood-framed picture of my parents stood out against the blank canvases and jugs of oil paints lining the shelves. The photo was the only thing of importance I'd brought from home. I figured they would probably like to know how my first *official* school function had gone.

Then I realized I *did* want to go to the party, though not to see Brent. *But perhaps I can* accidentally *bump into Dean.*

Chapter Two

THE HEAVY BEAT OF CLUB music thumped in my ears as we reached the ballroom. A large mass of teenagers clustered on the dance floor. Some onlookers stood around the edges, and a few students were off in the corners doing... well, each other. Aside from the gold-flaked columns and the red floral, stained-glass ceiling, which looked as if someone had hacked down a rose bush and flung it up there, the ballroom looked like any other high school dance.

If it had been any other high school dance, I would never have gone. I would have chosen the solace of my studio, or perhaps a quiet evening alone with Clark Gable, over the incessant chatter and commotion of a large party. I'd always imagined myself growing up to be Vivien Leigh, though not in the spotlight of Hollywood's golden age.

"There he is." Travis grabbed my hand and dragged me across the room to introduce me to Eric, a senior performing arts student who was currently directing the next school performance of *Othello*.

Eric's dark Creole skin both clashed with and complemented his ice-blue eyes. His burgundy polo stretched across his muscled chest as he inched closer to Travis, almost as close as the kids who were dancing. I picked at a speck of vermillion paint on my thumbnail, waiting for a chance to excuse myself, but they were obviously too engrossed with each other to notice me, so I headed for the bar.

I circled the outside edge of the dance floor, scanning faces. My heart sank when I didn't see Dean amongst them. *You're being ridiculous, Libby. So he looks a little familiar. So what?* What did I think I was going to do, ask him if I'd known him in a past life? Or maybe if he happened to pop in and out of paintings, particularly mine? No, I wouldn't have the guts to ask him anything.

Someone grabbed my arm, startling me.

"Sorry. I didn't mean to scare you," Brent said over the music. He released my arm. He'd changed out of his tuxedo into a gray button-down shirt and black slacks.

"It's okay," I said, though the hairs on the back of my neck still stood on end.

"Did your friend come with you?" he asked.

I nodded toward Travis. He and Eric walked hand in hand to the dance floor.

Brent looked in that direction. "Oh." The proverbial light bulb came on over his head. He turned back to me. "Would *you* like to dance?"

I bit my lip. Just *looking* at the dancers gave me heart palpitations. "I need a drink." I motioned to the bar.

He tilted his head, leaning down and putting his hand on my arm. "May I join you?" He pulled away but left his hand on my elbow for a second.

"Sure, but you're not allowed to have red punch."

He laughed. "Agreed."

I shivered when Brent put his hand on my back, and he guided me across the room. Tucked away in the corner, the bar served anything non-alcoholic someone might want. As far as schools went, Aldridge Academy was pretty laid back, but not *that* laid back.

"So why are you here at Aldridge?" I asked Brent after we'd ordered our drinks—Sprite for me, club soda for him.

He twisted his lips, seeming to think hard about his answer. "I'm what you'd call *undecided*."

"Oh? Well, what did you put on your enrollment application?"

He downed the final swallow of his drink then took my not-quite-empty glass from me. "Actor," he said as he tossed both cups in a nearby trash can. "Come on. Let's dance."

My knees quivered, and my throat seized up. I tried to say no, but he took my hand and dragged me into the mob of hormonal dancers before I could protest. Standing in the middle of the crowd, I tried to act as if I knew what I was doing. I kept my arms tight at my sides so they wouldn't shake and I wouldn't be in danger of hitting anyone. I moved my feet as best I could to the music, hoping my legs wouldn't give out completely.

I didn't recognize the song or the singer. My iPod housed mostly classic rock and alternative music. Brent seemed to know the song well and mouthed the words as his body expertly moved to the electro-funk rhythm. While dancing, he let his exterior formality fall away. His posture became more relaxed, and his eyes brightened. I knew I looked ridiculous. After the song, I stopped dancing and turned to walk away.

Brent tugged my hand. "You really don't like to dance, do you?"

I tried to look apologetic. "I'm better with a paint brush."

"I bet." He laced his fingers with mine. "Would you like to get some air?"

"Uh..." My adrenaline kicked into high gear. The new song was a slow one. Was the lesser of two evils being alone with a boy I'd met only hours ago or slow dancing with him in a crowded room? "Some air would be great."

Brent led me out of the ballroom into a dimly lit corridor. "Better?"

I gulped in the cool air. "Much." *Because I don't have to dance.* I released his uncomfortably sweaty hand and pointed at an arbitrary piece on the wall. "This painting here is interesting." The style was too abstract for me. It resembled a Chagall, and if I squinted, it looked like a spotted cow smoking a pipe.

He nodded. "All the artwork in the school are the final pieces of the students who graduate, except two."

"Really? Which two?"

"Don't you know?" He gave me a little frown. "They're the only two pieces in Madam Harris's office. One of them is yours."

I leaned against the wall for balance as my head swirled. "I didn't realize... I mean... I didn't know. It must be the one I submitted with my application." I tried to take slow, even breaths. "Madam Harris liked it enough to hang in her office? I thought it would be in storage or something."

"No." He leaned over me, close enough for me to feel his body heat. "Usually they're returned to the students," he said in a hushed tone.

I put my hand on his chest, intending to push him away. "Who painted—"

"Brent." The deep voice echoed in the hall.

I dropped my hand and jerked my head to the right. All my efforts to slow my heart rate flew out the window. And if I thought my knees had been weak earlier, it didn't even compare to how flimsy they became when I saw *him*. A bead of sweat trickled down my neck, and my stomach did a flip as if I'd been caught cheating on a test.

"Yes, Dean?" Brent said, though he didn't step away from me.

"Who's this?" Dean's voice was definitely American and, at that moment, the most beautiful thing I'd ever heard.

"Ah, where are my manners? Dean James, this is Libby Tanner." Brent finally gave me some space, and I realized I was acting exactly like one of the teenage girls I'd griped to Travis about earlier—flustered and ogling a boy. *Okay, not just any boy, young Marlon Brando's doppelganger.*

I didn't know if Brent noticed, but Dean's eyes doubled in size, and he swayed ever so slightly. At the same moment, Neely stepped out from behind him.

"And this is Neely." Brent sighed. "Now that we're all acquainted, is there something you wanted?"

Dean's eyes flicked to Brent then settled on me again. "It's time to go," he said, as if he wanted me to go with him. Then he looked back at Brent. "We have early practice tomorrow."

"And I don't want to have to prop you up if you wear yourself out with *her* tonight." Neely arched one of her perfectly shaped eyebrows at me.

Brent smirked. "Yeah, you would know about—"

"There you are. I've been—" I turned my head in time to see Travis's face pale. "Sorry. I'm heading up."

"I'll come with you." My voice jumped an octave on the last word. "Well... um, thanks." I scooted away from Brent.

Brent ran his hand through his hair. "Yeah. I'll see you."

I grabbed Travis's arm and pulled him down the hall, sparing a single glance over my shoulder. I saw Dean turn a corner and disappear.

Travis barely gave me time to shut the door when we got to my room. "All right, I thought my night was exciting, but wow. And by the way, you're a terrible dancer."

I groaned and flopped onto my bed. "I'm pretty sure Brent was taking pity on me by getting me out of there."

"Yeah, pity." Travis sat down by my feet. "*That's* what he was doing."

"Besides"—I rolled onto my side—"he told me something really interesting."

"He wants you to paint him nude while he wears that Heart of the Ocean necklace?"

"Really? *Titanic?*" I threw a pillow at him.

"What? Leonardo DiCaprio was hot. Not young Paul Newman hot, but still."

"Fine, I'll give you that, but that's not what Brent said. He told me the piece I submitted with my school application is hanging in Madam Harris's office, along with only one other painting."

"Oh." Travis yawned and hugged my pillow. "Who painted the other one?"

"I don't know. We were interrupted by Dean before Brent could tell me."

"Did Dean want you to paint him nude too?" He waggled his eyebrows.

I glared at him. "Travis."

"Come on, Libby. Have you seen Dean's arms?" He held his left hand out over his right bicep as if to show the magnitude of Dean's muscles. "I'd sculpt either one of them nude if they'd let me."

"That is *so* off topic," I said, lying on one of my other pillows.

"Ah, you *did* notice his arms."

"I am not talking about Dean's arms." I put my own arm over my eyes. "I'm talking about my painting."

"All I'm saying is he has great arms." Travis moved to lie next to me, and I uncovered my face. "But that's cool"— his eyelids drooped—"that Madam Harris liked your painting so much."

"Maybe I could ask her about it." I waited for his reply, but he appeared to have fallen asleep. I brushed his bangs away from his forehead. "I'm not supposed to let boys in my room, so I probably shouldn't let you sleep in my bed."

"Mmm hmm." He gave a sleepy sigh.

I leaned over and kissed his temple. "Don't you want to tell me about *your* night?"

His eyes flew open, and he sat up. Apparently, his evening had been very *magical.* He divulged every detail, telling me how he danced with Eric and how he already knew what a great kisser the guy was. "My night may not have been as juicy as yours, but I'm happy." He snuggled in next to me.

"I'm glad, sweetie, but I'm not interested in seeing either Brent or Dean again."

He narrowed his eyes. "I don't believe you. And Brent still has your dress."

"Shit!" I buried my head in my pillow. "I forgot."

Hunched over my laptop at my desk, I stared at my algebra assignment, while a stray part of me wondered which was worse: the knot at the base of my neck or the throbbing between my eyebrows. Most of my credits had transferred from home with no problem, but I had to double up on math and history in order to qualify for graduation. I needed to get the algebra homework to my advisor in the next few days, or I would fall further behind.

I leaned back and swiveled in my seat. My eyes never tired when I painted—pain of any kind didn't seem to exist then—but looking at a computer screen made them burn. I didn't know how my dad could stand it all day.

Thinking of Dad reminded me I still needed to let my parents know how dinner had gone the other night. I knew they missed me terribly, but coming to Aldridge was the opportunity of a lifetime, and they'd never deny me that. I clicked open my school e-mail—that and the community phones in the student lounges were our only sources of communication—and sent them a note. I told them the food was great, and I'd met a few performing arts students, but I left out the part about my dress and the dance. I knew I owed them something more, but there were too many thoughts and feelings I couldn't put into words.

After hitting Send, I stood and stretched before heading into my studio. Painting seemed to be the best remedy for homesickness. The only problem was it also made me think about my mystery boy, which led to me thinking about Dean.

I picked up a brush and twirled it between my fingers as I gazed at my current piece. "Where are you? Better yet, *who* are you?" I sighed, wishing the canvas could give me the answer.

I jumped when someone knocked on my suite door then shuffled out of my studio and through the bedroom. When I opened the door, I had to blink a few times before my eyes adjusted to the light in the hall. Kari, a cute brunette with golden brown eyes, lived in the suite right across from mine. "Hi, Kari."

"Hey. Did you still want help with that math assignment?"

"Oh, yeah. I..." My eyes went directly to the box she was holding. It was white and tied with a green silk scarf. "Did you bring me a present?"

She giggled and held it out. "This has been outside your door for most the day. I thought you might want it."

I took the box and smoothed the loose end of the scarf out with my fingers. It was a shimmery emerald green, like leaves after a heavy rain, with fine black flowers that had to have been embroidered by hand. The scarf was edged all the way around with the same black thread as the flowers.

"The scarf is beautiful," she said. "It looks vintage. Whoever it's from must really like you." I glanced up at her, and she flushed. "Sorry, none of my business."

"Thanks for coming over. I could really use the help with math. I would have asked Travis, but algebra isn't his thing either."

"Yeah, sure." She beamed as if I'd given *her* a gift.

I let her in and shut the door. On the way to my desk, I dropped the box on my bed.

"Aren't you going to open—" She put a hand up to her mouth. "Sorry. Again, none of my business."

"It's fine. I'll open it." I sat on the edge of the bed and untied the scarf. After pulling several sheets of tissue paper from the box, I uncovered my cleaned red dress and a small note.

Meet me at 8 tonight. —BH

On the flip side of the paper was a map with directions to a room in the performing arts wing.

"A scarf *and* a dress," Kari said, bouncing on her toes.

"The dress was already mine. Brent got it cleaned for me."

"Well, the scarf is still beautiful. What does the note say?"

"He wants me to meet him." I glanced at the clock on my desk and gasped. "In twenty minutes!"

"You should go. He's so cute."

I *wanted* to get some of my assignment done, but I at least needed to thank him for the gift. "You're right. I think I'll do that, but I'll still be mathematically inept later. Rain check?" I winced. I wasn't sure that was the best example of good manners. A cell phone would have solved all my problems, at least at that moment. I could have texted a 'Thank you' and saved myself the trip.

"Of course." She grinned then went to my door. "Have fun."

"Thanks," I said as she left.

I hung my dress in the closet and grabbed Brent's note. It didn't take me long to get to the performing arts wing, but finding the correct room was a challenge. I'd never explored my own side of the school, let alone that section. When Travis said I was practically a shut-in, he wasn't wrong. When I finally came across the right hall, a door opened ahead of me, and Dean stepped through it.

He slowed as we neared each other, and I stopped when his expression turned from contentment to confusion.

"Libby?"

"Hi. I... I'm looking for Brent."

A scowl was his only response.

"Do you know where he is?"

"Through there." He pointed at the door he'd exited, Studio 121. "But you shouldn't go in there."

"Why not?"

He tilted his head. "You won't like what you find on the other side."

"How would you know what I like?" I put my hands on my hips.

"Suit yourself." He walked past me down the hall.

I blew out a breath. "Wait." The minute the word passed my lips, I wished I could pull it back.

He spun around. "Yes?"

"How... how do I know you?"

He rubbed his left hand against his leg then slipped it in his pocket as he'd done before. "You don't." Then he turned away and continued down the corridor.

Dumbstruck and alone in the hall, I wrapped my arms around my middle, trying to shake the feeling he'd lied. But why would he? And why had he made a face when I said I was looking for Brent? *Shoot. Brent.*

Realizing it must be after eight o'clock, I hurried to the door. A blast of cool air hit me as I flung it open, making me shiver. In the far corner of the empty room, Brent leaned against a ballet bar that stretched across a long wall of mirrors to my left.

"You decided to come," he said with an easy smile as he pushed away from the bar. "I'm glad."

I forced up the corners of my lips, relieved he wasn't bothered by my tardiness. I wondered briefly if I should have worn the red dress. I was a little underdressed in my fairly clean Fleetwood Mac T-shirt and dark jeans, compared to his navy polo and khaki pants. There was no denying the boy was ridiculously handsome.

I shrugged off the thought and stepped into the room. "I wanted to thank you for the scarf."

"You're welcome. I think it was... meant for you. Are you ready for your lesson?"

"My what?" I rubbed my arms, glad I'd worn the jeans but wishing I'd worn a sweater as well. "What lesson?"

Grinning, he strode across the room until he stood inches away from me. "You seemed uncomfortable at the party the other night, so I thought I'd give you a dance lesson."

He's out of his mind! I should have listened to Dean.

My whole body seized up. I couldn't breathe. No matter how cute he was, I wanted to retreat, mortified at the idea of dancing in front of him again.

"Brent, I appreciate the offer." I took a step backward, desperate to leave. "I'm afraid dancing is not my thing though." I inched back some more, but he put his hand on my shoulder, trapping me. "I mean, you're probably not good at painting. Nobody's good at everything, right?"

"I'd like to teach you." He let his hand drop. "But if you really don't want to learn, I won't force you."

I saw the disappointment in his eyes and felt a pang of guilt. "I want to learn. I don't want to hurt you though. All I'll do is crush your toes."

He took my hands in his. "My toes can take it, and you'll hurt me more if you leave."

How could I turn him down? So even though all my instincts told me to run, I stayed.

"I'm sorry," I said for about the hundredth time, one apology for each stomp on Brent's toes.

He was trying to teach me the waltz, but the lesson wasn't going well. Every time he took my hand or put his on my waist, I shivered and couldn't concentrate. I tried watching which direction he stepped, but I couldn't get the message from my brain to my feet.

He ran his hand through his hair, causing it to stick up. "It would help if you let me lead."

"Sorry," I said again.

"She's never going to learn like that." Dean leaned against the doorjamb with his arms crossed over his chest. His posture caused his gray T-shirt to stretch over his biceps, reminding me of Travis's comment the other day. And with his worn jeans riding low on his hips, he was the picture of rugged casual.

"Thank you for the observation," Brent said. "But I don't bloody well need your help."

I cringed at his harsh tone and thought I should say something, but Dean beat me to it.

"I didn't mean anything by it." Dean stood up straight and held up his hands in surrender.

I took a step forward. "Of course you didn't, but if you think you can do better..."

Dean kept his expression guarded as he looked from Brent to me. I figured he'd shake his head and laugh if he'd actually seen my lesson with Brent. Surely he wouldn't want to take over.

"Would you mind?" His tone was much warmer than earlier in the hall.

"Oh!" I glanced at Brent, but he'd turned away, his head lowered and hands braced on the ballet bar. "No. I... umum, Neely won't mind?" I sputtered.

"No." The corner of Dean's mouth twitched. "She won't."

"Really?"

"Well, it is just a dance lesson."

"Oh... right." I looked over at Brent again, half expecting him to jump in. When he didn't, I faced Dean but avoided direct eye contact. "Uh, okay." Hesitantly, I put my arms in the position Brent had shown me. "Be warned, you're going to get your toes squished."

"I'll take my chances." Dean smirked, moving two big steps toward me. "Now put your arms down."

I followed his directions, mostly because I couldn't speak with him standing so close. It was hard enough just to breathe, and that sense of familiarity was overwhelming.

"Shake them out and let them hang loose at your sides." He demonstrated, and I followed. "Good. Now I want you to keep them as loose as you can for the moment."

Biting my lip, I looked down at my feet. My arms may have been loose, but the rest of me was tense, and my stomach did its own little waltz. I spotted Brent from the corner of my eye. He hadn't moved.

"Look me in the eyes," Dean said.

Yeah. Right. Easier said than done. But I raised my head anyway.

When our eyes locked, his face blanched. "I-I'm going to put your arms where I want—" He stopped, took in a deep breath, then recovered his composure. "I'm going to put your arms where they need to go, but keep them loose." He reached for my right arm, and I immediately tensed. "Loose, remember?"

I forced myself to relax as he trailed his hand down my bare skin, leaving a trace of warmth everywhere he touched. He curled his fingers around mine and raised our arms. Taking a half-step closer, he placed my right hand on his shoulder. The second his palm pressed against my waist, I had to hold in a gasp as a jolt of heat surged through my midsection. Dean reached for my left arm, and again, he started at my shoulder, trailing his hand down to my fingertips and cupping my hand in his.

"I want you to lift your right elbow slightly, but try to stay relaxed."

My frazzled nerves twitched and did all sorts of things I'd never experienced, but I nodded and complied.

"I'm going to step forward with my right leg, and I want you to step back with your left, but keep your chin up and your pretty green eyes on me."

I couldn't have looked away from him if I'd wanted to. And I didn't want to, even though the magnetic force of his gaze sent my heart into overdrive. I fought off a moan when his grip tightened on my waist. With one of his hands fitting perfectly in the curve above my hip and the other wrapped protectively around my fingers, I was encased in warmth. *Thank goodness I didn't wear that sweater.*

As if they didn't belong to me, my feet moved more gracefully than ever before. The smell of him—mint tea and fabric softener—made my head swim as he pulled me closer, guiding me effortlessly around the room. I released the breath I'd been purposely holding, suddenly realizing… *I'm dancing? With Dean.*

I had no idea how long it lasted—a minute, an hour? However long, it wasn't long enough. We didn't stop moving until the bang of a slamming door echoed in my ears. Dean released me, and my arms fell heavily to my sides. Surely blushing, I forced myself to look away from him. Then I noticed Brent wasn't in the room anymore.

"How did you do that?" I glanced back at Dean and was saddened by how far away he was, his hand reaching for the door. "I can't dance."

He paused. "You obviously couldn't dance with *him*. I wonder why that is. Don't you?" Then he swung open the door and was gone, leaving me to feel abandoned, yet again.

I tried to find Brent but got all turned around on that side of the school. When I finally came to a hall I recognized, I decided it was best to return to my suite. I felt bad about upsetting him, or at least, I thought I'd upset him. I had no idea I'd get so carried away with Dean.

I was sure Brent hadn't intended for my lesson to end up like that. But it did. The only other time I felt so completely focused was when I painted. When I held a paintbrush in my hand, the rest of the world melted away.

Just like dancing with Dean.

By the time I made it to my floor, dragging my feet in a slow shuffle the whole way, it was almost ten o'clock. A figure sat with his knees bent and back against my door. Brent. As soon as he saw me, he jumped to his feet.

"What are you doing here?" My tone was harsher than I'd intended.

"Wondering if I'm wasting my time." He shoved his hands in his pockets and looked at me expectantly.

"Brent, I didn't intend to hurt—"

"It wasn't your fault. The bloody tosser can't leave well enough alone." He stopped and ran his hand through his hair, somehow making it look neater than it did a second ago. Then he mumbled, "I have no idea what Neely sees in him."

I do.

"Would you let me take you on a proper date?" Brent's abrupt question jarred me out of my thoughts.

I said the first thing to pop into my head. "A date? We're not allowed off school grounds without a chaperone."

He laughed. "Are you accepting?"

"Um, I..." I looked down and picked at my nails. I hadn't come to Aldridge to date. I'd come to paint.

"One date, that's all I'm asking," he said when I didn't finish responding.

"Okay." I shrugged, looking up at him again. "I guess." I wasn't sure what I was getting myself into, but the guy I really wanted to get to know had a girlfriend, and who was I to turn down a charming, well-dressed English boy?

"I'll take that as a yes." He grinned. "And you can leave the details to me."

Goose bumps coated my arms as I watched him walk away. I rubbed at them to ease the chill. And then a thought crossed my mind... *I hope he doesn't plan on taking me dancing.*

Chapter Three

As the angry red display of my digital clock clicked from 2:56 to 2:57 a.m., I kicked at the tangle of blankets twisted around my legs and struggled to my feet. Even as exhausted as I was, sleep eluded me. I staggered across the room to my studio and sank down in front of the canvas I'd been working on.

The piece wasn't turning out the way I expected. I wanted to give up on it, but for some reason, I couldn't. Delicate pink blossoms originally coated the trees, but I'd changed them to apples ripe for the picking. I pecked away at the grass and the sky, but something remained wrong with the image.

A bead of sweat trickled from the damp curls clinging to my neck and ran down my collarbone to soak into the thin cotton strap of my tank top. As long as I stayed in my suite, I was at the mercy of an unpredictable hundred-year-old radiator. Desperate to flee the inferno, I stashed some supplies in a pouch and picked up the canvas. Many students used a studio near the supply room on the main level of the school to work in groups or get help from the faculty. I almost never worked in public places, but I couldn't paint another stroke in that heat.

Thankfully, the room was empty when I arrived and much cooler than the blaze I'd just escaped. I set up my canvas and paints on an unoccupied easel. My hand moved instinctively, adding deep brown to enhance the bark on the trees and a smattering of mint green to lighten the grassy orchard floor, as well as enough red to make the tree branches hang low to the ground, weighted down with apples.

A few hours later, nails once again dappled in color, I'd finished. The dewy sweet smell of the orchard wafted from the canvas, and a smile spread across my face. Under one of the trees, holding a bright red apple, sat my mystery boy. He stood, tossing the fruit aside and rubbing his hand on his pants. He always seemed more lifelike than the rest of the painting, though his *exact* features were indiscernible. I opened my mouth to say something to him, but then he waved and was gone.

"What the hell?" The voice came from behind me.

I jumped, knocking the painting off the easel and onto the floor. "Dean, you scared the crap out of me! What are you doing here?"

"How did you do that?" He pointed at the painting as I picked it up.

After checking to make sure the boy had disappeared, I set the canvas back on the easel. "I'm a painter," I said. "I paint."

He moved closer and glared at me. "Most paintings don't come to life."

"I suppose that depends on how much you like what you're looking at."

I busied myself with putting away my supplies, but he stepped even closer, placing his hand on my arm. My pulse raced beneath his fingertips as I turned to face him. The smell of his aftershave mingled with the scent of the orchard, and my brain fought against my body's urge to lean into him.

"Libby," he said, his tone changing to hushed and pleading, "where did he go?"

Could Dean see *him? Is that even possible?* I told him the truth. "I have no idea."

"Yes, you do." He rubbed his coarse thumb over my bare arm.

My attire hadn't crossed my mind until then—barely dressed in a tank top and pajama pants—as he pulled me to him, pressing us together. I was amazed I didn't pass out, between my heart pounding in hyper-drive and the heat radiating between us.

"The boy in your painting ... where is he?"

All at once, I regained my composure and yanked free of him. I picked the canvas up off the easel and gave Dean a good view. "*This* is an apple orchard. Do you see a boy?"

He put one hand on the top of the painting, lowering it, and scowled at me. "He was there."

"I didn't paint any boy." Again, I was telling the truth, though I knew he wouldn't understand.

He grumbled and turned to leave. "I know what I saw, Libby," he said over his shoulder as he shoved open the studio door and left.

With shaky hands, I tried to finish collecting my things. Dean *had* seen the boy, and he'd seemed... angry? Upset, maybe? Why and *how* was that possible? *Nobody else has* ever *seen him.* My fingers fumbled, and I dropped a brush on the floor. When I reached for it, my hand grazed something else. I picked up a deep-red life-sized apple and stared at it.

He'd been holding an apple.

Then he tossed it aside.

The sound of fist on wood woke me.

"Go away," I shouted, covering my head with a pillow.

"Nope," Travis yelled. "Get your cutie patootie out of bed and open the door."

"No boys allowed!"

"As if anyone follows *that* rule."

"I do."

"Liar."

Without lifting my head, I scooped a shoe from the floor next to my bed and chucked it at the door. "Consider that me giving you the boot."

"If I know you, it's a paint-spackled sneaker from the floor beside the bed. We can do this all day, but I'll win. You can't resist me. I may be gay, but you're still my girl."

After I resigned myself to the fact that he wasn't going away, I flung off my covers and stomped to the door and opened it. Through my blurred vision, I could see him curl his lip slightly.

"You look like—"

My hand shot up between us. "I didn't get a whole lot of sleep last night." I shuffled back to my bed and re-covered my head with the pillow.

"Painting or partying?"

I shifted the pillow and peeked up at him. "Both, sort of."

"No wonder you're still in bed at"—he grinned and nodded toward the clock—"ten 'til two in the afternoon. I came by earlier to get you for breakfast, but you must've been so sound asleep you didn't hear me. More bagels for me, thanks for the carbs. Wanna tell me what happened last night?" He made himself comfortable at the end of my bed.

I sat up, pulling my knees to my chest, and told him everything up to when Dean came into the studio.

"So Dean just showed up?" Travis asked.

I nodded and yawned.

"What was he doing? Did he say anything to you?"

"He... um, sort of said some stuff." I picked at a blob of red paint on my left ring finger, in the same shape and color as the apple I'd found. I didn't need the extra reminder of last night's incident. The paint flakes sprinkled onto my comforter, and I brushed them away, still not making eye contact with Travis. "He was upset about something."

"Okay." He dragged out the word. "Was it something about Brent?"

"No, about my painting." I pointed at the canvas I'd left sitting out.

Travis shook his head. "Why would he be upset about an apple orchard?"

"He was upset about the boy in the orchard." I buried my face in my knees.

"Libby, maybe you need more sleep, or maybe Dean does, but I don't see a boy. Did you paint over him?"

"He disappeared," I said with my head down.

Travis tapped my shoulder. "Sweetie, you need to speak up if you want me to hear you."

"This is so hard." I shook my head then looked up at him. "I've never told anyone before."

"And?"

"The boy... in my painting. He disappeared, right after chucking the apple." I pointed at the red fruit sitting on my desk.

His gaze shifted to the apple, then to me, then to the apple again. He seemed to be deciding if he should be worried or should believe me about the vanishing boy who threw apples into the real world. "Hmm. Would you mind repeating that, please?" he finally asked.

Capturing my bottom lip between my teeth, I continued to pick at my nails. "This boy has shown up in my paintings since I was little. He stays for brief moments, then he's gone and never returns to the same painting twice."

"So... a vanishing boy appears in your paintings?"

"Yes," I whispered.

"Who is he?"

"You believe me?" My voice hitched. "You don't think I'm crazy?"

He nodded. "I *do* think you're a little crazy, but not about this. Trust me, I've seen stranger things."

"Stranger than art coming to life?"

"Well, pretty close to it."

I flung my arms around his neck, hugging him so tightly I expected him to accuse me of assault. "You have no idea how good it feels to tell someone this."

"Obviously." He laughed. "So tell me about this mystery boy. Is he cute?" He waggled his eyebrows as I let him go.

"I suppose so, but I like my guys more three-dimensional. And I've always thought of him more like a muse, I guess." I hoped he wouldn't press me for a serious answer. "I'm always busy wondering who he is or why he doesn't stay."

"He doesn't come to all your paintings?"

"No. Sometimes I think he might show up, but I'm often wrong. And yesterday was the first day we ever interacted."

Travis sat up straighter. "What do you mean 'interacted'*?*"

"He waved at me right before he vanished." *Of course, he could've been waving at Dean, who was standing behind me.*

"And what's up with the apple?"

I glanced over at the fruit. "He tossed it. Actually, I knocked the painting off the easel when Dean startled me, and it's possible the apple fell out."

Travis leaned back again, making himself comfortable. "Has anything else ever come out of your paintings?"

"No." I pulled at a loose thread on my blanket. "But some of my paintings... come to life."

He eyed me carefully. "To life?"

I nodded, still tugging at the thread. "Like one turned from day to night and another made my studio at home smell like the beach. Once, I painted a waterfall, and I heard the water splashing against the rocks."

Travis glanced at the orchard again. "Do *all* your paintings come to life?"

"No, and they don't stay that way either. It's like when I complete one, it takes one deep breath, showing me that moment in time, then freezes there. And I don't have any control over which ones do and which ones don't. Though, the ones that come to life are always clearer in my mind when I start to work on them, and I usually finish them much faster."

"Usually?"

"Well... the orchard is the first one that came to life that took me more than a few days to paint. I have no idea why though."

"I guess I get why you're so private about your work," he said more to himself than to me. I wasn't used to his uncharacteristically calm demeanor. He put his hand over mine. "Does anyone else know about this?"

"No." I sighed. "Not even my parents. Except... Dean saw the boy. I tried to deny it, but I'm sure he didn't believe me."

Travis scratched his head. "Well, I'd steer clear of him, for a while at least. Let him cool down."

"That would make Brent happy. He was upset over me dancing with Dean."

"Yeah, about Brent..." Travis arched an eyebrow. "Are you two a thing?"

"No. I mean, I don't think so." I fell against my pillow.

Travis laughed. "You have way too many men in your life for someone who 'just wants to paint.'" He made air quotes with his fingers

I stretched my limbs. "Painting *is* all I want to do."

"First..." He stood up. "You need to take a shower and eat. And since I'm such a great friend, I'll go make you something while you get cleaned up." He pulled me to my feet and gently shoved me toward the bathroom.

"Travis?" I reached for his hand.

He squeezed my fingers. "I know, Libs. I love you, too." Then he slipped out the door.

A short time later, I found him at the end of the hall, in our floor's kitchen, putting the finishing touches on a turkey sandwich. He sat very still and quiet next to me, his hands folded in front of him, while I ate. "Is something bothering you?" I hoped what I'd told him earlier wasn't the cause of his unusual silence.

"No." He looked around and then back at me. "Well, sort of."

"I'm sorry if I laid too much on you earlier."

"It's not that."

"Okay." I swiveled on my stool. "Are you going to make me guess?"

He took my empty plate then washed and dried it before answering. "Would you mind coming with me for a minute? It won't take long."

"Of course not." I hopped off my stool.

He led me across the hall to his room, which was set up almost exactly the same as mine, though his was much tidier. There was no need to step over clothes or smooth rumpled blankets. He made his bed and put his clothes away daily, two tasks I rarely performed. His bedspread and curtains had a southwest pattern, deep red rust accented with brown and tan. On his desk, a small gold frame held a picture of a pretty blonde.

"Is that your sister?" I asked.

He picked up the frame and handed it to me. "Yeah, that's Theresa... Tess."

"She's pretty. How old is she?"

"Fifteen. She's *exactly* two years younger than me. We have the same birthday. She was pissed when I came to school here, but she understands now. I hope."

"It must be nice to have a sister." I returned the frame to him. "But my parents had enough trouble adopting *me*."

He looked at the picture for a second then set it down. "Yeah, they can be a real pain in the ass sometimes, though." He chuckled. "Anyway, what I want to show you is through here."

We went through the door to his studio. One wall was lined with shelves holding pieces of clay in varying stages of completion. Another had a window overlooking the woods behind the school, and the wall to my right had all sorts of sculpting tools neatly arranged by size and style.

He moved to the center of the room and pulled a sheet off a large, smooth block of stone. When he swiveled it around, the image protruding from the other side was both beautiful and grotesque. Arms and legs stuck out in all different directions with the joints at angles they should never go.

"I have a secret too." He ran his hand along the edge of the stone.

A moment later, the limbs moved. They silently gripped and kicked, rolling in on themselves until the stone smoothed out again. Travis spun the form around again. The side that had been smooth was covered with faces. Seven different—frightening—expressions glared out at me. He re-covered the stone and glanced up.

"I don't even know what to ask first," I said, looking into his gloomy eyes. "How...?"

"It's a long story. My parents are less than thrilled about having a gay son. In fact, they practically shoved me out the door when I got accepted here. It's easier to tell their friends I'm studying in Europe than to admit the truth." He stuffed his hands in his pockets, rolling his shoulders. "I haven't had any communication with them since I got here, partly thanks to Aldridge's no cell phone rule. I call Tess from the school phones as often as I can, but..." He shrugged again and looked away.

"Oh, Travis, I'm so sorry." I couldn't imagine being estranged from my parents.

"I haven't told you the worst part yet." He let out a deep sigh. "A year and a half ago, they thought I was *confused.* They kept inviting over friends from their club who had daughters my age. They encouraged me to take out the girls and basically told me I should try sleeping with them."

I gasped, bringing my hand to my mouth. "They... but why?"

"I won't go into all the details, but they thought I didn't know what I was missing so they *provided the opportunity*. Forget that it was sick of them to offer these girls up like prostitutes then have their parents to dinner the next night. Of course, it didn't work, and we had several arguments, one of which ended with my fist slamming into a piece I was working on. Instead of breaking my hand or the piece crumbling to the floor, it turned into the exact image I had in my head." He looked ashamed for a brief moment, and I could only imagine what shape the stone had formed.

"Is it any stone or that one specifically?" I pointed at the sheet-covered block.

"Most stone. But I can't change someone else's sculpture."

"Do you think...?" I bit my lip. "I mean, can other students, you know?"

"I suppose it's possible. It seems a bit fated that we both ended up here at Aldridge, but I'm not going around asking. And if someone else asked me, I'd deny it."

Travis was right. I would never voluntarily tell some random student about the mysterious vanishing boy in my paintings or that some of them came to life. I shuddered at the memory of telling Dean the truth... sort of. Any inkling I had that *he* was the boy in the painting was gone. *So why does he still seem so familiar?*

"I didn't mean to freak you out earlier," Travis said, interrupting my thoughts. "Sometimes the images in my head are pretty graphic."

"It's okay. I wish you could see one of my paintings come to life though."

"Someday." He wrapped his arms around me. "Thank you. I'm glad we're friends."

"Me too."

When I returned to my room, I moved the orchard painting into my studio. I had no way of knowing which piece my mystery boy would appear in next, so my only choice was to keep painting until he appeared again. I would keep painting until I knew who he was... and what he wanted.

And after learning of Travis's talent, I wondered if I was the only painter my mystery boy visited. *If not, who might the others be, and do they know who he is?*

Do they know who I *am?*

Chapter Four

Brent beamed at me as I approached him in the main hall. "You look fetching, Miss Tanner."

I wasn't too dressed up, but for a change, I also wasn't covered in paint. I'd put on a pale blue top with little white flowers on it and a pair of cropped tan pants, which happened to match his pressed khakis. "You too, Mr. Henderson," I said, feeling a blush come to my cheeks. "I almost thought I was silly for bringing this outfit since it's been so cold."

He carried a picnic basket and had blanket draped over his arm. Originally, when he'd said he wanted to go on a picnic, I thought he was crazy. It had rained almost every day since I'd arrived at the school. But Mother Nature had decided to shine down on us.

"Well, aren't I lucky I get to see it?" He offered me his free arm as we stepped outside.

The sun lit the flawless cerulean sky, and a warm breeze washed over me. Walking through the English garden with Brent hugging tight to my arm, I felt like Elizabeth Bennett from Jane Austen's *Pride and Prejudice*. The air smelled more like spring than fall, even though some of the trees had already turned a vibrant golden orange. Except for some late-blooming Asters with bright yellow centers contrasting against purple, finger-like petals, most of the garden had gone dormant.

A row of hedges stood like sentries along a high stone wall, where five steps took us down to a wide green lawn that stretched for a few hundred yards before ending at a heavily wooded lot. At the far edge of the lawn, he spread the red and black wool tartan blanket under a shady tree and motioned for me to sit.

I took a seat and watched him unload the basket. "Did you make all this?" I asked, amazed at the selection of food. There was pasta salad, several kinds of mini-sandwiches—the only one I recognized was cucumber—and pudding with fruit. I picked up a plate and began filling it.

He poured a glass of lemonade and handed it to me before making a plate for himself. "No. I know some kids who like to cook. I gave them an excuse to use their skills."

"That was nice of you," I said, sniffing one of the mystery sandwiches before taking a bite.

"So, Libby Tanner, tell me something about you I can't find on the Internet." He stretched out on his side and propped his head up with his hand while taking a bite of pudding.

Balancing my plate carefully on my lap, I sat with my outstretched legs crossed at the ankles and tried to think of something to say that wasn't *too* revealing. "Well, since the school has blocked just about everything but Netflix and iTunes, and you can't believe half of what you read on Wikipedia, why don't you tell me what you do know, since you've obviously looked me up? Then I'll know what's still a secret."

"Fair enough. I know you grew up in the United States. I know you started painting when you were seven, and by the time you were ten, there were already galleries asking to show your work. By fifteen, you'd made enough money to... well, enough to pursue anything you wanted. And you recently decided you'd had enough of your"—he leaned forward and grinned playfully—"vulgar Yankee ways and came to live here in jolly ol' England. Where, I might add, you've met a handsome chap you're starting to like but are still unsure of."

I laughed. "I'm pretty sure that last part isn't on the Internet."

"Maybe. Maybe not." He winked.

"Didn't I just say you can't trust Wikipedia?"

"So none of it's true?"

"Hmm." I took another sip of lemonade before answering. "Let's just say that last part wasn't the part I was referring to."

He sat up and moved a bit closer. "Tell me what is true then."

"Okay." I set my empty plate and glass off to the side. "Well, my full name is actually Olivia Bea Tanner. My parents called me Livy when I was little, but I couldn't pronounce it, so turned it into *Libby*, and I guess the name stuck. And more specifically, I grew up in southwest Michigan, where my parents still live. At three, I painted my first recognizable picture with one of those kid watercolor sets: a lone tree against the background of a bright blue sky. Everyone thinks I was seven when I first started to paint because that's when one of my art teachers displayed my painting of the Saugatuck lighthouse. I'd captured it at sunset when the colors were at their most saturated. Several people offered to buy it." I didn't mention anything about the money. The galleries set the prices, not me.

"And now our little Miss Tanner is adored by many around the globe. So what brought you here?" He laid his hand over mine on the blanket.

My first instinct was to pull away, but I resisted. *This is normal date behavior.* "The school mailed me some information a few years ago, but my parents thought I was too young to be so far away from home. It was hard enough to convince them to let me come this year."

He reached up and pushed a strand of hair from my face. "I'm glad they changed their minds."

"Me too," I said. "Now it's your turn. Tell me about the *undecided* British actor I agreed to go on a picnic with in October."

"Ah. I'm afraid you'd find it very boring." He shifted away from me and stuffed a mini sandwich in his mouth.

"Boring? Maybe I'll have to Google *you.* Will I find some deep dark secret you don't want me to know?"

He stopped eating and stared into my eyes for a moment. I wondered if my teasing had hit a nerve when he let out an uneasy laugh. "I suppose I do have some secrets," he said, perfectly straight-faced. Then he cracked a wide smile. "But fortunately for me, *you* don't believe what you read on Wikipedia."

We both laughed before he picked up our used dishes, placing them neatly in the basket.

He stood up and held out his hand. "Would you like to walk with me?"

"Sure."

We left the picnic basket and blanket there and walked the tree line.

"I grew up in London," he said.

"Oh, I would love to paint the Thames one day."

"It's beautiful." He turned and smiled at me. "Lots of things to see and do in London, especially theater. My family loved the theater, so I was forced into dancing and acting lessons at a young age."

"You make it sound as though you don't like to act."

"I..." He glanced at me and then away. We walked in silence for a bit, and I grew sure he'd never finish the thought. "I prefer to be myself."

"I think that's why I like to paint so much. To be myself, I mean."

"Yes, you are an amazing artist. Something about the way your paintings come to life on the canvas."

I stopped, my mouth falling open as I dropped his hand. I wondered if Dean had told Brent what he'd seen. "What... what makes you say that?"

"Sorry, I meant it as a compliment." He held his hand out again, and I took it, forcing a smile.

After another quiet moment, I cleared my throat, "Brent?"

"Yes?"

"The other painting in Madam Harris's office... you never told me whose it was."

He tensed for a moment. "A student, but he didn't stay to graduate."

"Did you know him? Why did he leave?"

"I met him once or twice." He shrugged. "He left due to some... family matters."

I sighed. "That's too bad."

"I suppose."

"What's the painting of?"

He shook his head. "Madam Harris's office is off limits to students. I only know about the paintings because I overheard her telling a maintenance person to hang yours in there across from his. Sorry..." He looked at his watch. "I almost forgot I have practice this evening. I should probably get going."

"Oh. Okay. I had a nice time today," I said, though I wanted to ask more questions about what he'd overheard.

"Yes, I'll have to think of something for our second date." He spun around, leading me back the way we'd come.

"We're going on a second date?"

"Sorry." He stopped. "Would you like to go out again? No pressure this time."

"Hmm." I squinted at him then squeezed his fingers. "Yes, I'll go out with you again."

We reached our picnic spot, and after gathering up what was left, we walked hand in hand toward the school building.

At the door, I let go of his hand. "So I'll see you later?"

He nodded, stepping away slowly. "You will definitely see me later."

I headed to my room, happy I'd decided to go out with him in the first place. But my good mood faded fast when I noticed Dean near the steps, leaning against the railing. Was he waiting for me?

"Hello, Libby. Did you have a good time with Brent?"

I rolled my eyes. "How is my social life any of your concern?"

He pushed away from the railing and moved closer. "I was *trying* to be polite since the last time we met I... wasn't."

"Which time?" I crossed my arms. "When you snubbed me in the hall? Or when you barged into my dance lesson? Wait. It must be when you scared me half to death while I was trying to paint in peace."

"I see. Though you're the one who asked me to dance." Then he ducked his head and turned away.

Each step he took away from me felt like a hundred pound weight on my shoulders. "Dean?"

He spun around. "Yes?" Somehow, he seemed closer than he'd been a second ago. His eyes changed as well. The stone façade crumbled away.

"I... I had a nice time with Brent, thank you for asking." *Shit! That was so stupid.*

He nodded then left without another word. I shuffled my feet as I went upstairs. The hall seemed busier than normal, and I was glad Travis answered his door right away.

"Libby," he said, sounding surprised. "Come in." He stepped to the side to let me by.

"Hey. What are you up to?"

"Um..." He looked down at his clothes, which were covered in dried bits of clay. "Working. I thought you were on your date."

"I was." I sat down on his bed. "But Brent had to go to practice, and I'm not ready to go to my room yet."

He perched on the edge of his desk chair. "Is that good or bad?" Gray pieces of clay smudged on his hands and cheek, but even that couldn't take away from his obvious good looks. His vintage Johnny Cash T-shirt and muddied jeans added to the retro-cowboy look.

"The picnic was nice."

"But?"

"I ran into Dean. I think he was waiting for me after my date."

"Oh." Travis's face fell. "Are you all right? Did he bug you about the painting again?"

"Yes... no..." I shook my head. "I'm fine. I think he was trying to apologize, but I didn't give him the chance, and I was sort of mean to him."

Travis laughed, a big belly-shaking laugh.

I glared at him. "It's not funny."

"It's extremely funny." He continued with his hysterics, and I pouted until he got it under control. "I am so glad I do not have the drama you do."

"This year was not supposed to be this crazy. I was supposed to paint. That's it!"

"So tell Brent you don't want to see him and tell Dean to leave you the eff alone. You can lock yourself in your suite and paint away. Become the next van Gogh and never deal with the outside world."

"That is *not* helpful." I gripped the edge of his bed.

Travis shook his head. "All I'm saying is that it's okay to have a *little* drama. It may even be good for you. It could inspire you to paint something amazing. Not that you don't already, but it might help."

"Maybe." I shrugged, picking at my nails even though there was nothing on them since I'd scrubbed them clean before my date.

He leaned forward in his chair. "Obviously something else is bothering you."

"Yes... sort of..."

"This is like pulling teeth, Libs. *Spill.*"

"Well, we had a nice time while we ate, and I told Brent about me and painting when I was little, but when I asked about him, he clammed up. All he said was that he grew up in London and his family pushed him into acting."

Travis leaned back again and put his hands behind his head. "Pretty minor stuff to be worried about, I'd say. Maybe he's embarrassed and doesn't like to talk about himself."

"Actors aren't usually known for their modesty, but that's not all." I breathed out heavily. "When I asked him about the other painting in Madam Harris's office, he seemed to get... edgy."

"I think you're reading way too much into this. He was probably nervous. Painting is your thing, not his."

"Yeah, I guess. But he did say the other painting was by a student who dropped out."

"Huh." Travis stretched out his legs. "It's probably by that Ryan kid."

"*What* Ryan kid?"

"I never met him, but a few months ago, he up and left school. Everybody said it had something to do with his family, but no one heard from him after he left, not even Neely, who was dating him at the time."

"Wait!" I sat up and clasped my hands. "*Neely*, Dean's current girlfriend, was dating some guy named Ryan?"

"Yep. Actually, she made a big deal about the whole thing, saying the school was lying and that Ryan wouldn't have left without saying good-bye."

"You mean he just up and left?" I waved my hand in the air. "She didn't have his home address or anything?"

Travis shrugged. "Apparently not."

"That is odd. But it doesn't explain why Brent would care."

He closed his eyes then opened them and leaned forward again, putting his elbows on his knees. "Libby, this was, like, six months ago."

"And?"

"Well, at the time, Brent *liked* Neely. A lot. And he was happy Ryan left."

"What?" I stood up. "Don't you think this is something you should have told me *before* I went out with him?"

He sat up and crossed his arms. "As far as I know, he got over it, and now he obviously likes you. So be happy. Enjoy going out with him. Besides, like, a month after Ryan left, Dean started here. He's been with Neely ever since, and she dropped whatever issue she had about Ryan."

"Great." I flumped down on the bed again. "Brent liked the girl Dean's dating. That sort of explains why he acted the way he did when Dean took over my dance lesson. I'm not even sure Dean's that great a catch," I lied, though I don't know whether it was to myself or to Travis.

"I'd catch him anytime." He waggled his eyebrows.

"Travis!"

"Sorry." He held his hands up in surrender. "Off topic, I know. Anyway, I'm sure if Brent didn't like you, he wouldn't be pursuing you like he is. You're not exactly *accessible.*"

I threw my arms in the air. "What do you mean by that?"

"Look, I love you, sweetie, like I love my own sister. But you tend to keep people out here." He stretched out his arm then dropped it and took my hand. "And sometimes you go into this whole other place in your head where no one else is invited. So if Brent is willing to work at getting to know you, then more power to him. I also don't think you need to worry too much about Neely. She and Dean are tight." He squeezed my fingers then let go.

"*Tight,*" I said in a huff. "Am I really that bad?"

"Well, I wouldn't change your name to *Vincent.*" He nudged my foot with his.

I did my best to smile, but I was sure he saw right through me. "Should I still stay away from Dean? I mean, I do think he was trying to be nice today."

"From what I hear, Dean is a good guy, and I don't think he'd try to hurt you or anything. But I wouldn't go flaunting your paintings in front of him either."

"You know, you're almost as bad a gossip as Maggie Bates," I teased.

"No." He shook his head and smiled. "Maggie will talk to anyone about anything, anytime. I'm talking to my friend, who happens to have snagged the interest of Brent Henderson, the most eligible guy here and third hottest male student."

"Third hottest?"

"Well, yes, considering Dean would be the second."

"Okay, I can't believe I'm asking this, but..." I put my hand over my face, peeking through my fingers. "Who is possibly hotter than Dean?"

Travis grinned. "Me. Of course."

Chapter Five

FOR MY SECOND OFFICIAL DATE with Brent, we went to see a movie. The school had set up a projector in the auditorium showing *On the Waterfront*. Unfortunately, I spent the entire film contemplating how much Marlon Brando reminded me of Dean. After the movie was over, we wandered out into the gardens. The weather had cooled considerably since our picnic, and the chill pricked at my bare face and hands.

"Personally, I like Cary Grant better than Brando, but that's because we're both from Bristol, and we grow better actors there." Brent jutted out his chin and held up his hands, striking an overly dramatic pose, as he quoted in a bad American accent, "'I couldah been a contendah.'" He laughed as we passed a row of wilted rose bushes. "Bloody wanker. I have no idea what women saw in him, even before he became a fat arse."

I stopped and stared at him for a moment, then shivered, wondering where that rant had come from and also thoroughly disagreeing with him. Brando was pretty hot back then.

He frowned. "You're cold."

I rubbed my bare hands together. "I'm okay."

"Do you want to go inside?"

"No, I'll be fine once we walk a little." I took his hand, hoping to steal some of his body heat, but he was colder than I was, so I tugged him forward to keep moving. "I thought you said you grew up in London?"

"I did. I wasn't born there. And I haven't been to Bristol in a long time."

"Why not?"

"No reason." He turned his head toward the tree line and got quiet.

My teeth began to chatter, and he put his arm around me.

"Why don't we go inside?" he said. "We can listen to music or something."

"Um..." I wondered *where* inside he wanted to go since we weren't *technically* allowed in each other's rooms, and I feared that was what he hoped for. "Maybe another time?"

"Sure, another time." He squeezed my shoulder, and we headed toward the warmth of the school building. Right before we reached the door, he stopped walking, twisting his lips to the side and wrinkling his nose.

"Is something wrong?" My voice shook as my teeth continued clacking.

He shook his head as if dismissing a thought and then gave me a kiss on the cheek. "No, nothing." He ushered me inside.

I wasn't sure if I should tell him thank you, or give *him* a kiss on his cheek. He certainly wasn't as forward as the few boys I'd dated at home, but I liked that about him. "Thanks for the movie," I finally said, looking down at my nails but forcing myself not to pick at them.

"You're welcome. Would you like me to walk you to your room?"

"That's okay. I'll see you later?"

"Yes." He nodded. "Good night, Libby."

"Good night."

Veering from my usual path, I ambled down a dim hall, admiring the work of students who'd come and gone before me. Stopping in front of one painting in particular, I found myself mesmerized by its striking resemblance to my own style, both in content and color. The subject was a small pond with ripple rings flowing out from the center, as if a stone had been tossed into it. The soft russets of the pond's bank and the lush greens of the overhanging trees made me wonder if I hadn't actually painted it myself. Several of my pieces had a water element to them, and the brush strokes of that one were almost identical to my own.

The painting also made me think of my mystery boy. I hadn't been able to paint anything worthy of his presence since the orchard. Though not too unusual, his absence made me worry he wasn't coming back, maybe because Dean might have seen him. I reached up to touch the surface of the pond, almost wondering if I might feel the wetness of the water.

No, this couldn't be mine. But how uncanny.

"I wouldn't do that if I were you."

I gasped and spun around, surprised to see Dean sitting on the floor a few feet away, but then again, not surprised at all. "You know, I really wish you'd stop stalking me."

He grimaced, then pushed to his feet. A few long strides brought him almost right next to me, heat radiating from him in waves. "I was here first. You were too busy looking at the artwork to notice." He motioned toward the pond. "You wouldn't want to disturb the fish, would you?" Then he pointed to a black box with a red light on the edge of the frame. "Alarms. All the paintings have them."

"Oh." I glanced at the little box. "What are you doing down here anyway? Where's Neely?" I didn't really care where she was. But I did care that she wasn't with him.

"She's playing cards in the lounge. They were getting loud, and I wanted to read." He held up a book I hadn't noticed before: *A Short History of England, Ireland, and Scotland.*

"Studying?"

"No, I like history... and the quiet."

"Yeah, the quiet's nice." I bit my lip. His warmth, combined with the smell of mint tea and fabric softener, beckoned me closer, making me want to curl into his arms. "I should go," I said, forcing myself to step away from him.

Something flashed in his eyes, but it was gone almost instantly before he pointed to the painting. "Strange that this one isn't marked like the rest of them."

I examined the edge of the frame again then looked at a few around it. Every other piece had a little gold nameplate. "Yes, strange." I looked up, but he'd already gone.

I really wish he'd quit doing that.

I avoided Brent for several days, not because I didn't want to see him, but more because I was afraid of seeing Dean. I wasn't afraid of *him* or for my safety but rather deeply concerned for my sanity. When he was around, I lost my capacity for rational thought, and he seemed to show up whenever I was with Brent.

Twice over the course of the next week, Brent came by, but both times I used my painting and schoolwork as an excuse. He wanted to see what I was working on, but I told him I didn't like to show anyone my unfinished pieces, which was only *mostly* true. On his third time to see me, I knew I couldn't ignore him any longer without him feeling completely rejected. I also kept hearing a little voice in my head, one that sounded an awful lot like Travis, saying I needed to get out more and be more social. He was always telling me to act my age, and dating Brent would at least show I was making an effort to fit in with my peers.

"I'm glad I finally convinced you to come out of your room." His lips spread into a wide grin as we walked toward the main dining hall.

"Me too."

"Who knew poetry readings would do the trick?" he said, entwining his fingers with mine.

"It's not really the poetry."

"Not the poetry, huh? You must have missed my dashing good looks." He straightened his shoulders.

I couldn't help but laugh. "Yes, that was it. That and the coffee."

He laughed too, squeezing my hand. When we reached the dining hall, I could see the faculty had gone to a lot of effort to make it look like a real coffee shop. Small round tables with candles on them were scattered around the room, as well as a few chairs and couches. A large coffee bar sat adjacent to a small stage near the front, where students could perform by giving a poetry reading or singing.

I waved at Travis and Eric, who sat on a couch near the stage. Eric's dark arms were wrapped around Travis from behind, while his chin rested on Travis's shoulder. Like a cup of chamomile tea, Eric calmed Travis in a way I rarely saw. They were the perfect complement to each other, which was probably why Eric was able to convince Travis to do a poetry reading, the other reason I'd decided to go out that night.

Brent and I found an empty table close to the back, but before we could sit, a student I didn't know tapped Brent on the shoulder.

"Hey, Madam Harris is looking for you again." The guy had a slight southern drawl.

"I'll be right back," Brent said. "What flavor coffee would you like?"

"A vanilla latte, but I can get it if you want."

"No. Sit. I'll just be a moment." Then he walked away.

He couldn't have been gone more than a minute before Dean and Neely came over to our table.

"Oh, look. Libby's by herself." Neely's long black hair was pulled into a beautiful loose braid, and she tossed it over her shoulder, nearly smacking me in the face. "She won't mind if we sit here. No one else is."

I shifted my eyes from her to Dean, but he seemed to be looking at anything *but* me. "Um, Brent will be right—"

"I'm sure it will be fine. He'll probably appreciate a more stimulating conversation." Neely took a seat and pulled on Dean's arm for him to do the same.

He glanced at her and nodded, though I couldn't quite read his expression with his face turned to the side and the lighting so low in the room. Neely, the picture of beauty with her heart-shaped face, smiled warmly at Dean. My insides rolled when I noticed his shoulders relax after he gazed into her almond-shaped eyes. He always seemed to be tense around me, and watching them together, I understood why he liked her.

"How do you like Aldridge?" she asked.

Her attempt to make small talk made me uncomfortable, and I squirmed in my seat, wishing Brent would hurry up. "I like it," I mumbled around what felt like a mouth full of cotton. "It's nice to be able to paint as much as I want."

Dean dragged his attention away from Neely to look at me. "What are you working on?"

My stomach began its little waltz, and my knees shook. "A meadow," I said as evenly as I could.

He shifted his weight and his knee brushed mine under the table. "Did you finish the one you were working on a few weeks ago?"

The already small table suddenly felt as if it belonged at a toddler's tea party, and I had to lean back to take a breath. His sweet mint smell was intoxicating, especially mixed with the coffee aroma. I wondered if he'd told his girlfriend about our early morning encounter and the orchard painting—or our dance, for that matter, and the other times he'd stopped me *alone* in the hall.

"Which painting was that?" I tilted my head like a confused puppy.

He scowled. "The orchard."

I had to hold in my giggle at his annoyance. "Oh, I didn't like that one." I clicked my tongue. "I put it with some others to go to the incinerator."

"You did what!"

Neely and I jumped in startled unison, and a couple at the next table whipped around to look at us.

"Libby, do you have any idea what could happen? You have to get it back before it's destroyed."

Neely put her hand on Dean's arm. He didn't seem to notice. But I did, and the waltzing in my stomach erupted into a mosh pit.

I had only been joking, but his overreaction irritated me. Forcing myself to lean forward again, I narrowed my eyes at him, our faces only inches apart. "It's my painting. I'll do what I like with it." We were so close I could feel his breath on my face and see the rise and fall of his chest as he clenched his fist on the table.

"Libby." Neely's voice broke the tangible tension that had grown in the air. "Perhaps someone else would like it."

"I won't sell or display paintings I'm not happy with." I drew my eyes away from Dean to look at her, and thankfully, she removed her hand from his arm before my nausea became a real problem. "If I don't like them, they're destroyed."

"But—" she started.

"I see we have company." Brent handed me my coffee then moved his chair closer to mine before he sat down. "Did I miss anything exciting?"

"Libby was telling us how much she enjoys it here at Aldridge," Neely answered.

I was curious as to why she didn't tell him what we were really talking about, but more than that, I was thankful for Brent showing up when he did and for my stomach beginning to settle.

Brent looked at me and smiled then whispered in my ear, "I hope that has something to do with me."

I put my hand over his and nodded. "Thank you for the coffee, too." Half-expecting Dean to get up and leave right then, I took a sip of my vanilla latte.

But he didn't. He just settled in his seat and watched the first performer take the stage.

His words kept running through my head. *"Do you have any idea what could happen?" What did he mean by that, and why does it matter so much to him?*

The only performance I was able to pay any attention to was Travis's. He'd memorized a poem about wearing figurative masks.

By the end of the evening, I couldn't tell who was more uncomfortable: Dean or me. When the final performer went on stage and did an overly dramatic reading of *The Raven,* I inched closer to Brent and asked him to walk me back to my room. He nodded with a goofy grin. When the lights came up, we all stood, and Brent took my hand.

"Big plans, you two?" Neely asked as she and Dean followed us out of the dining hall.

"Nothing thrilling," I said. "Though I do have some more paintings to destroy."

Dean snapped his head around to glare at me, but I tugged on Brent's arm and walked away.

"What was *that* all about?" he asked when we were a good distance away from them.

"They were upset because I said I would incinerate one of my paintings."

"Well, that's one way to get rid of your work. Why do they care?"

I stared up at him, a little surprised. "It wouldn't bother you if I *burned* my art?"

"They're your paintings. You have the right to do whatever you want with them," he said as we approached my door. "So you'll come to the party with me after the performance?"

Some of the performing arts students were putting on a show that featured a collage of dances. It was one of the school's mandatory events, which also meant there'd be a party afterward.

I forced a smile. "Yes."

He leaned in closer, and I had to catch my breath, unsure if I *wanted* him to kiss me or if I hoped he wouldn't.

"Good." He kissed my cheek, but when he pulled away, he had a strange look on his face, almost a grimace. "I... had a nice time with you tonight."

A shiver ran across my shoulders. Our third date. Maybe Travis was right. Maybe Brent really *was* nervous. Maybe he thought I'd be as bad at kissing as I was at dancing.

I contemplated opening my door and letting him in my room, but said, "I had a nice time, too," deciding *not* to open it. "I meant to ask you, what did Madam Harris want from you earlier?"

"Oh, um... she needed my help with a... project."

"Something for the performance?"

"Uh, yeah, the performance."

"Okay. Well, I'll meet you after then?"

"Great." He hesitated as other students passed by us. Some, including nosy Maggie Bates, gawked openly. "I'll see you later," he added then walked away.

I went inside, closed the door, and pressed my spine to it. "Why didn't you let him in? He's cute. He's nice to you. He's..." *There's just something... missing.*

I kicked the door with my heel then jumped when someone knocked on the other side. I opened it, expecting to see Brent or Travis. But it was neither.

"I have nothing to say to you." I spit the words out at Dean. Unfortunately, I hadn't taken the time to notice his expression. His dark eyes were tired, or sad maybe, and his shoulders drooped as if they carried a heavy burden.

"Sorry." He blinked once slowly then took a step back.

"Wait." I sighed. "If you've come to ask me not to burn the painting, then you might as well know I was bluffing. I'd never destroy my art like that, especially not that one."

His eyes seemed to brighten, and he put his hand on the door jamb, leaning toward me.

"Don't assume that means I'm going to let you in to look at it. I know what you think you saw, but some..." I had to work at keeping my voice even, and I hoped he didn't notice my hands shaking. "Some of my paintings I don't share with others. That's one of them."

"I..." He paused as if trying to choose his next words carefully. "I apologize for my intrusion." He pushed himself away from my door but hesitated again.

"Did you want something else?" I asked, desperate to know if the painting was all he'd come for and hoping it wasn't.

He took a long time to answer. "I hope you have a pleasant evening." Then he retreated down the hall.

"You too," I whispered, my heart sinking as I watched him go.

Chapter Six

Travis and I fought our way through the throng of people filling the auditorium to near capacity as several faculty members helped students and visitors find seats. I waved at Kari across the aisle before noticing Madam Harris close to the stage. She was speaking with an elderly couple and pointing at a couple of empty chairs in the second row. Loud chatter filled my ears like white noise, disorienting me. Travis clutched my hand and ushered me down a middle row to a vacant seat. The cacophony of voices finally stopped when Madam Harris took the stage to welcome everyone, but it still took several seconds for the whispers to trail off.

The first performance was a Celtic tap dance. The black-and-emerald-clad dancers moved with the rhythmic cadence of a drum, tapping their feet with calculated chaos. Next was a ballet, the pretty pink dancers graceful and flowing like a Degas set in motion. When the ballerinas left the stage, three petite girls dressed in long white kimonos and holding traditional Asian fans entered. It took me a minute to register that the girl in front was Neely, and she was clearly the best of the three. She flipped her open fan in the air, tapping it with her fingers to make it spin and turn several times before snapping it closed at the precise moment the music ended.

The stage darkened. Clapping and stomping started, and the lights blazed on, displaying performers in bright reds and oranges. The crowd cheered as the rhythm increased, and the pulsing sound of pounding feet became so heavy I thought they might break through the floor. When the music and stomping reached its climax, the stage went to black again, and everything was quiet. The crowd erupted in cheers, only to be silenced by the next set of performers.

A jazz group came on, then swing dancers took the stage. The guys lifted the girls high into the air then swished them down and through their legs. I hadn't seen Brent yet, but all thoughts of him rushed out of my head when the swing music ended and a deep blue glow emanated from center stage. I sat up straighter in my seat to get a better view of Dean standing alone like a shadow in the light. Black nylon pants hugged his hips and thighs, flaring slightly at the knee, and a black long-sleeved shirt clung to his lean, muscular form. From a standing position, he jumped straight up into the air, tucked his lithe body, flipped once, and came down without a sound, flawlessly in the exact spot he'd started.

"You're drooling," Travis whispered.

And I was. *Because he's magnificent.*

I'd been so focused on Dean that I hadn't noticed the other dancers entering the stage around him, and I couldn't believe he hadn't hit any of them when he landed. Dean flipped again, spinning and twisting in the air as if suspended by an invisible line. Except there was no line, just him and the quiet swiftness he possessed. The other dancers advanced, circling and imprisoning him. He fought to break free, finally thrusting his hands into the air and scattering them across the stage as they ripped his shirt away, revealing his chiseled muscles.

Magnificent and *gorgeous.*

The music morphed into a Latin beat, and the other dancers retreated from the stage. The hairs on my neck and arms stood on end as Dean swept his body low, looking for another attacker. He swung to his right at the same moment Brent came bounding onto the stage with his fist aimed at Dean's back.

"Ouch," Travis yelped when I clamped his hand to keep from screaming.

Brent narrowly missed Dean, who'd rolled out of the way. But he advanced again, sweeping a kick in Dean's direction. Dean curled his stomach away before Brent's foot connected.

I can't breathe.

Dean somersaulted forward, and Brent leapt backward, arching his spine and placing his hands on the floor before returning to a standing position. The two of them advanced and retreated with legs and arms and bodies, twisting and fighting in time to the music.

I'm going to pass out if this doesn't end soon!

The murderous expression on Brent's face as he stalked Dean across the stage caused a lump to form in my throat and my heart to come to a screeching halt. When Brent kicked both legs at Dean after coming out of a handstand, almost slamming Dean in the face, my still heart took off as if trying to pound its way out of my chest. But Dean spun, stretching out his legs and forcing Brent back again. Though only a performance, the animosity between them was palpable.

They seemed to be at a draw, moving around each other, gauging their next attacks. Watching, waiting for what was coming, was pure torture. Brent took a step away, preparing to swing at Dean, but the music changed again, and a girl in a barely-there silver dress came onto the stage. The two fighters backed away from each other in awe of the seductive figure moving between them. They both neared her, but she shoved at Dean, clearly choosing Brent as her partner for the next dance.

All the air rushed out of me, and I sank into my seat as Dean disappeared, seemingly unscathed, from the stage.

"I won't tell Brent you wanted Dean to win," Travis whispered.

I snapped my head around to look at him.

He narrowed his eyes at me. "Hmm, then again, maybe the right guy *did* get the girl."

Returning my attention to the stage, I watched through dazed eyes as Brent and his partner began a tango so intimate and sensual it bordered on provocative. His hands roamed her body, sliding down to her thigh and lifting it up to hold it tight to his hip. He pressed into her, arching her back and sweeping her low before pulling her back against him. She buried her face in his neck for a moment before turning to face the audience.

I gasped. *Neely.*

The dance continued to grow in intensity from provocative to carnal. Neely wrapped her arms around his neck then leaned away and grazed her hands down his chest, hips, and legs until she was kneeling on the floor in front of him. He bent at the waist, touching her lightly on the shoulder. When she gazed up at him, the anguish was clear in her expression. He lifted her to stand, and she placed her hands on his face. They twirled around once more before coming to a dead stop in center stage.

The last beat of the music sounded. Their lips locked. And the lights went out.

The crowd rose to their feet, clapping and calling for an encore.

"That was *hot,*" Travis said over the applause. "I don't know about them, but I think I need a cigarette, and I don't even smoke."

Every muscle in my body was tense, making it painful to move, but I had to get out of that theater. Pushing through the mass of people to get to the exit, I left Travis somewhere behind me. A cool rush of air hit my face when I staggered into the hallway, shaking and jittery. Some of the performers were emerging from a side corridor, so I went in that direction. I scanned the endless stream of faces then realized I was searching for one in particular.

Dean came around the corner, his clean hair still damp and a gray Henley covering the sculpted muscles I'd seen on stage. Our eyes locked, and he seemed startled at first, but his expression quickly turned to a schooled nonchalance. I froze in place, my heart refusing to give up its tantrum as he came closer. In an effort to calm my nerves, I took in a deep breath, but all I got for it was a nose full of his intoxicating fresh scent.

He stopped in front of me. "Are you looking for Brent?"

"I... um... you're bleeding! What happened?" I instinctively reached up to wipe the blood from his cheek. "Are you all right?"

He didn't flinch away. In fact, he leaned his warm face into my palm. "It's just a scratch, but I'm better now."

I held my hand there longer than necessary, enjoying the heat passing between us, which somehow calmed me. Finally, I pulled back my hand.

He reached for it, turning it so the palm was up. "Now my blood is on you."

"It doesn't bother me. Are you sure you're okay?"

He smiled, but then his face hardened. "It will bother *him*," he said, dropping my hand.

"There's my girl." Brent came up next to me and gave me a peck on the cheek.

I wiped my hand on my pants as Dean took a small step away.

Brent put his arm around my waist and grinned. "Did you enjoy the show?"

"Yes, it was a lot of fun, and a little surprising." I glanced at Dean out of the corner of my eye. He hadn't moved any farther away, and a crease had formed between his eyebrows.

"Sorry I didn't warn you about the whole tango thing," Brent said.

"It's okay." I shook my head then noticed a red splotch on Brent's cheek. "What happened?" I asked, touching my fingers to the mark that looked like a hand print.

"Nothing." He waved it off. "A minor misunderstanding."

"Oh." I looked between him and Dean. "So how did Neely end up dancing with *you*? Why not Dean?"

Brent glanced at Dean then smirked and dipped me low enough that I had to grip him tightly to keep from falling over. "Because I'm better," he said loud enough for Dean to hear. Then he pressed his lips firmly against the base of my throat.

My insides clenched when I saw the look in Dean's eyes as Brent raised me back to a standing position. Brent chuckled then turned away when someone came up and congratulated him on the performance.

Dean's hand brushed my fingertips. "He's lying," he whispered. His lips grazed my ear, sending a pleasant tingle down my spine. "I just prefer the waltz."

An unexpected smile came to my face, but when I turned to look at him, he'd already disappeared into the crowd. My smile quickly faded along with the warmth of his presence.

A short time later, all the students were gathered at the party. Brent convinced me to dance to a few songs, but after I had stepped on his toes several times and nearly elbowed him in the eye once, we both needed a break. We headed to the bar. He kept his arm locked around me the entire time. I barely had room to move, let alone breathe.

"So does that fighting dance have a name?" I asked after we got our drinks and he'd finally given me some space.

"Yes, it's called *capoeira*. It's Brazilian."

"It seemed extremely intricate. Do you ever actually hit each other?"

"Once in a while in practice, or by accident."

"Accident?"

"Yes, the whole thing is choreographed down to the slightest detail. If either Dean or I move an inch in the wrong direction, we're likely to get hurt. But don't worry, I can take it." He puffed out his chest and rolled his shoulders back.

My mind drifted to the blood on Dean's cheek, and I briefly wondered if Brent had been the one to cause that. And if it had been an *accident.* "I have to admit, when you told me you were enrolled as an actor, I thought you meant a play actor."

"I did." He scanned the crowd. "I like to dance, too, though. Like I said, undecided." Then he leaned in and whispered, "But I'm not undecided about you." He sat up and smiled coyly. "Do you want to get out of here?"

Do I? I gulped down my fears. As much as I would have rather retreated to my room, I knew I should spend some time with him. But it would be on my terms, not his. "Why don't you show me some of those dancing skills you used on stage? Maybe I'd be better at the tango."

He laughed then set our drinks aside and led me to the dance floor. After a few more songs, we decided to call it a night. He didn't ask again to go to one of our rooms, and I headed to my suite alone. On my way up, I saw Eric slip into Travis's room. I was happy Travis had found someone he shared that kind of connection with. I liked Brent, but I wondered if or when I'd ever feel as strongly about him as he seemed to feel about me.

A chill came over me, and I found myself wishing for the warmth I'd felt earlier near Dean, and I wondered where he was. My night seemed incomplete without my seeing him one more time.

So what if I don't see him? We're not even friends.

Still, even after a few minutes, I opened my door and scanned the hall. But it was empty.

Chapter Seven

"You really don't have to stay," I told Travis as he handed me a box of tissues.

He sat down on the end of my bed and patted my leg. "Don't be ridiculous. You can barely lift your head. Besides, I've taken care of Tess plenty of times when my parents were too *busy* at the club to bother with their own daughter."

"But I don't want *you* to get sick." I blew my raw nose then put the dirty tissue on the nightstand.

He shook his head and stood up. "Don't worry. I never do. My immune system is a force field. You can shoot at it all you want, but it doesn't come down." As if to prove his point, he grabbed my discarded tissue and went into my bathroom.

As he walked out carrying a wastebasket, there was a knock on my door. I started to get up, but Travis held up his hand to stop me before going over to open the door.

"Oh hey, Brent," he said, still holding the large can full of my dirty Kleenex.

I started to say something, but I couldn't get the words out before sneezing, loudly.

Brent recoiled and halted before stepping over the threshold. "You're sick," he said, looking a little ill himself.

I wiped my nose. "Yeah."

He took a long step back. "I'll come by another time." Then he practically ran away.

Travis shut the door, affecting the air of a proper British butler. "Apparently *he's* never taken care of a sick sister before." He plopped the wastebasket down next to the bed.

I closed my eyes and laid my head on a cool pillow, too tired to respond... or to care that Brent was a germophobe.

When I hadn't gotten better after several days, Madam Harris brought a doctor to my room. He said I had a severe cold—I could have told them that—but nothing time, rest, and chicken soup wouldn't heal. Our headmistress seemed frantic. I thought she just didn't want any other students catching what I had until I realized her concern was all for me.

"I'll let your parents know what the doctor said. Is there anything I can get you before I see him out?"

The kindness in her voice made me want to ask her to sit with me, just until I fell asleep, or to get me a spoonful of sugar to help the medicine go down. And I had the odd feeling she might, but I knew she had an entire school to run. "No, thank you." I rubbed my eyes, dizzy from sitting up while the doctor examined me.

For a second she looked disappointed, and I thought maybe I *should* have asked her to stay, but then she patted my leg and left with the doctor. I stayed awake for a few minutes wondering why she was being so attentive. Maybe she was that way when any of the students were ill... maybe.

Brent came by after a few days, but I wouldn't let him in, even though I was insane with boredom. I told him I didn't want him to get sick, and he seemed more than okay with that. Travis made sure I ate and stayed in bed, per the doctor's orders. He also helped me keep up on my schoolwork. Unfortunately, he still couldn't help me with math, and no one could help me paint. I doodled in my sketchbook, but the only things I could think of was the shadowy figure of my mystery boy and the midnight eyes of Dean James, both images more frustrating than healing.

Madam Harris stopped in twice, once to tell me she'd contacted my parents. I wished I'd had the chance to talk to them, but I knew they'd only feel helpless, being so far away while I was sick. I longed for some of my mom's specially brewed tea and to watch old home movies with my dad. On her second visit, Madam Harris said she would be away for a while, but the school nurse would update her on my recovery.

"Do you think it's strange how concerned Madam Harris seems to be?" I asked Travis. "I mean, hasn't any other student been sick before?"

"Well, you are her favorite... and mine."

"No fair teasing me when I'm sick." I coughed, the force of it painfully rattling my chest as if I were gargling gravel. "By the way, I never thanked you for the sculpture you gave me." I gestured at the foot-tall statue of two faceless forms wrapped in an embrace standing on the corner of my desk.

He handed me my medicine and a bottle of water. "No need to thank me. It was just a get-well gift."

I popped the pills into my mouth and swallowed, wincing as they grated on my sore throat.

"How about a movie?" He opened my laptop and pressed the power button. "I'll even let you pick which Hepburn we watch."

"Definitely Katharine." I slid over on the bed, letting Travis climb in next to me with the computer.

"So you're choosing the brash American over the cultured Brit?" He'd barely gotten the words out when I heard a loud knock at my door.

Travis hopped off the bed and set my laptop on the desk before scurrying to the door. He opened it, positioning himself between me and whoever was there, blocking my view. "Let me check if she's up to visitors." He shut the door again and turned back to me. "Do you want me to let Dean in?"

"What is *he* doing here?" I sat up and grabbed a tissue from the box next to me.

Travis laughed. "I haven't seen you this alert in days. Maybe he wants to make you *feel* better." Travis waggled his eyebrows.

My eyes watered, but I wasn't sure if it was from the cold or from the shock that Dean had come to see me. "How do I look?"

"Well... at least we'll know if he's shallow."

"Thanks for your honesty." I sighed. "You can let him in, but would you shut my studio door first, please?"

Travis poked his head into the hall. "Just give us a sec." Then he closed the door, picked up my dirty tissues, and shut my studio door. "You ready?"

"I guess." I smoothed the blankets over my legs.

Travis gave me a quick kiss on the forehead then went back to let in Dean. "She's all yours."

Dean gave Travis a polite nod as they passed each other. Then Travis turned and winked at me before closing the door behind him.

Dean was wearing faded jeans and a long-sleeved, cream-colored thermal shirt. I couldn't smell anything with my nose plugged, but the memory of his scent was enough to spike my temperature.

I held up a limp hand in warning. "Don't get too close."

He nodded but took two steps toward the bed anyway, then leaned his shoulder against the wall. "Sorry you're not feeling well, especially today." His tone was friendly and oddly comforting.

How could he possibly know it's my birthday when I haven't told anyone? "It's not so bad." I dabbed at my tender nose with a tissue. "Except I don't feel like painting."

He glanced at my closed studio door. "I'm sure once you're better you'll paint something that will leap off the canvas."

I knew full well what he meant, but I didn't have the energy to play that game. "Was there something you needed?"

"No, I just heard you were sick." He pushed away from the wall and rubbed his hand on his dark-washed jeans. He made a face as if he wanted to say something else. He seemed... nervous. *That's strange for him.*

I wanted to ask him where he'd been the other night after the dance performance. But I couldn't work up the courage or fight past the remaining fogginess in my head to think how to word it.

"I should probably go. You need your rest." He stepped toward the door but stopped before opening it. "I hope you feel better soon." Then he was gone.

Without knowing it, he'd given me the best—and worst—birthday present ever. He'd come to visit me, and then he'd left before I could ask him to stay.

Moments later, Travis returned and settled back on the bed next to me. I didn't make it much beyond the halfway mark in *The Philadelphia Story* before I stopped fighting the need to sleep. I think I might have muttered a tired "You're on your own" to Travis.

At first my dream was serene, peaceful even. Wearing my red dress, I sat under an oak tree, playing with a leaf and studying the delicate veins running through it. A shadow fell over me, and I looked up. My mystery boy stood there, holding out his hand. But when I moved to take it, he vanished. The space around me morphed into the orchard from my painting. He was there again, in the distance. I jumped up and ran toward him, but the faster I went, the farther away he got. Then I slammed into a giant wooden door.

I woke up with a start, shaking and drenched in sweat.

"Shh," Travis said, wrapping his arms around me. "It's going to be okay."

I hoped he was right and curled into him as he rocked me. "I'm so glad you're here."

"I know, sweetie. I know."

When I was feeling well enough to get out of bed for a while, I went to my studio and stared at a blank canvas that seemed destined, for the moment, to stay pristine. On top of everything else, I was homesick. The weather had turned cold, and it was Thanksgiving in the States. I'd called my parents, but talking to them only made me miss them more. They were going to a friend's house for dinner since I wasn't there, and the thought of missing my mom's pumpkin pie made my mouth water. Eventually, I gave up staring at the canvas and crawled back in bed. Trying to paint while thinking about food was never a good combination. On the plus side, my nails hadn't been so clean in years, and maybe my dream self could at least get a little turkey and stuffing.

The next day, I felt well enough to get out of my room and be among other people. The timing actually worked out well since Travis and I were going to the opening night of *Othello*.

"You're looking much better," Travis said as he led me into the auditorium. "You could use a little meat on your bones, but at least you're upright and walking."

"Yeah, too bad they don't celebrate Thanksgiving here. I might have eaten a whole turkey by myself."

"I don't know where you'd fit a whole... hmm, don't look now," Travis said, "but Mr. Hottie is headed this way."

My mind jumped from stuffing to something even more enticing, and my palms began to sweat. I hadn't seen Dean since he'd come to my room when I was sick, but when I turned around, it wasn't Dean coming toward us.

"I am not sitting here by myself," Travis whispered in my ear.

I shooed him away as Brent approached. "I thought you'd be busy backstage." I forced a smile.

"You have no idea how happy I am to see you're feeling better." He leaned over and kissed my cheek.

"Me too, and lucky for you, I'm no longer contagious."

"Do you think you might be up to coming to the cast party after the show?" His eyes were hopeful, and I was happy I wouldn't be disappointing him.

"I was actually already planning on it."

"You were? Ah, yes." He nodded at Travis. "I keep forgetting that you know Eric."

Dean came up behind Brent. "They're ready," he said, stealing a glance at me then looking away.

"Hmm." Brent frowned then took my hands and pulled me closer to whisper in my ear. "I've missed you. I'll be waiting...

impatiently." He pushed my hair aside and kissed my jaw, sending a cool chill down my neck before he turned and slapped Dean on the shoulder. "Shall we then?" he asked, walking away.

For a second, Dean stood there, unmoving. I opened my mouth to speak, but no sound came out, and a moment later, he was halfway down the aisle, headed for the stage. I collapsed into my seat and glanced up in time to see him hesitate before going behind the curtain. He turned and caught my gaze, but he quickly shoved the heavy red cloth out of his way and disappeared.

Travis cleared his throat, obviously exaggerating the sound.

I rubbed my forehead with my fingertips. "What?"

"You do realize they will both be at this party, right?" Travis whispered.

"Yeah, I know." I still hadn't figured out how I was going to handle that, though.

The lights dimmed, and the play began, giving me a much-needed distraction.

Afterward, Travis and I fought against the crowd and found our way backstage. Behind the curtain, the world went dark, but the light shining from farther ahead was enough to help us see around all the props and set pieces.

"There's Eric," Travis said when we reached the doorway to the greenroom.

Eric waved, and Travis immediately ditched me, leaving me standing there like an outcast. Luckily, Brent spotted me and pushed his way through the throng of people.

When he came near, I said, "Hey, the show was wonderful!"

He wrapped his arms around me. "Thank you. I'm glad you're here." I could hear the grin in his voice.

"It... um... didn't seem like there were this many people in the cast." I pulled away, trying to breathe normally as claustrophobia set in. I hated crowds.

There were at least fifty people in the room, along with props and furniture filling up the remaining space. On the walls were a mixture of photographs from different performances and signatures of people I assumed were past students.

He settled his arm around my waist. "You really don't like crowds, do you?"

"Is it that obvious?"

Someone bumped me from behind, and Brent pulled me closer. Then, with his free hand, he tucked a strand of hair behind my ear. "We don't have to stay," he murmured.

I was pretty sure his offer wasn't entirely out of concern for my comfort. "Where would you like to go?"

He wrapped his other arm around me. "How about—"

A sardonic voice interrupted, "Is this the girl you've been jacking off to? I can certainly see why. I know *I'll* be thinking of her next time."

Brent dropped his arms and shoved me behind him, his body blocking me from the wiry boy standing in front of us. "How dare you talk to my..." He shook his head. "That's highly inappropriate, Joel. You'll do well to keep your comments, and your thoughts, to yourself."

"Aren't you going to introduce us? I'd like a name to go with the face. You know, for later." Joel leaned to the side to leer at me with his beady brown eyes. "In fact, you should introduce her to everybody. Pretty girl like that should be passed around."

"Bugger. Off." Brent's clipped tone was harsher than I'd ever heard from him. "Let's go." He faced me again, the crease between his eyes softening as he took my hand. "I'm not going to make a spectacle of you."

Joel laughed and walked away as Brent tugged on my arm to leave.

I didn't budge. "You know what? Why don't we stay for a little bit? I'd like to meet some of your *nicer* friends."

He laced our fingers together and gave me a questioning look. "Are you sure?"

I nodded and squeezed his hand. I wasn't going to let a jerk like that run me out of a party I was invited to, no matter how uncomfortable he'd made me.

Keeping either his arm around me or holding my hand the entire time, Brent led me around the room and introduced me to one person after another. The rest of his friends seemed very nice. After a while, hip-hop music blared through some speakers, and several kids began to dance with more coordination and style than I would ever have. Amy, a cute blonde I'd met moments earlier, tapped Brent on the shoulder and summoned him to the dance floor.

"Go ahead," I said. I only hoped he wouldn't drag me out there with him.

He hesitated. "We can still leave. I don't want to make you uncomfortable."

"I'll be fine." I gave his hand a squeeze then let it go. "I'll go get something to drink."

"One dance and I'll be right back."

I watched as he took his place on the floor. He seemed to instinctively know what steps to take, completely in his element. He waved to me before the dancers all turned to face the opposite direction and start the whole sequence of steps over again. I took that as my cue to head to the drink table.

But I didn't make it that far. An embarrassing amount of tingles surged through me when Dean's hand pressed into the base of my spine. I was so focused on the warmth of his palm and each slightly splayed finger that he'd steered me most of the way to the backstage area before I even noticed. He removed his hand, and I shivered, only to flush once again when he stepped toward me. A shadow cast on his face obscured his features.

I retreated until my back was against a large foam set piece, one of the changeable courtyard walls from the play, but he kept advancing. The distance between us became wafer thin.

"He's no good for you. You shouldn't date him." Dean's voice was rough and low, his minty breath feverish against my cheeks and lips as he leaned over me.

"Let me get this straight..." I placed my palms against the set piece, bracing myself as my knees threatened to give out from under me. "First, you tell me we don't know each other." A bead of sweat formed at my nape. "Then, you take over my dance lesson." I took a deep breath, purposefully wanting to inhale him, his smell and warmth like a towel fresh from the dryer. "Then, you accuse me of painting something I didn't." I tried to sound angry, but my shaky voice betrayed me. "And now, you're telling me who I can and can't date?"

"We'd never met before the other night." He leaned down farther, his hand flat on the heavy foam wall near my shoulder. In that moment, I became hyperaware of my own body—and his. "He's not the right dance partner for you." He stared into my eyes as he moved inconceivably closer. His knee pressed between mine, rubbing my lower thigh. "I know what I saw in that painting."

I swallowed. The space between our lips was imperceptible. In fact, I couldn't tell if they were lightly touching, or if I only wished they were.

"And I'm very serious in saying that Brent is not what you need."

My heart sped up even more, if that was even possible, when I caught myself about to ask him what it was he thought I needed. "It's really...." His proximity fogged my brain. Why didn't *Brent* make me feel this warm? Dean's sculpted shoulders blocked out the light, but I closed my eyes anyway, desperate to collect myself. His hand trailed up my arm and brushed my hair from my shoulder, exposing my neck and burning me where he touched.

"You were saying?" His lips touched mine, officially, undoubtedly, for the briefest of moments. He was too close... *and* too far away.

I was saying... I was saying... what? I was about to say I needed him. *No, that's not right.* "I was saying that I'm the one who gets to choose who is or isn't good for me."

I felt, rather than saw, the smile that came to his face. "Yes, you should." But instead of doing what I wanted him to do, he pulled away, and the chill returned. "The song's over," he said in a heady voice.

"It is?" My voice squeaked as my eyes snapped open.

We stood there for a moment before he offered me his hand as though he was going to walk me back. But he dropped it back to his side, taking another slow step away. "I..." He shook his head. "You should get in there." Then he disappeared into the blackness.

If Brent's no good, why are you letting me go to him?

I shivered again then bent down and put my hands on my knees, taking a few deep breaths before pushing away from the wall. The last thing I wanted to do was to go into that greenroom. But I lifted my leaden feet across the backstage floor anyway. From the doorway, I could see Brent surrounded by people patting him on the arm or shoulder, trying to get him to dance to another ear-assaulting electric beat. I hoped he would; I needed more time to recover. Unfortunately, he caught my eye and headed right for me.

"That looked like fun," I said, trying unsuccessfully to remove thoughts of Dean from my head. "You really are a good dancer."

"Thank you." He panted, catching his breath. "You didn't get your drink?"

"Oh, um..." I averted my eyes. "I guess I got... caught up in the moment."

"Well, let's get one together then, shall we?"

We found an unoccupied wrought-iron bench in a quiet corner. The slightly curved seat forced our legs to press together, and the uncomfortable angle made me wish Brent would go dance with the other kids again. Instead, he ignored their calls to join them and put his arm around me. His body clammy against mine, he pointed out people I hadn't met earlier.

I probably should have paid better attention, but when Dean crossed in front of us, headed for the exit with Neely close on his heels, I blocked out everything else. Neely put her hand on Dean's arm, stopping him before he was out the door. He spun around, his eye catching mine for a split second before he looked at her. His expression gave nothing away, but my guilt and yearning washed over me in waves. I wanted to look away when Neely took his hand, but my muscles wouldn't respond to my command.

Travis walked up a moment later, blocking them from my view and saving my sanity. "I'm beat. I'm gonna head up."

"Okay." I jumped up. "I'll go with you."

Brent grabbed my hand. "I can walk you later."

"Thanks. But I'm still recovering, and I probably shouldn't stay up too late." I twisted out of his grasp.

"Yes, that's true." He stood and hugged me. "Before you go, I wondered if you'd like to go to London next weekend for dinner and a show. Some of the drama kids are organizing a trip, and I'd love it if you'd accompany me."

"London sounds great." I glanced at Travis, and Brent picked up my hint.

"You and Eric are welcome to come, of course," Brent added.

"That would be great," Travis said. "Thanks."

Brent kissed my cheek. "I really am glad you came tonight. I'll see you Saturday."

I nodded, and Travis and I made our way toward the exit. Unfortunately, that meant we had to walk right past Dean and Neely. I tried to avoid looking at them, but Neely made it impossible.

"Leaving so soon?" she said as we approached the doorway.

My eyes shifted to hers, and for a brief moment, my guilty conscience imagined her reaching out and slapping me. "Yes, it's late, and it's been an eventful evening," I said, eager to escape her scrutiny before my face gave away my emotions.

"Eventful evening? I guess so when you're used to watching paint dry." She flashed the fakest smile I'd ever seen.

"Don't mind her. She's just tired," Dean said. "I should probably get her to bed."

I didn't respond. Still too stunned from our earlier encounter, my lips couldn't form words while in such close proximity to his. Besides, the only words I had for him couldn't be spoken in front of others, especially his girlfriend. Instead, I shoved Travis through the doorway ahead of me with more force than necessary.

At the end of the hallway, Travis stopped and started coughing in front of a painting of a woman being shattered to pieces, the Daliesque image a little more real than surreal at that moment. "Are you going to tell me what that was all about *and* what possessed you to go backstage with Dean earlier?"

"Oh, my God, Travis, do you think Brent saw? And why are you coughing?" I examined him, looking for any signs that he might be getting sick.

"Just a tickle in my throat from the dancing and the dry air. I'm parched. Don't worry about it. And don't worry about Brent either. He was too busy shaking that cute ass of his to notice. But obviously you're concerned that he *might* have."

I knew a leading statement when I heard one. I just didn't know how to respond. "I don't want Brent to get the wrong idea. Dean wanted to... talk."

"Okay." Travis held up his hands. "I'm just making sure you know what you're doing."

"Of course I don't know what I'm doing." I spoke way too loud and a few students in the hall looked in our direction. I put my hands over my face and started walking again. I lowered my voice to almost a whisper. "I meant to say that I like Brent. He's sweet and cute and—"

"And what about Dean?"

My shoulders drooped. "He's with Neely."

Chapter Eight

THE EARLY AFTERNOON SUN CASCADED in through the bare window as I sat alone in my studio. The hazy golden glow surrounded me, warming my face. We'd already gotten a few inches of snow, but the crisp white blanket dappled with a jewel-like shimmer inspired me rather than chilled me.

I'd almost finished a snowy bridge scene. The honey-colored stone pillars and iron railings of the bridge blended effortlessly with the trees in the background, glistening in the burnt-orange sunlight. With a final dab of dark purple, the painting was complete. Hope bubbled inside me when delicate white flakes began to float down inside the canvas. I shivered, then held my breath until the last snowflake fell, but my mystery boy never came, and the painting went still once again.

"As if I didn't have enough going on right now." I smacked my paintbrush down on the easel. "You couldn't show up just this once when I'd really like to see you."

You're losing it, Libby. Or maybe it's already gone?

It'd been over two months since I'd painted the orchard and seen my mystery boy, and I sometimes wondered if the magic was lost to me. Even my classwork lacked… something. My mind was so unsettled and my painting so sporadic lately that I ached deep inside. I was so disconnected… from him.

When I was sure nothing more would happen within the bridge scene, I set the whole thing aside and gathered my paint-soaked brushes. The colors spilled down the drain as I washed the brushes, wishing the murky swirl would carry my sorrow away with the pretty hues. I glanced over at the picture of my parents. If I'd been in the same mood at home, my mom would force me out of my studio. We'd go get ice cream and pedicures, and when we got home, an empty canvas would be waiting for me on my easel.

I intended to walk away and do something else for a while, but I couldn't. Without someone there to distract me, I was a slave to the canvases lining my wall, waiting to be painted. I placed one of them on the easel then dragged my fingertips across the clean, taut cloth.

It shimmered like the sun setting in the horizon, with vibrant pinks, yellows, oranges, and even some purples. I jerked my hand away, and the canvas went blank again.

That's never happened before.

My pulse quickened as an image formed in my head. I rushed to open my paints and fumbled with the brushes as I set to work. As if the image would be lost if I didn't go fast enough, my hand flew from my palette to the canvas and back again.

By the time I was done several hours later, my hands and neck were stiff, and my jeans and T-shirt were ruined. But I didn't care. All I cared about was that he was there, leaning against a tree.

The tree's leaves had turned burnt sienna and ocher where it stood at the edge of a wide creek. The iridescent water in the creek glided over the rocks in its path, determined, flowing to an unknown destination. In the distance, the sandy slopes of a hill rose just high enough to allow the sun to shine down on the tall grass.

I reached out and brushed my fingertips across the painting. It shimmered as the boy looked up, his eyes widening in surprise. Then he scowled and shook his head. He pushed away from the knotted trunk of a massive walnut tree, turned his back to me, and vanished. The leaves on the tree rustled, and the ground beneath it quaked. The large tree came crashing down inside the painting, falling directly over the creek. Then everything froze, as if I'd painted it that way.

My heart sank, and tears pricked my eyes. I wanted him back. I wanted to know why he seemed so miserable. And most of all, I wanted to know why he was in my paintings in the first place.

A knock from the other room startled me. I rubbed at my eyes and left my studio. When I wrenched open my suite door, I was greeted by the last person I wanted, or expected, to see. "Neely?"

"Can I come in?" She slid her way past me, not waiting for my answer. Dressed in navy jeggins and a long white sweater and moving with the poise of a dancer, she made me feel incredibly inadequate.

"Um, yeah. Sure."

"I know we don't really know each other, but I wanted to talk to you, artist to artist."

I closed the door. Her opening didn't give me the feeling that I would enjoy the upcoming conversation. She was probably going to tell me to stay away from her boyfriend, even though he was the one who had crossed the line. Okay, so maybe I didn't discourage his attention, but who could blame me?

"What is it you'd like to talk about?" I asked, picking a splotch of ocher from my thumbnail.

"Brent."

"Hey, I... wait. What?" I stared at her. "Why do you want to talk about Brent? Do you like him or something?"

She crossed her arms. "No. I despise him."

"You *do*? But you two looked so comfortable together on stage and everything. I mean... you kissed him."

"I did *not* kiss *him*. That was not part of our routine, and I let him know it."

Oh! That's how he got the mark on his cheek.

"Listen," she said, dropping her arms and stepping closer to me. "Dean would be pissed if he knew I'd come to talk to you, but Brent is dangerous. You need to be very careful around him."

My head clouded, and I needed to sit down. "I... I really don't understand."

"Just trust me, okay?" She put her hand on the doorknob. "And I'd appreciate it if you kept this conversation between us. Dean isn't pleasant when he's mad."

I opened my mouth to speak, but I couldn't think of anything to say.

She opened the door. "Oh." She paused before leaving. "Looks like Dean and I are riding with you guys to London tomorrow." Then she waved and was gone.

What the hell was that? I was not looking forward to the London trip, even though I really wanted to see the city. But going for a night on the town with Brent, Neely—who apparently hated Brent—and Dean—who made my heart and stomach compete against each other for attention—did not sound like an enjoyable evening. At least Travis would be there to save me.

"You are not allowed to be sick," I said. "You told me you never get sick."

"I know. I'm sorry. I obviously underestimated your ability to get past my defenses. I guess it's time for maintenance on my force field." He blew his nose with a sound like a trumpeting herd of elephants.

"No. I'm sorry." I plunked down in his desk chair and sighed. "I feel horrible that you caught my cold. Is there anything I can do for you?"

Travis coughed, honking like a choking goose, reminding me of my plans to someday visit the London Zoo.

Eric—wearing a scuba mask, snorkel, and bright yellow kitchen gloves—said, "I've got it covered." He picked up Travis's discarded tissues with a pair of tongs.

I poked him in the arm. "You certainly do, Scuba Steve."

"Hey, don't knock it. I've seen *Outbreak*. I know how these things spread." His gray-blue eyes sparkled behind the Plexiglas of the mask.

Travis let out another hacking cough. "I'll be better before you know it."

I patted him on the hand. "I hope so. I hate seeing you so sick."

"No worries. I'm in good gloves... err... hands."

I had to hold in a laugh since Eric really was being sweet. "What do you think I should do about London?"

"I think you should go," Travis said. "But you could always fake a sneeze in Brent's general direction, and then he'll bolt."

"No. I can't. He's looking forward to this."

He tried to sit up a little farther. "So you don't believe Neely?"

"I don't know. The whole thing is so messed up, and it's not as if Neely or Dean have given me an actual *reason* to stay away from Brent." I rubbed my eyes with the heels of my hands. "I kind of wish all three of them would leave me alone."

"Yet you're choosing to go to dinner and the theater with them." He wadded up another pile of used tissues, and the man in the mask reached out his tongs.

"Ugh. Yeah. I don't want to miss out on seeing London, and I really am trying to live outside my studio."

He patted my arm. "Well, I'm proud of you."

"Thanks." I got up and gave him a kiss on the forehead. "You're sure there isn't anything I can do for you?"

"Positive. But I want to hear all about London when you get back."

I climbed into one of the school's sleek black town cars, feeling somewhat like a mafia princess, not to mention a pawn in a three-way chess match among Brent, Neely, and Dean. The car wasn't exactly a limo, but the back seats faced each other. Brent patted the spot beside him, and I settled in across from Dean and Neely. The inside of the vehicle was a sauna, engulfing me in Dean's fresh linen scent almost to distraction. Only the low whisper of a violin's melody drifting from the speakers could rescue me from his pull.

Brent skimmed his hand over the hem of my red Marilyn Monroe dress, brushing my knee in the process. "You look beautiful tonight. I'm glad I spilled punch on this, or we may never have met."

"I'm glad you got it cleaned. It's the only one I brought." I forced a smile as I crossed my ankles to shift my legs away.

"Is that the scarf I gave you?"

"Yes." I tucked the emerald silk under the collar of my black wool dress coat. It wasn't meant to be worn for warmth, but I didn't have another scarf and, despite my new reservations about Brent, I thought he'd like to see me wear it at least once. And my mother would have told me it was the right thing to do.

He stared at me, making me even more uncomfortable, and I could feel the blush blooming on my cheeks.

"It matches your eyes," he finally said.

"Yes," Neely said. "How very *American* of you to wear such bright, festive colors. It's nice that you get to see a bit of London. You've been here what, three months now?" Though she spoke to me, she looked toward Dean.

"Yeah, three months," I said.

"Have you painted since you've been feeling better?" Dean asked.

"A little." I played with one of the buttons on my coat. "I did finish a still life of one of Travis's sculptures."

"It's too bad Travis couldn't join us," Brent said.

I nodded. "Yeah. I wish he hadn't caught my cold."

Brent squeezed my hand and kissed my temple. I bit my lip and suppressed the instinct to cringe at his proximity. Neely turned to stare out the window, but Dean glared at Brent as if in silent challenge, though Brent was too busy looking at me to notice.

We arrived at a French bistro, along with the other students from our school. We were seated at a table together, and as the waiter took our orders, I prayed I'd get food poisoning and be forced to end the evening early. But with my luck, it wouldn't hit until *after* the show we were going to see, and I'd be forced to suffer through the remainder of the evening *and* the puking.

"Libby," Neely said, pulling me from my thoughts, "which side of your family do you get your talent from?"

Dean shot her a look I couldn't read.

"I'm not sure." I shrugged. "My dad's a computer genius, but he couldn't draw a stick figure to save his life. My mom's a nurse, and the only thing she can draw is blood."

Brent laughed, but the other two didn't seem amused. Usually that joke worked to get people off the topic of my genetic background, but Neely wasn't giving up that easily.

"Oh, maybe it skips a generation," she said.

"Maybe," I agreed. "Or maybe I was switched at birth." I tried to make it sound like a joke, but it wasn't far from the truth.

"Would you like to know who your talent came from?" Brent asked as if he could give me the answer to that question.

I smiled at him. "I like to think I'm unique."

"What's your favorite thing you've painted?" Dean asked.

The Dock. "A portrait of my parents." *Let him chew on that for a while.*

He clenched his jaw. "You're not known for your portraits."

"I've only done the one."

He looked as if he might say something else, but the waiter arrived with our dinners, and the conversation changed to schoolwork and the upcoming holidays.

It was dark when we left the restaurant, but London was aglow with holiday lights trimming every street corner. Couples huddled together to keep warm as they walked, avoiding the splashes of slush from passing cars. Brent pointed out some of the sights as we drove through town to the theater. Big Ben loomed in the distance, and my mind conjured images of Peter Pan and Wendy flying by on their way to Neverland. A few drifting snowflakes danced in the lights of the city as we crossed the Tower Bridge.

A foot nudged mine as I leaned over Brent's shoulder to gaze out the car window. I turned to see whose foot it was, and Dean's eyes immediately drew me in like the dark water of the Thames below. He held my gaze like a warm embrace, and it took me several moments to remind myself I was supposed to be on a date with Brent.

We arrived at the Playhouse Theatre about an hour before the performance was scheduled to begin. The restored Victorian building had a rounded façade of light gray stone with *Wicked* in neon lights ablaze above the entryway. The lobby was decorated with posters and props from previous season's performances, including *La Cage Aux Folles* and *Spamalot*. I wished we were seeing one of those, since I really could've used the humor.

After we checked our coats, I excused myself to the ladies' room but told the others not to wait for me. When I came out of the restroom, several other patrons were still mingling in the halls, including Dean, who was looking at one of the marquees.

He noticed me and stepped away from the wall, directly into my path. "You and I need to talk," he said.

"I think we need to find our seats." I tugged at my skirt, wishing I could pull it over my head and hide as I did when I was little.

"We have time." His face and tone were unreadable.

"Look, I admit I was impressed by your dance performance. I appreciate you coming to see me when I was sick, and as far as the other night..." I shook my head. "Anyway, I can't think of even one other thing we might have to talk about, except maybe your girlfriend coming to my room yesterday. Apparently, she feels the same way you do about Brent—which, by the way, is still none of your business. Or hers."

"She did that?" At last an expression: shock.

I crossed my arms. "Yes."

His granite countenance returned. "Well, she's right. But she's not my girlfriend."

"She's... not?" My words caught in my throat, and I couldn't hide the smile that came to my face as my arms fell to my sides.

He took a step closer to me, effectively removing any personal space between us. "Neely and I are close, but not like that." The stone look on his face crumbled away, leaving contentment in its place. Even his eyes relaxed, losing their severe gaze.

I wiped the smile from my lips. "Well, I still don't know what else we could discuss." I needed to regain my composure and get control of the conversation. "And I really think we should find our seats."

"We need to talk about your paintings."

"If my art bothers you that much, then don't look at it. I may have to come watch your"—*Incredible. Exciting. Jaw-dropping. Heart-stopping. Sexy*—"dance performance, but no one is making you look at my paintings."

I attempted to step around him, but he reached out and put a hand on my arm. A blast of warmth shot though me. My heart beat so fast I thought it would burst right out of my chest. Almost instantly, my mind flashed to that secret moment with him backstage, the same level of awareness of his body and mine.

He smirked as if he'd read my thoughts, but there was no malice in his eyes. In fact, he looked amused. "Does Brent know you were watching me on stage and not him?"

"No. I mean..." My cheeks burned.

The lights in the hall blinked off and on, alerting us it was time to take our seats.

He leaned down and brushed my hair off my shoulder. Then he whispered, "By the way, I thought your painting was amazing. I can't wait to see more." His lips grazed my skin, his breath warm on my neck, causing an embarrassing whimper to escape me.

When he pulled away, I grabbed his hand. We stood there, staring at each other, for a long moment. I knew he was holding something back. He had that look on his face often, an expression that said he wanted to tell me something else but couldn't. The lights flickered again. If we didn't take our seats, we wouldn't be allowed in the theater.

Why don't we stay out here together? I don't have anywhere else to be... for the rest of my life.

He released my hand and stepped away. "We should go," he said. "I'm sure Brent is waiting for you."

Crestfallen, I made my way into the auditorium. Dean followed, and I refused to let myself look at him. When we got to our seats, I slid down the aisle past Neely, taking my seat on the other side of Brent, while Dean sat on the end beside Neely.

Brent smiled and leaned over to me as the orchestra began to play. "I was getting worried," he whispered, taking my hand.

The sensation of Brent next to me didn't even compare to what I'd felt with Dean. There was no warmth, no desire to be close to him. The only thing I felt was full from dinner.

"I got lost," I said, pulling my hand from his to retrieve a tissue from my purse. I dabbed my nose then placed my hands in my lap to keep from holding his again. "Dean found me, though."

Like he always does.

Chapter Nine

"That's awesome, Libby." Travis wrapped his arm around my shoulders.

I'd been working on painting a still life of the sculpture he'd given me. Inspiration had eluded me since my trip to London the weekend before, but at least I was painting something.

"Thank you, but it's not as amazing as the actual sculpture."

"I am pretty gifted, aren't I?" He puffed out his chest and tried to keep a straight face, but he couldn't hold it, and we both laughed until he started hacking out a cough.

I scowled at him. "You are gifted, but you *should* be in bed."

He nodded and headed toward my bedroom. "Do you want to eat with Eric and me later?"

I followed him. "Yeah. You can send Scuba Steve to come get me."

"Laugh all you want, but he didn't get sick." He swung my door open to find Madam Harris on the other side. "Uh, hello, ma'am. I was just leaving."

"Mr. Weston, you are in violation of house rules."

"Yes, but Libby's virtue was as safe as if she'd been in a room with my aunt Ruth." He smirked. "On second thought, Libby's virtue was probably *safer* than if she'd been in a room with my aunt Ruth."

Madam Harris continued to stare at Travis until his smirk faded. He shuffled his feet, cleared his throat, and then mumbled an excuse before practically sprinting away.

"I hope I'm not intruding," she said to me from the doorway.

"No. Not at all." I bit my lip. "Would you like to come in?"

She flashed a cheerful smile and stepped into my room but left the door open behind her. "I heard you were feeling much better and joined some of the other students in visiting London. Did you have a nice time?"

"Yes. It was wonderful."

Because I found out Dean isn't with Neely. And it's all I can think about. Even if I don't know what to do about that now.

"A place you could see yourself in the future?" she asked, folding her hands in front of her.

"Absolutely," I said, thinking about Dean, then shook my head to clear the thought. "I mean London is a great place to visit, but I wouldn't want to live there."

"Oh." She looked disappointed. "Well, I hope you visit often once you're done here at Aldridge."

We stood there in an uncomfortable silence for a second, and I thought perhaps the time was right to ask about the painting in her office. But in the extra moment of hesitation, I lost the opportunity.

"Our holiday art show is coming up, and I've come to *insist* you contribute. I'd like to see what you've been working on."

"Uh, sure. Just come back here." I led her into my studio. "This is one of Travis's sculptures." I pointed to the still life on my easel.

"That's beautiful, Libby. If Travis doesn't mind, we could display them together. And how about this one?" She gestured at the bridge scene painting.

"It's not my best," I lied, desperate to steer her away from any paintings that had come to life. "I'd rather select another one."

"But it's quite stunning in its color and composition. I think it will look nice with some of the other pieces. It's decided." She turned, and I hoped she was about to leave without choosing any others. Then, she stopped. Her hand went to her mouth, and she paled. "Where did you get that?"

My insides plummeted when I realized she was pointing to my creek painting. I'd hidden the one with the fence and the orchard behind some other canvases, but had left that one out.

"I painted it a few weeks ago, but I can't display it." I stepped in front of the painting, trying to block her view.

She nudged me out of the way. "But this is exquisite."

I balled my hands into tight fists at my sides.

She turned to look at me. "I really *must* insist." Her voice was stern.

"Yes, ma'am," I said, defeated. I didn't have a choice anyway, since anything I painted while attending Aldridge was technically school property until I graduated.

"Thank you. Now, I should get going." She brushed past me, heading for my bedroom and the open door. "I'm so glad you're feeling better," she said with a final nod. Then she was gone.

I resisted slamming the door, instead closing it gently. I leaned my back against it and slid down to the floor, burying my head in my knees.

So much for feeling better.

In the days leading up to the show, I did little else but worry about my paintings going on display. What if they came to life again? What if my mystery boy showed up while someone else was watching? It was a ridiculous thing to obsess over since it'd never happened before, but I couldn't help it.

The dining hall was set up to look like an art gallery. The pieces were grouped by style, impressionists on one wall, modern art on another, and so forth. One of Kari's drawings hung near the entry, depicting a waterway in Venice, done all in shades of gray as if a cloud had fallen over the city. She drew with colored pencils, and from the few of her pieces I'd seen, she was exceptionally talented. The colors and details were so vivid her work looked more like re-touched photographs than drawings.

My paintings hung on three separate walls. The one I'd done of Travis's sculpture was on a wall above his actual piece and near the other sculpted pieces. The bridge was by the front of the room on a wall with other similar scenes, but the creek stood alone in the center of the room.

A showpiece. The last thing I wanted for one of my "alive" paintings.

I wandered around the outside edges, looking at everyone else's work. Through a break in the display walls, I caught a glimpse of Dean and Neely standing in front of my creek painting. Based on Neely's scowl and Dean's rigid posture, they weren't in the mood to be interrupted. I almost turned away but stopped when Neely pointed at my painting and then to Dean. He'd said they weren't a couple, but by the way she was scolding him, they appeared to be having a lovers' quarrel. *Over my painting?*

"I'm glad you let Madam Harris display the creek," Brent said, coming up next to me.

I let out an embarrassing squeak of surprise.

"Oh, sorry. I didn't mean to scare you."

I fumbled for a response. "No, it's fine. I just didn't see you walk up."

He slipped an arm around my waist. "It really is the best piece in this entire room. It looks like you could step right into it, right onto the tree, cross the creek, and get lost in the woods forever."

"Thank you." I forced a smile, doing my best to hide my discomfort at the thought of other people looking at it. *Someone is lost in those woods.*

We walked around the room for a few minutes, but he seemed distracted and eventually excused himself. Seizing the opportunity, I went to see if Dean and Neely were still arguing. When I peeked around the display, Dean was standing in front of the painting, alone.

The unyielding set of his shoulders and hard line of his jaw gave him the appearance of something strong and unbreakable. Approaching him slowly, I wondered if he liked that painting as much as the one of the orchard. When I reached his side, he turned to look at me. Immediately, his face softened and a small smile came to his lips.

"The most beautiful in the whole room," he said, then reached and brushed my hair off my shoulder, trailing his hand down my arm, making my nerve endings go haywire.

"Thank you." I gulped, unsure if he was talking about me or the painting.

"You didn't want to display this one, did you?" His fingers lingered on mine for a second before he dropped his hand to his side.

"How did you know?" I looked at the base of the fallen tree where my mystery boy had stood. "This one is... personal," I heard myself say. I hadn't decided to, yet there it was.

"Like the orchard?"

There was a double meaning to his statement, but I answered truthfully. "Yes, *exactly* like the orchard."

"I guess I'm lucky I got to see that one then." He watched me with his unnerving indigo eyes.

"You can see lots of my paintings." I picked at my clean nails. "Just look online."

"I'm not interested in those, Libby. I want what you don't share with others."

Are we still talking about art?

He looked over my shoulder. "Brent's coming. I'll see you later." Then he stepped away, taking his warmth with him.

"Promise?" I whispered loudly, surprising myself with the question and already missing him as he strolled toward the door.

Dean gave a slight nod just as Brent reached my side.

"Are you ready to head to the party?" Brent asked.

I bit my lip. "I think I'm going to go back to my room. I'm not feeling well."

He took a half-step away. "You're not getting that cold again, are you?"

"No, no. Just a headache."

"Good. Want me to keep you company?" He took my hand, but I twisted out of his grip.

"Why don't you go and enjoy the party? You can stop by my room in the morning, say ten o'clock?"

He ran his hand through his hair and stared at the floor. "You're sure?"

"Yeah, my head. I'm just not up for company. I'll see you tomorrow." I inched closer to the door, eager to find Dean.

Brent finally gave up and headed toward the ballroom while I left in the opposite direction. The chill of the marble-tiled floors leached through the bottoms of my shoes and into the soles of my feet. I hugged my arms tight to my chest, hoping to conserve any heat I had left as I strode toward the stairs. I spotted Dean coming down a side hall. The sight of him was enough to warm me through to my core, washing away every trace of chill.

"There's something I want to show you," he said as he approached. "But we don't *exactly* have permission to see it."

"What is it?" My voice quivered, both from the sight of him and the excitement of doing something a little mischievous.

He took my hand then looked at me as if to ask if it was okay. I entwined my fingers with his in response, fitting them together like puzzle pieces. His palm was warm against mine, and the hint of a smile crossed his face.

He led me to the main hall and into the gym area. There were several treadmills, ellipticals, and assorted weight machines lining one wall, and frosted glass doors led to the pool and changing rooms. I was about to ask him again where we were going when I heard voices coming from close by. He quickly pulled me through a side door and pressed my back to the wall. Then he shut the door, plunging us into darkness.

Wherever we were, the air felt heavy and smelled of wood. But that was secondary to the feel and scent of him so close to me. He tried to adjust around me, and I felt the push of his hip against mine. Letting go of my hand, he braced his arms against the wall on either side of me. My eyes were taking a long time to adjust, and I reached out, searching for something tangible, and ended up pressing my hand to the smooth planes of his muscled chest.

More voices and giggling came from outside the door, and I felt his body tense, his heart beating rapidly beneath my fingertips. My heart beat just as fast as his, but not because I was afraid of being discovered.

"Dean?" I slid my hand up to his neck then grabbed a fistful of his shirt with my other hand.

"Shh."

Fine. If you don't want to talk, we don't have to talk. I pulled him to me with both hands and pressed my lips to his. He was probably as shocked at my forwardness as I was, but then his mouth relaxed on mine, and his arm came down from the wall to encircle my waist, crushing me against him.

I had known he was strong, but I'd never imagined him as gentle. So when his other hand cradled the back of my head and he weaved his fingers into my hair, I let out a little moan. My toes curled, my stomach danced, and my arms trembled around his neck. Of the few times I'd been kissed, it had never been like that. I felt completely exposed yet totally safe at the same time.

Too soon, he pulled away. I slowly lowered my hands and rested them on his sides, just above his hips.

He trailed his fingers up and down my arm then leaned closer, his hot breath on my ear. "You surprised me," he whispered.

"Was it a good surprise?" I asked, hoping I hadn't made a huge fool of myself.

He dragged his lips from my ear and ran them gently across my cheek, leaving a sizzle in their wake. "Yes," he said, just before his mouth met mine again.

The second time he pulled away, he did it reluctantly. "As much as I'd like to stay here with you..." He let out a heavy sigh then took my hand.

I wanted to stay there with him too, enclosed in our private cocoon, but I knew it wasn't possible.

He opened the door to the tiny room, which I realized was a one-person sauna, and looked around before leading me away. It was hard for me to pay close attention to where we were going since my head was still foggy from our kiss and thinking about when we would kiss again, but I knew we were exiting the gym on the opposite side and entering a tucked-away hall. We stood still for a second before he looked down at me with a soft expression and put his arm around my waist. Then he ushered me across the hall and through a door on the right.

"Where are we?" I whispered.

He pointed at a door beyond the one we'd just come through. "Through there is Madam Harris's office."

I bounced, tugging on his arm like a child. "Is it locked?"

He reached in his pocket and pulled out a small ring with a single key. "Not for long." With a quiet click, he opened the door.

There was my chance to see the other painting, so why couldn't I seem to move my feet? They were rooted in place, and as much as I wanted to move forward, I couldn't connect that message from my brain into my legs. Then, as if he knew exactly what was going on, Dean put his arm around me, gently nudging me ahead.

The first thing I saw was a mammoth mahogany desk, but behind that was the painting I'd submitted with my application. I stared at the image of the heavy, dark wooden door with its curved black iron handle on the right side and a small square caged cutout near the top for peeking through. My eyes darted over the stone stoop and frame, seeking out what felt different.

I knew that piece. I remembered working on it. And if memory served, I'd finished it rather quickly before packing it up to ship. Then it hit me. "Dean, this isn't mine."

"What makes you say that?" He moved to stand at my left.

"The door." I pointed at it. "It's closed. I painted a similar scene, but I painted mine with the door slightly ajar."

He hung his head as if defeated. Then he took my shoulders and spun me around to look at the painting on the wall behind us.

It's the exact same image!

"I don't understand. How can this be?"

"We should go. We don't want to get caught in here."

He had to drag me from the room. We didn't go back through the gym. Instead, he took me through another maze of hallways that eventually led to a set of stairs. "This will take you up to your floor." His hand abandoned mine, and he stepped away.

"Where are you going?" My entire body shook, rattling my teeth like a winter wind blowing through me. I couldn't bear the thought of him walking away and leaving me alone in the cold.

"To the party." He moved closer and rubbed my arms.

I shivered again and goose bumps pebbled my skin, but not from the chill. "You're not going after… after… I mean, you've got to explain."

He took my hands, swirling his thumbs across my wrists. "Do me a favor." He kept his voice low, and I found myself transfixed by his dark, pleading eyes, completely out of character for him since he always seemed so in control. "Break things off with Brent and stay away from him."

I continued to stare into his eyes until I remembered what I'd said to Brent earlier. "I told Brent to come find me in the morning."

"Do not let him in your room or near your paintings." Dean put his hands on my cheeks, his eyes shifting from pleading to severe. He kissed my forehead then wrapped his arms around me. "I'll keep an eye on him, but I don't want him to know. Just be as safe as you can, okay?"

I melded against him, soaking up the warmth pouring through his soft cotton shirt. I nodded into his chest then felt him kiss the top of my head. He let go of me and disappeared into the dark hall. Gulping air into my lungs, I raced up the stairs and went directly to Travis's room. I had to knock several times while bouncing up and down. Just when I'd decided to walk away, I heard him flip the lock.

Travis opened the door wide enough for me to see he had a serious case of bed head. "Hey."

"I really need to talk to you," I said in a rush.

"Um…" He looked behind him, over his shoulder. "It's sort of not a good time."

"Oh? *Oh.*" I grimaced, realizing Eric was probably in there with him.

"It's all right," Eric said from within the room. "Sounds important."

Travis opened the door wider.

Eric put on his shirt and walked over. "I'll see you later." He kissed Travis on the cheek then looked at me. "He's all yours." He winked then patted my shoulder and left.

"I'm really sorry," I told Travis as I went into his room.

He closed the door. "It's fine, Libs." He waved it off then coughed lightly.

He'd gotten better much faster than anyone I'd ever known. Vitamin E for Eric, maybe, and apparently Eric didn't feel the need to wear a hazmat suit anymore. "What's going on?"

I sat down on the end of his bed, and the whole evening's events came tumbling out of my mouth in a rush. "You have to tell me what to do!" I put my face in my hands.

He chuckled and wrapped his arm around me. "Don't you think it's pretty obvious what you should do?"

"I know," I said, dropping my hands to my lap then picking at my nails. In the past few months, they'd been cleaner than ever, but only because I'd been nervous more often. "Brent's never done anything bad to me, though. He's always been really sweet."

"Yes, but you've always kept him at a distance. How many times have you told me there's no spark? He's initiated everything... often. Tonight, *you* initiated things with Dean."

"You're right." I sighed then snuggled into him. "I'm really sorry for busting in on you and Eric."

"Your timing was tragic, but I forgive you." He rubbed my arm, and I closed my eyes, thankful for my one uncomplicated relationship with a boy. "Oh, I want to give you something."

We both sat up, and he leaned over to open his top desk drawer. Something crinkled in his hand before he pressed a strip of condoms into my palm.

"And why are you giving me these?"

He settled back on the bed and put his arms behind his head. "Better safe than sorry."

"I think my real question is why are you giving them to me now?"

"Well, I was pretty sure you wouldn't need them with Brent. But with Dean..." He waggled his eyebrows suggestively.

"You think you know me so well." I shoved the strip in my pocket then plopped down next to him.

He laughed. "I don't *think*. I *know*."

The morning of December 23rd, the school emptied out quickly as students and faculty left for the holidays, but several others, including Travis and me, remained. It was easier for him to deal with his parents from a distance, and while I missed mine, we'd decided that I shouldn't risk getting sick again from being on a plane. Also, it would be a lot of travel for too little time together.

Unfortunately, staying meant I had to deal with the business of breaking up with Brent. Travis was right. Brent had initiated most everything in our relationship, and I had just been along for the ride. Passive. Whether or not what Neely and Dean said about him was true, I didn't want to waste any more of Brent's time or mine by sleepwalking through a relationship that would never go anywhere.

Three sharp raps on my door pulled me from my thoughts. I didn't want to embarrass Brent by breaking up with him in the hall, so I made sure my studio door was shut before I answered the knocking.

"Let me in, quick." Travis pushed into my room before I could get a word out.

"What are you doing? Brent will be here any minute."

"I know. He's on his way up. I'll hide in your studio while you break up with him."

"Travis, what are you—"

Another knock cut me off.

"Don't let him stay too long and don't tell him I'm here," Travis said in a low voice then went into my studio and hid before I could argue with him.

"Libby, are you in there?" Brent said.

"Um... yeah..." I opened the door in a mild state of shock at Travis's behavior.

"You look pretty this morning." Brent stepped into my room and leaned in to kiss my cheek, but I shied away from him. "Uh oh, what's wrong? You're upset I went to the party."

"No." My mouth went dry as though I'd shoved a roll of paper towel in it.

"Okay." He leaned against the wall. "What is it then?"

"I don't think we should see each other anymore." I blurted out the words, more flustered by the fact that Travis was listening to the whole exchange than by the conversation itself.

"What?" His eyes filled with fury. He pushed himself away from the wall, and I realized I'd taken a step back. "Bloody hell, Libby! Do you know how much work I've put into this? I thought—" He stopped and held up a finger. "That tosser, Dean, finally got to you, didn't he?"

I flinched then crossed my arms. "I'm not talking about him with you."

"Fine, I understand." He flung my suite door open so hard it bounced off the wall. "Merry fucking Christmas." He slammed the door behind him.

I could have handled that *better. But it's done.*

I sat on the end of my bed just as Travis stepped out of my studio. "Good riddance," he said.

"What on earth is going on with you this morning?"

"Come on. We have to go."

The hall was filled with students as Travis dragged me toward his room. He opened his door and shoved me right into Dean's arms.

"What took you so long?" Dean's voice was strained. "Are you okay? Did he hurt you?"

"I wouldn't have let him." Travis shut the door and stepped around us to walk over to the bed.

"I'm fine," I said, utterly confused but glad Dean was worried about me. "Brent didn't do anything. Wait," I pulled back a little. "Why are you in Travis's room?"

"Libby," Travis said, "I think you'd better sit down."

Chapter Ten

"WHY DO I NEED TO sit down?" I looked between Travis and Dean. "What's going on?"

Before either of them had a chance to respond, someone knocked on the door. Dean and Travis both froze in place. *As if I wasn't already on edge.*

Dean stepped around me and opened the door.

Neely sauntered in without an invitation. "He went to the weight room," she told Dean as she brushed past him. "He'll probably be there for a while."

"Are you talking about Brent? Why are you watching him?" I looked at Travis. "Do you know what's going on?"

Travis came over and took my arm. "You really need to sit." He led me to the edge of his bed and sat down next to me. "I'm only this much ahead of you." He held up his thumb and forefinger about a centimeter apart. "I promise."

Neely glanced at me with her perfect almond-shaped eyes then moved across the room with a ballerina's grace and sat down in the desk chair. I wasn't sure what annoyed me more, the fact that I had no idea what was going on or that Neely *did*. I'd never had a clique, posse, or circle of friends before, and so it was weird to realize I had one at the academy, yet I was still somehow out of the loop. Dean shut the door then hesitated for a moment before standing across from me and leaning against the wall. A sinking feeling came over me when he didn't sit next to me or kneel in front of me, or anything to let me know he felt the same way I did, especially after last night.

"I'm sorry we've had to be so secretive," Dean said, hooking his thumbs in his jean pockets as though he was attempting to be relaxed but failing. "Brent really is dangerous, especially to you." A little hope bloomed when he looked at me with the same worry on his face as when I'd come into the room.

"You keep saying that," I said, "but why?" It was like being left out of my own secret.

"Because if he gets the chance, he'll trap you like he trapped Ryan," Neely said.

"Wait. Ryan?" I looked at her then at Dean again. "You mean the kid who left school?"

"He never actually *left*," Dean said.

I shook my head, more frustrated than I was a second ago. "I have no idea what you're talking about."

"You see"—Dean shifted his weight from one foot to the other—"Ryan is a painter with an unusual talent, much like yours. Brent is a painter too, but not nearly as good as you and Ryan."

"A painter. He said he was *undecided,* but I thought he meant between acting and dancing." *Painting, wow.*

Neely crossed her arms. "Well, he's awfully good at acting."

"Brent has many talents," Dean said. "But his jealousy of others gets in his way, which is why we think he wants to trap you. We think he's pretending to like you so he can get close to you, get you to trust him."

"Stop." I put up my hand. "What do you mean by 'trap me'? And it sure didn't feel like he was pretending." *Unless that's why he never kissed me.*

"Like I told you..." Neely shuddered. "He's a good actor. BAFTA worthy."

"Neely!" Dean said, but she just rolled her eyes. "As I was saying..." He glared at her then went on. "Ryan's paintings are a lot like yours. They come to life, and in addition to that, Ryan knows how to *enter* them. He's been able to travel from painting to painting for a long time. Brent somehow found out what Ryan was doing and discovered a way to make it so he couldn't get out."

"Uh... paintings are inanimate objects, in case you hadn't noticed." I tried to arch one eyebrow and radiate concern and skepticism. I probably just looked crazy.

"Sweetie..." Travis put his hand over mine. "I think it's okay if you tell them. In fact, I think they already know." He gave me an encouraging, best-friend smile.

"Fine," I said. "Some of my paintings come to life, but I can't go *in* them. At least, I've never tried to."

"And the boy?" Neely snapped.

Dean pressed his palm to his forehead. "Neely, could you please chill out?"

"You might as well tell her." She waved her arm in my direction. "Dragging it out isn't going to make it better."

Dean dropped his arm to his side and looked at me. *This is it. He's finally going to say what he's been keeping from me all this time.*

"Wait a second," Travis nearly shouted, startling me. "You think...? Holy shit."

And then it hit me too, and a pit grew deep in my stomach. "You think Ryan is the boy you saw in the orchard?" I asked Dean.

Dean nodded slowly.

"For God's sake, Dean," Neely said. "Tell her already."

"I... I don't know how that could be." I studied the beige flecks in the rug. "I've never met Ryan, and you said he could go into his own paintings, but you didn't say anything about going into other people's. And even if he could, why mine?"

Dean shuffled his feet. "I said he could move from painting to painting, but not just anybody's—yours specifically."

I stared up at Dean. "You still haven't told me why!"

"I can't prove this"—he cleared his throat, clearly stalling—"but we think Ryan is... your twin brother."

My head spun. The whole room went blurry, and I had to grip Travis's hand to keep from fainting. "I don't have any siblings," I said, though my mouth had trouble with the words, and I was sure they hadn't come out clearly. "I'm an only child."

"But your mom and dad aren't your biological parents, are they?" Dean asked.

I jumped up and pointed at him. "You don't know the first thing about me."

Dean pushed himself away from the wall and looked down at me. "I *know* I saw Ryan in that orchard. I know he's been in other paintings of yours. And I know both of you painted the exact same wooden door in those paintings hanging in Madam Harris's office."

I wasn't a crier, but my eyes began to sting, and the tears threatened to fall. "No one knows I'm adopted, except..." I looked at Travis.

He held up his hands. "I didn't say anything. I swear."

"I know you wouldn't," I whispered as I sat down beside him again. He wrapped his arm around my shoulders.

"And there it is," Neely said triumphantly, then looked at Dean. "Are you happy now?"

"That's enough," he said to her.

"No, it is *not* enough! I've been waiting for months for you to say something, and I'm tired of it. I just want Ryan out of that damn painting." Her voice cracked, and she turned away. I'd forgotten about Travis saying Neely was Ryan's girlfriend, but it all made sense. She and Dean were close because they both cared for Ryan.

I took a deep, shuddering breath. If what Dean was telling me was true, I needed to know more. "So about Ryan," I said as calmly as I could. "Why do you think he's my brother?"

A hint of a smile played on Dean's lips as he leaned against the wall again. "Ryan and I were both orphans, foster brothers I guess you could say. *Not* biological. Shortly before he came here to the academy, he saw a picture of you outside an art gallery. He said he thought he recognized you from painting popping—that's what he calls it. At first, he thought maybe you just had the same gift as him, but not long after that, Madam Harris saw him painting in a park and offered to waive his tuition if he'd come to school here. Once he was here, he sort of became obsessed, and that's when he started saying you were his sister. He mailed you the school's information and went into as many paintings as he could to see you. I kept telling him he shouldn't, but every time he saw you, he was more and more convinced you were related. Then, almost ten months ago, your painting of the door arrived. Ryan wanted to see if he could go into it the same way he could go in his own. I told him it was a bad idea, but..."

"He did it anyway," I finished for him.

"Ryan's never been able to go into anyone else's paintings, Libby. And believe me, he's tried." Dean reached into his pocket and pulled out a piece of paper. "There's also this." It looked like it had been folded and refolded a hundred times. His hand trembled when he gave it to me.

"Where did you get this?" I asked, staring at the watercolor painting through more tears.

"Ryan painted that just before his fourth birthday. Do you recognize it?"

I nodded. The painting had rolling green hills, a blue sky with puffy clouds, and on one of the distant hills was a small tree. It was the same watercolor I'd painted when I was three, the same one that currently hung in a frame at home.

"That was the first picture Ryan went into," Dean said. "I was so scared when he disappeared. All of a sudden, he was gone."

"Hey," Travis whispered to me. "You're shaking."

"I'm... I'm just..."

"I know this is a lot to take in, Libby," Dean's voice was soft in a way I'd never heard it.

"This is the first picture I saw him in," I said, trying to keep my own voice even. "My parents thought he was an imaginary friend. I didn't see him again for a long time."

"He didn't paint again for a long time," Dean said. There was something more to his comment, but I let it go for the moment. "I'm sorry you got dragged into this. I told Ryan there had to be a better way to learn about you."

"It's okay. I mean, I understand him wanting to get to know me." I looked at Travis, and he hugged my shoulders tighter. "And this"—I held up the watercolor—"is awfully convincing evidence."

I returned the paper to Dean, and he carefully slid it back into his pocket. "Why now?" I asked. "Why didn't you tell me sooner?"

"I've wanted to tell you several times." He pressed his left hand to his thigh as if the muscle ached. "I almost did in London, but I couldn't be sure Ryan was right. I mean, until I saw him in the orchard, that is. But then, I wasn't positive you knew you were adopted. I also didn't think you trusted me."

"What changed?" I wondered out loud then saw the corner of his mouth turn up, and he raised his eyes to mine. "Oh." My cheeks warmed, remembering our kiss from the night before and happy that it made him look at me like that.

"Okay," Neely said. "We've established that Libby is most likely Ryan's sister and that they can both paint some crazy stuff. *Now* can we talk about rescuing Ryan? I mean, that *is* the whole point here."

"I understand that this is a lot to take in." Dean sighed and gave me an apologetic look. "But we need to figure out how Brent locked Ryan in that painting and keep him from doing the same thing to you."

"How do you know it was Brent?" Travis voiced the same question on my mind.

"We just know it was Brent, okay?" Neely said, though it was more of a mumble, and she quickly looked away again.

Dean glanced at her, his expression unreadable.

"Hey!" I sat up straighter on the bed. "*I'm* the one who dated him all that time. I think I deserve to know why you think he's behind all of this."

"I fucked him, all right?" Neely twisted around and looked right at me. "Though you may as well say *I'm* the one who got fucked. I knew Ryan was going into that painting, and when he didn't check in with me like he normally did, I got worried. I tried to find him, but he wasn't in his room, and no one had seen him. I don't know what I thought I was going to do, but I went to Madam Harris's office to try anything. When I got there, someone was climbing out of the painting. I thought it was Ryan, since I'd seen him do that before, but then I saw that it was Brent. I didn't know what to do. He said Ryan wasn't getting out and that I might as well forget about him. I knew Brent liked me, and I thought maybe if I... well, obviously it didn't work, since we're here and Ryan is still in there."

I closed my mouth when I realized it was hanging open. "I didn't—"

"Just forget it. I try to." She lowered her head. "I can't believe I ever liked him," she said so low I almost didn't hear it.

Everything clicked into place. I still disliked her, but I couldn't deny we had something in common—Brent had used us both.

"So..." Travis dragged out the word, breaking some of the tension. "Why did Madam Harris tell everyone Ryan left for family reasons if she knew his only family was you, Dean?"

"I think she's been hiding Ryan's disappearance because it would be bad publicity for the school. Plus she doesn't know my connection to Ryan."

"Why haven't you told her?" I asked. "Maybe if she knew, she could help."

"I, for one, don't trust her," Neely said sharply, still looking away from us.

"Yes, well..." Dean cleared his throat. "I didn't want it getting back to Brent that Ryan was my brother, and since I knew your painting was here, I figured you'd be coming too."

"That's when you decided to enroll," I said.

Dean nodded. "I moved to London after Ryan started school here. We didn't talk every day, but when I couldn't get in contact with him for over a week, I began to worry. I was working for a performing group in the city, and a guy there knew Madam Harris. He helped me get into the school even though I'm a little older than the other students. Ryan and I don't have the same last name, and we don't look alike, so no one would have guessed I knew him."

"You do look alike, though." Ryan's posture was ingrained in my head, and that was why Dean had always seemed so familiar. They both held their right shoulder a little lower than their left, and they had the same habit of rubbing their left hand on their leg then putting it into a pocket.

"We're not related, Libby," he said, but I couldn't tell if he meant him and Ryan or him and me. He slumped down to sit on the floor. "Anyway, I was able to enroll about a month after Ryan went missing. He'd mentioned Neely a few times, so I sought her out, and she told me about Brent trapping Ryan."

"Yeah," Travis said, "and I'm the one who pushed you into dating him."

"It's not your fault," Dean told him. "I'm the one who should have said something sooner."

I sighed. "Well, I know now."

Dean looked up at me from his spot on the floor, his eyes somewhat guarded. "Take as much time as you need with all of this." Then he shrugged. "Ryan's not going anywhere."

"Oh, I didn't mean it that way," I said, afraid I'd offended him. "I want to help, especially if he's my brother." I knew I'd need some time to process that. "I just don't know what I can do. I mean… I've never tried to actually go *into* any of my paintings."

"It's okay." Dean stood up again and stretched his long legs. "We'll figure it out. But for now, I think we all need to return to our normal routines. Brent won't get as suspicious that way."

"Um, about that…" I looked down at my hands and picked my nails. "Brent already figured out I broke up with him because of…" I glanced up at Dean.

He stood perfectly still. The stone wall instantly went up in his eyes, and his face hardened. His abrupt change in demeanor made my heart ache in a way I'd never experienced before, as if someone had ripped it out and stomped all over it, leaving a bloody mess on the ground and a hole where it used to be.

"You'll just have to keep a low profile," Dean said. "And don't go to the other side of the school unless you absolutely have to. How many paintings of yours have come to life while you've been here?"

"Four," I said, swallowing down the lump in my throat. "The creek, the orchard, the bridge, and one other."

"Hmm, the creek and the bridge are still in the dining hall, so try to avoid that too. Where are the others?" he asked in a very business-only tone.

"My studio."

"All right." Dean moved toward the door. "I'll walk you to your room and help you find a place to hide them. I don't want any chance for Brent to get you into one of them. Neely, could you go keep a lookout for him until I get back to our side of the building? And Travis, do you think Eric could help us keep an eye on things as well?"

"Yeah, I'll go talk to him now while you're stashing the paintings. I should also report Brent."

"For what? Being a first class asshole?" Neely stood to leave.

Travis laughed. "I agree with you, but no. For being in Libby's room."

"But I invited him."

Dean scowled. "Even though I told you not to."

"Again, you gave me no reason *why*. And I wasn't about to break things off with him in the middle of the hall."

"Fine." Dean lowered his eyes to the door handle. "But we can't report him since we may still need Brent to get Ryan out, so we don't want him getting expelled."

Travis and I stood up while Dean waited by the door, and Neely left without so much as a good-bye.

"It's all going to be fine," Travis whispered in my ear, clutching me to him.

My body had started shaking again as I nodded into his chest. Though I thought he was trying to convince himself as much as console me. I held him tightly then stepped away and went out the door with Dean. My stomach rumbled as we crossed the hall, and I could have sworn I heard Dean trying to hold in a laugh.

"We can stop in the kitchen," he said.

"I'm not really that hungry."

"You should eat though." He placed his palm on the small of my back and veered me into the kitchen.

His hand warmed me like a heating pad against my spine, both pleasant and painful at the same time. *I don't want to feel like this for him if he doesn't feel the same.*

I made a turkey sandwich while he stood in the doorway watching me and the hallway at the same time. The emotionless wall was still up on his face. Everything that had transpired between us before had been because he needed me to rescue his brother. *My brother?* How had I been so wrong?

When we got to my room, I set my sandwich down on the desk. He shut the door then followed me into my studio.

"I don't know where you want to hide them," I said. The orchard and the other painting were against the far wall. "I can't burn—"

"No, of course not. I don't want you to destroy any of your work. Ever."

I felt my stomach clench at the thought of my art going up in flames with my brother—*brother?*—perhaps trapped inside.

He stood in front of the two paintings and hung his head slightly. "That night," he said, "the night you said you were going to burn your paintings, then asked Brent to walk you to your room, I was so worried I wouldn't get to you in time, that Brent would trap you before I ever had a chance to..."

I held my breath. I wanted him to finish what he was saying. But when he did, it wasn't what I wanted to hear, and the wound in my chest ached even more.

"I was afraid I'd never get the chance to tell you about Ryan."

"I'll do what I can to help." I picked my nails, feeling completely humiliated for kissing him last night. Yesterday, I was a girl with two guys into her; today, I was un-datable.

"Libby"—he reached toward me then let his hand drop again—"I'm really grateful, and I'm sorry about all of this. I wish—"

"It's not your fault." I cut him off and grabbed one of the paintings. "Just like it isn't Travis's fault. We can hide these in my closet. There's a small gap between the wall and the built-in drawers where I think they'll fit."

He stood still for a minute and watched me, then picked up the other painting. The two of them fit nicely in the space and were covered by the clothes in my closet. When we exited the bathroom, he went to the door and paused there.

"You could stay," I said. "If you want."

"I forced Ryan to come here," he said abruptly. "He didn't want to leave the States, and I convinced him this would be a better life for him. So yes, this is my fault, and I'm not going to let my mistake ruin your life too." He left my room so fast I didn't even have a chance to respond.

Chapter Eleven

"MERRY CHRISTMAS, SWEETHEART," MOM SAID. "Did you open your gifts?"

Calling my parents on the phone certainly wasn't the same as being home, but it was at least a small amount of normalcy after the past few days of being on an emotional rollercoaster. First kissing Dean, then ending things with Brent, and of course, finding out about Ryan.

"They're perfect," I said. "I love the vanilla body wash. The stuff the school supplies dries out my skin. And I really needed some new jeans."

"Well, with all the painting you've been doing, I was pretty sure you'd ruined a few pairs by now."

"Yeah... painting."

"What's wrong? Not enough time to paint? That *is* what you're there for." I could hear the concern in her voice.

"I've had plenty of time, but some of the kids—"

"Aren't they being nice to you? I thought you were making friends. If someone is bothering you, you should talk to Ms. Harris. She seemed very kind when you were sick. I think she really enjoys having you there at the school." Somehow, she managed to spit all that out without taking a breath.

"No one is being mean, Mom." No one I could tell her about anyway. "And yes, Madam Harris is nice."

"Then tell me what's bothering you. Wait. I'm putting your father on the phone."

"Mom, I—" There was no use trying to stop her. She'd already called for my dad to pick up the other line.

"Merry Christmas! How's my favorite daughter?"

Usually his endearment toward me made me smile. Sure, I was his *only* daughter, so being his favorite was redundant, but I still liked it... normally. My parents and I rarely talked about my adoption, and they'd certainly never said anything about me having a brother out there somewhere. I'd like to think, if they'd known, they would have tried to adopt him as well.

"Am I an only child?" I blurted.

"Of course you are. Why would you ask such a silly question?" my mom retorted.

"I think what your mother is trying to say is that you grew up in this house with just us, so it's alarming to hear you ask that."

"I know. I know. It's just..." I had no idea how to explain what I was asking without coming right out and saying it, but I was almost afraid to hear their answer. Thank goodness they knew me well enough to read between the lines.

"Libby." My father used the voice he reserved for when I needed to pay strict attention to him. "We've never kept the fact that you were adopted from you, but due to the circumstances, there is no way for us to know if you have siblings out there. The man at the agency told us you were available for immediate adoption, and at the time, we were just so happy to have a baby we never even considered asking if you had any brothers or sisters."

"But if I had..." My voice squeaked.

"We most certainly would have kept you together," Mom said. "Is there a reason you're asking now?"

I hesitated. I wanted to tell them about Ryan in the worst way, but my mouth wouldn't form the words. And how would I ever explain the fact that my imaginary friend from my childhood was a flesh-and-blood person popping in and out of my paintings?

"Are you there, sweetheart?"

"Yes, I'm here. I should probably go, though. Some of the other kids want to use the phone." I was the only one in the student lounge, but I'd already said enough to ruin one Christmas morning.

"All right," Dad said in a softer tone. "Oh, did you get your mints? Your mom didn't think they would travel well."

"Yeah, I got them, and they taste perfect. Thanks, Dad. Love you. Merry Christmas."

"Love you, too, sweetheart. We'll talk soon."

"I love you, too," Mom said. "I miss you." Her voice cracked.

"I miss you, too. I'll call after New Year's, okay?"

"Any time. I'm always happy to hear your voice."

"Thanks, Mom. Bye."

"Good-bye, sweetie," and the line went quiet.

Great! I managed to freak my parents out on the first Christmas I've ever been away.

A little while later, Travis and Eric showed up wearing coordinating reindeer sweaters—Travis in green with a dancing Vixen and Eric in red with Cupid sporting a bow and arrow. They brought a white one for me with a blinking-nosed Rudolph, and I reluctantly threw it on with my new jeans. We spent the better part of the afternoon eating sugar cookies with frosting and watching all my favorite Christmas movies, including *It's a Wonderful Life, Meet Me in St. Louis,* and the original *Miracle on 34th Street* with Natalie Wood.

Eric also brought me an envelope from Dean. When I opened it, I found a Christmas card and an image of two young boys. The picture looked as though it came from one of those photo booths in the mall. Inside the card was written, *This was taken right before Ryan came to Aldridge.*

I recognized both of them right away. I knew their faces so intimately it frightened me. Dean was handsome, of course, but I could see the beginnings of the stone wall forming on his face. Ryan looked... like me. We had the same green eyes, only his were sadder than mine. And the longer I studied his face, the angrier I got at Brent. How could he have been so crazed with jealousy to hold someone hostage like that? I tucked the picture away where no one would happen upon it but where I could easily get to it if I wanted.

The next day, I retreated to my studio. I sat at my easel for hours trying to think of a way to get Ryan out. Sometimes I would paint, but other times, I would just sit and stare at a blank canvas. I tried to recreate the door painting, hoping it would give me the key to rescuing Ryan. My attempts were futile, though, since when I tried to repaint it with the door open like I had originally, it slammed shut on its own.

Travis practically moved into my suite, doing everything there except sleep and shower. I worried he wasn't spending enough time with Eric or getting any sculpting done, but every time I asked him, he said my safety came first and Eric understood that. He jumped when someone knocked on my door.

"Will you calm down? Do you really think Brent would just show up and knock?" I asked as I went to answer it.

"Yes, and you'd better ask who it is first." He stepped in front of me.

"Fine." I rolled my eyes at him. "Who is it?" I asked in a singsong voice, expecting it to be Eric but hoping it was Dean.

"Hey, it's Kari."

"Oh!" I opened the door. "Hi, come on in."

"Thanks. Hi, Travis." She walked in and stood by the bed. "It's pretty quiet around here with everybody still gone."

I shut my suite door. "You're back early, though."

"Yeah, my dad had business in Tokyo, and I didn't feel like hanging at home alone. He got me this awesome mani-pedi set. Well, I'm sure his assistant bought it, but I thought maybe we could do our nails together." She looked at me hopefully.

"I'd love to," I said, grabbing Travis's arm and pulling him toward the door. "Is now a good time? Travis was just leaving."

"I wasn't—" Travis started.

"Sure you were. You just didn't know yet."

He scowled, then his face softened, and he pulled me into a hug. "You win," he whispered, "but I'll be back soon."

A half hour later, Kari and I sat on my bed as we finished lacquering our toes with bubblegum pink polish.

"I can't tell you how much I appreciate you coming over."

She gaped at me. "Really?"

"Absolutely. Besides the fact that I needed a pedicure pretty badly, Travis has been a little clingy lately." I screwed the cap onto the polish and set the bottle on my desk.

"Did something happen between him and Eric?"

"No... um, between me and Brent."

Her mouth fell open for a second before she snapped it shut again. "Are you okay?"

I had no idea how to answer that question other than to lie. "I'm great." I blew on my nails to avoid saying any more.

"Well, that's good. I mean, if you're happy about it."

"Happy about breaking up with Brent? You have no idea."

New Year's Eve came and went, and other than a few messages relayed through Eric telling me Brent wasn't acting any different than usual, I hadn't seen or heard from Dean in days. I knew we were supposed to keep a low profile, but the whole scene was ridiculous.

I paced my room, waiting for an epiphany, something that would help me find Ryan, something that would bring me closer to wherever he was and hopefully closer to seeing Dean again. "Travis, I have to get out of here."

"Okay," he said while playing solitaire on my laptop. "Do you want to go to the kitchen or the lounge?"

"No, like out out."

He stopped playing his game and looked up at me. "It's the middle of winter, and it's been snowing for days. I don't really think you want to go outside."

"We could go see Eric," I said hopefully.

"Uh, *that's* not going to happen." He slammed the laptop shut. "It's too dangerous, and we don't know what Brent's doing right now."

"You mean after all the times you spent trying to get me out of my studio and into the real world, *now* you're okay with me locked up in here?"

"No, I'm not *okay* with it. And you *can* leave your studio. But I'm not letting you go to that side of the school."

"Please, Travis." I folded my hands in front of me and gave him my best pouty face. "I don't want to end up like van Gogh. I like my ears."

"You're killing me. You know that, right?"

I did know it, and I smiled. He'd spent so much time looking after me that he'd barely been able to see Eric, so the prospect of doing both things was irresistible to him.

"I suppose we could go help paint some sets for the winter play. There will be lots of people around, and I'm sure Eric would appreciate the help of a skilled painter like you."

I jumped up and hugged him. Then I stopped when a thought hit me. "Brent's not in the play, is he?"

"No." Travis laughed. "Eric wouldn't cast him."

Twenty minutes later, we were getting instructions from Eric, who did appreciate us coming to help. He set us up in the greenroom with six large panels and gave us the basic idea for the set, but he pretty much left it up to me to create something. They were doing a production of *Enchanted April.* It was mostly set in an Italian villa, and there was a whole thing about the wisteria.

I set out to create an elegant flowered backdrop. Twisted limbs formed trellises dripping with the lavender and milky white flowers, while fountains sculpted with cherubs dotted the lush green lawn.

When I finished the second panel, I needed more green and blue paint, so Travis ran to the supply area to find some. He wasn't even gone a second when I felt someone in the room with me. I looked around, thinking it was another worker, but when I glanced at the first panel I'd finished, I saw Ryan sitting on the bench I'd painted.

"Ryan!"

He smiled and nodded as if he could hear me and was happy I knew who he was.

I checked to make sure no one else was coming, not wanting to look like a complete nutcase while talking to a piece of painted foam. "Dean told me everything, and I'm really trying to help, but I just can't seem to get anything right. And since I have no idea how you got in there, I feel like I'm just going in circles and—"

He held up his hand to stop my rambling, and I snapped my mouth shut. Then, *he* talked to *me*. It was broken and garbled, but his mouth moved, and I could make out some of the words.

"Wait," I said. "What about a key? And what pond? I haven't painted a pond."

But he vanished again.

"I *thought* I heard you," a voice said from behind me.

I turned around and gasped when I saw Brent standing a few feet away. "What are *you* doing here?"

"I could ask you the same thing." He leered. "And where's your entourage?"

"What entourage? I came to help Eric."

"You and Dean have a tiff?"

"Not that it's any of your business, but I haven't seen Dean in days." I stepped back to create more distance between us.

He narrowed his eyes, scrutinizing me. "Then who were you talking to?"

"Myself. Artistic temperament."

Brent opened his mouth to reply, but Travis appeared in the doorway loaded down with paint cans.

"I think I got every—" His eyes fell on Brent, and all the cans crashed to the floor as Travis rushed to step between Brent and me. "She doesn't have anything to say to you, so I suggest you leave."

"She has plenty to say, and we were just having a friendly chat that I'd like to continue someplace more… private." He held out his hand as though he expected me to take it. "Would you come with me?" His voice was almost pleading.

"She's not going anywhere with you." Travis slapped Brent's hand away. "Libby, go find Eric."

I backed up more, but Brent advanced and Travis shoved him. Brent stumbled a little then raised a fist. My stomach dropped to my toes, and I screamed as his fist connected with Travis's cheek. Instantly, the room swarmed with people. Two large guys tugged Brent back, and another guy and a girl were on the floor helping Travis, who was trying to say something, but I couldn't make out what it was. My vision went fuzzy, and there was such a commotion I almost didn't see Neely across the room. She caught my eye, though, and gave a short nod before disappearing through the doorway.

"Libby," Travis said, breaking me from my daze. Eric crouched over him as he sat on the floor. His cheek had already begun to swell. "Are you okay?"

Tears filled my eyes. *I'm so not used to that.* "Don't you dare worry about me. You're the one who's hurt, and we need to get you to the nurse."

"Where is he?" Travis tried to see around me.

My eyes panned the room and caught the back of Brent's head as two faculty members escorted him away. "He's gone. Come on," I said, and Eric assisted me in helping Travis to stand.

When we reached the office, the nurse shooed Eric and me out. I was in a daze as he walked me to my suite then left again to go wait for Travis. Alone in my room, I locked the door and crawled into bed. The whole thing had lasted less than a few minutes, but it continued to play in my head in slow motion. To keep my mind off the image of Brent's fist heading at Travis, I tried to remember exactly what Ryan told me. Was there a key to the door? Or was the pond the key? Or in my haste to make sense of things, had I really heard him say anything at all? A pounding on my door made me jump.

"Libby, open up."

Chapter Twelve

As soon as I turned the handle, Dean burst into the room and slammed the door behind him. "What the hell were you thinking? You shouldn't have been anywhere near that theater."

"And you can't just shove your way into my room and tell me what to do!"

"I'm not telling you what to do. I'm trying to protect you, yet you choose to walk right into the lion's den."

"Protect me? You don't even know me." I threw my hands in the air. "And I haven't seen you in a week. Do you expect me to stay locked up in my room like a prisoner in isolation?"

"No!" He clenched his jaw, balling his hands at his sides. "But I also didn't expect you to act like a selfish child."

I was so scared of Brent and upset about Travis and mad at Dean that I just lost it. Before I even registered I was doing it, I flung my hand toward his face. He caught my wrist millimeters before I connected with his cheek. Our eyes locked on each other, both of us breathing hard.

He lowered my hand, but didn't let go, and the anger slowly receded from his face. "You have no idea how scared I was."

"I'm sorry," I whispered, wondering if he was waiting for me to release his hand or if he was just holding it to make sure I didn't try to slap him again. "I talked to Ryan," I said, louder, not knowing what *else* to say.

"When?" He dropped my wrist. "How?"

I sat down and inched myself to the head of my bed, pushing my spine against the headboard. "In the theater, he appeared sitting on a bench in one of the set pieces I was painting. I couldn't understand all of it, but he said something about a key and a pond. Then he vanished again. That's when Brent showed up."

Dean seemed uncomfortable standing there in the middle of my room, as if he didn't know whether to come closer or step farther away. Finally, he did both by pacing my floor, then stopped abruptly, looking through my open studio door. "How did you get that?" He went into the other room.

I climbed off my bed and followed him. "I painted it," I said, glancing at the large painting of the wooden door on the easel.

"I mean, how did you get it from Madam Harris's office?"

"I didn't. I thought I could just paint the door again, only this time leave it open."

"It's closed."

"Obviously," I said. "It's actually my second attempt." I pulled the first one I'd tried from behind some blank canvases.

He took it from me and held it up. "I… I'm sorry." Dean set the painting down and pivoted to face me. "I didn't realize…"

"I want to help Ryan. But I need a little freedom."

He nodded. "I should check in with Neely, and I want to make sure Travis is okay."

"Would you tell him I'm worried about him?"

"Of course. After that… is it all right if I come back?" He sounded more timid than I'd ever heard him.

"I'd like that." I didn't want him to leave in the first place.

We went out of my studio, but before he reached my suite door, he stopped and turned to face me. Slowly, he reached out and put his palm to my cheek. My heart threatened to give out, and heat cascaded from my face to my neck and over my shoulders. Afraid he might pull his hand away before I was ready, I put mine over his.

He moved closer. "You pick at your nails when you're nervous. And if that doesn't help, you bite your lip."

Realizing I was doing exactly that, I stopped immediately.

He gave me a small smile. "You don't like crowds and would prefer a quiet evening alone—or maybe with a friend—over a loud party. You like butter on your sandwich, not mayonnaise or mustard. You're a bit messy, but that's okay because making the bed is overrated. You hate to draw attention to yourself, which, by the way, is impossible since you're so damn pretty, especially when you're covered in paint."

He ran his thumb over my cheek. Every cell in my body worked against me to stay calm. My pulse continued its frenzied pace, and my stomach flipped like a gymnast. I wanted to say something, anything, but my mouth was as dry as Death Valley. *Please, I want to hear more.*

"Painting calms you," he said, thankfully getting my message. "It's how you block things out, how you focus. And you're an incredible artist but a terrible dancer... without the right partner. You're soft and sweet and have a big heart, such a big heart that you're trying to help someone you've never met, and it bothered you to break up with Brent when he hadn't actually done anything to you, yet. You also have a thick skin, but it keeps you from letting people in because underneath you're afraid they'll see something you're ashamed of, though I have no idea what that could be." He cupped my face with his other hand. "I'm sorry if you ever felt like I was abandoning you. That was never my intention, and I hope you understand how important you are to me."

My eyes stung as I dragged in a ragged breath. He'd been right on every point. I'd accused him of not knowing me at all. *I was so very wrong.* Leaning forward, I put my hand on his waist. I was pretty sure my heart stopped because I couldn't breathe.

He hesitated for a moment before bending down and kissing me softly, his lips trembling against mine. Too soon, he pulled away, letting me go. "I'll be right back," he said, opening the door to my suite. "Please lock this." Then he disappeared behind it.

My body moved as if coaxed by puppet strings. I locked the door then went to my studio and sat down to stare at the painting on my easel. When I couldn't look at it any longer, I took it down and put a blank canvas in its place. I started to paint without really paying attention to what I was doing. Then, true to his word, Dean returned, accompanied by Travis and Eric.

Travis pulled me into a hug. "I heard you were worried."

"I'm so, *so* sorry. This is all my fault. If I'd just stayed in here like you wanted me to, this wouldn't have happened. Does it hurt a lot?" I asked him, examining his swollen, plum-colored cheek.

"Stop blaming yourself. I'll be fine. Besides, they gave me some pretty strong pain-killers, so no, it doesn't hurt at all."

"Well, I'm still sorry." I gave him another hug.

"It's really not your fault, and at least now we know Brent is a total douche bag."

Dean chuckled. "And we know I need to teach you some blocking skills."

"Yes, *please*," Eric said.

Travis rolled his eyes then winced.

"Are you hungry?" I asked. "Can I make you something to eat?"

He laughed. "Not unless you're trying to finish me off."

"There must be *something* I can do." *I need to do penance.*

"Yes, you can find Ryan," he said with a smile. "And I should go before I pass out, right here and now."

Travis and Eric hugged me again before they left, and while there were fewer people in my room after they were gone, the space became infinitely smaller with just Dean and me standing there. I started to pick my nails, but stopped when I remembered he knew that was a nervous tic of mine.

"Do you want to play cards or watch a movie or something?" I asked, having no idea what he liked to do in his free time. I'd yet to accumulate the same dossier that he had on me.

He smiled and stepped closer. "Would you mind if I rested here while you paint? It's sort of been a long day." He reached up and brushed my hair off my shoulder before trailing his fingers down my arm, and finally holding my hand in his.

The sensation was like taking all my favorite things in the world and giving them to me as a gift in that one simple act. I'd bottle that feeling up and carry it with me all the time if I could.

I shook my head, not able to speak with the way he was looking at me. Then I glanced at my unmade bed and cringed.

"It's okay." He smiled again and squeezed my fingers, sending a shockwave up to my shoulder then down into my stomach. "I don't mind." He let go of my hand, leaving it feeling cold, then went around me and sat down, kicking off his shoes.

I had to stand there for a second to make sure my knees would work. When I was pretty sure I could step without falling, I went to my desk and pulled out a handful of mint chocolates. "Something you didn't know about me." I took one and left the rest on the desk for him. "I love Andes mints." Then I went to my studio and started painting again. I heard him unwrap a few of the candies, then after a little while, I turned around to find him with his eyes closed. He breathed slow and deep. Contentment swept over me as I continued to work.

The afternoon sun gleamed in through my studio window, creating a geometric pattern on the floor. I absentmindedly added grays and browns to the canvas, intending to paint a pond with the thought that it might help me get closer to Ryan. But after a few hours, I actually looked at what I was doing. Without realizing it, I'd painted another closed door.

I snatched a box cutter blade off a shelf. *If I can't paint it open, I'll slice it open.*

But I never got the chance.

I didn't even know Dean was awake before he grabbed my arm, pinning me with his hips to my studio wall. Heat flared over my entire body. He raised his free hand to brush a strand of hair from my face then traced my jaw with his fingertips and rubbed his thumb on my cheek, making my knees wobble. If he hadn't been holding me there, I probably would have collapsed.

He leaned down and rested his forehead against mine. "I can't let you go."

"So don't," I said, right before his lips crashed into mine and my whole body ignited again.

I barely registered the thud of the box cutter hitting the floor. I wrapped my arms around his neck, and his tongue had swept across my lips, causing them to part. He tasted like chocolate and mint. I couldn't get enough of him.

Hot oil flowed through my veins as he lifted me with one hand and pressed the other into my back, holding me against him. Using the wall and his shoulders for leverage, I wrapped both my legs around his hips. Our lips never parted, and his tongue caressed mine as he pulled me away from the wall and carried me across the room.

Without stumbling, we made it to my bed, and he gently tugged off my T-shirt before resting my head on a pillow. Gripping the hem of his shirt, I pulled it off as well. I wanted to feel his skin, wanted the heat of it next to mine. I smiled as he trembled under my touch when I traced the formed muscles of his back and chest. I moved my fingers to the waistband of his jeans and helped him slide them off. His hands roamed over my neck and my collarbone, then down to my arms and across every inch of my bare skin. I was completely lost in him.

"Libby?" he asked between kisses.

"Mm hmm..."

He stopped for a second and looked at me. "I don't have a..."

"Oh! I have... um... a friend gave—"

He smiled then crashed his lips to mine again. I'd been kissed before, but never like that, and I knew I wanted more, wanted him closer to me than he already was. He kissed me everywhere his hands had been, my jaw, my shoulder, and lower until he kissed his way back up again. There wasn't much left to the imagination at that point, but neither one of us was pulling away.

Until someone knocked on the door.

I kept kissing him, trying to ignore it, but the knock came again, and we couldn't ignore the voice that came with it.

"Olivia," Madam Harris said, "are you in there?"

Dean looked at me, his eyes still full of hunger. "You should probably answer that," he said hoarsely.

I hesitated then decided he was right. "*You* should probably hide in my bathroom."

He nodded, grabbing his clothes while I threw on my T-shirt and jeans. When he was safely out of sight, I opened my door wide enough to see Madam Harris, but not quite wide enough to give her a full view of my room.

"Ah, good, you are here." She smiled, and a look of relief washed over her face. "There is something I'd like to talk to you about. May I come in?"

"Um, I was just lying down." She didn't need to know I wasn't doing it alone.

"Oh, I'm sorry to have disturbed you. But I *do* really need to speak with you. Would you mind meeting me in the gallery in say, twenty minutes?"

"Yes, ma'am. I'll see you then."

She smiled again then nodded and walked away. I opened the door to my bathroom to find Dean fully dressed, bracing his hands on the counter.

"Are you okay?" I put my hand on his back, but he flinched. "Sorry." I wrapped my arms around myself, wondering what I'd done wrong.

"Why does she want to talk to you and why in the gallery?" he asked, but didn't look at me as he placed his hands on the counter again.

"I don't know." I shrugged. "She probably wants to hear what I have to say about Travis getting punched. And she doesn't let anyone in her office, so the gallery may be the next best place."

"It's also where your creek painting is."

"You don't think Madam Harris has anything to do with this, do you?"

"She's been lying about Ryan disappearing, so I wouldn't put it past her." He finally looked at me, but the granite was back in his eyes. "I should get going," he said, as if he couldn't get away from me fast enough. "I'll send Neely to the gallery. It's getting late, so maybe she can camp out with you tonight, just in case. I'll come by in the morning."

"You don't want to stay with me?" I asked, a little surprised. I shivered. The warmth I usually felt around him—and the heat from moments ago—was completely gone.

He studied me as if memorizing my features. "I don't think that would be a wise choice."

"Oh, okay." I tried to hide my disappointment. "Did I do something wrong?"

"No, you didn't. I just don't think we..." He left the sentence hanging, then took a step forward but couldn't go any farther, since I stood between him and the door.

With a sigh, I stepped out of his way, allowing him to pass.

"Please be careful," he said, just before leaving me... utterly alone.

Chapter Thirteen

NEELY AND I CROSSED PATHS just outside the main dining hall, where the gallery was still set up. I groaned inwardly at the thought of her being my babysitter. Even from across the hall, I could feel her patronizing glare. She gave me a slight nod, and I was happy to avoid talking to her before I entered the dining room and went to find Madam Harris.

There were so many beautiful pieces of art in the room. Kari's drawing for one, and even Maggie's watercolor of a Tuscan hillside was as stunning as any Cezanne I'd ever seen. I didn't have to look far for our headmistress. Guessing correctly, I found her standing in front of my creek painting.

"Madam Harris?"

She turned slowly, her gaze unfocused. She usually wore a suit or dress, but that night, she had on skinny jeans with a cute three-quarter-sleeved, pale-blue sweater, an outfit I might have picked for myself when I wasn't painting. As I approached, her eyes softened, and she smiled at me. She reached out as if she might hug me, but then seemed to decide against it and put her hand on my shoulder instead.

"I'm glad to see you're okay," she said, then lowered her hand.

"I'm fine. I assume you're referring to what happened to Travis?"

"Yes, would you mind recounting the incident?"

"Um, no, but could we sit?" I pointed at a bench off in a corner.

She glanced at my painting one more time then motioned me ahead of her.

When we were both seated, I said, "It all sort of happened really fast. I was in the greenroom, painting, and Brent came in. He wanted to talk, but... see, Brent and I were sort of... dating."

Shock crossed her face, and she winced. "I had no idea you were involved with Brent Henderson," she said as if it were her business to know. "I suppose I've been too distracted to notice."

"Well, I don't know if *involved* would be the right word. I mean, we went out a few times, but..." *Why am I telling her this?* I shook my head. "Anyway, I broke things off with him a few weeks ago, and he's not very happy about it. Travis came into the greenroom just after Brent got there and tried to get him to leave. When Brent went to grab me, Travis shoved him. That's when Brent hit Travis, and everyone else came rushing into the room."

"Brent didn't hurt *you,* though?" she asked. I shook my head, and she let out a heavy sigh. "Well, at least you're all right. I am sorry about Travis, though. He seems like a very good friend. And as for Brent, he's under supervision tonight while he calms down. The matter will be dealt with further once I have all the information I need. But for now, I would suggest sticking to your side of the building and near other students."

That had a familiar ring to it. "Yes, ma'am."

"So are you seeing someone else now?"

I fidgeted. It seemed like an awfully personal thing for her to be asking, and I didn't really know what was going on between Dean and me.

"I'm sorry," she said. "I don't mean to pry." Thankfully, she let it drop. "You wouldn't remember this, but several years ago, I went to a showing of yours in the States. It was in a beach town, Suga...?"

"Saugatuck. It's near my hometown."

"Yes." She paused as if remembering something. "That's it."

"You came all the way to my show, and you didn't introduce yourself?"

"Oh, well..." She folded and unfolded her hands in her lap. "I was in the area on another matter, and you were busy with other guests. But I did have a chance to meet your parents. They're very proud of you."

"Yeah, they're great," I said, though I was more interested in what the other matter was that would have brought her to Saugatuck, Michigan.

As if reading my mind, she added, "I was there to meet another student."

"Oh." I tried to seem interested, but not too much. "I didn't realize another student here was from Michigan."

"He's not... here now. But maybe I can introduce you someday."

"That's too bad. Someday, I guess."

She tried to smile, but it didn't touch her eyes.

"Well, it was nice talking with you, Madam Harris." I stood up, biting my lip. "But I think I should get some rest now. It's been a long day."

"Yes, I understand." She stood as well. "Libby... is it all right if I call you Libby?" I nodded. "I hope you know you can talk to me anytime, if you need to."

Sure, I'll come talk to you, as soon as I figure out how you're involved in Ryan's kidnapping.

"And when we're in private," she added, "away from other students, you can call me Celeste if you like." She shrugged as though she wasn't sure of what she was saying.

Neither was I. "Thank you, Mada... I mean, Celeste," I said, the sound of it strange to my own ears. How the conversation had turned from discussing Brent and Travis to me calling her by her first name, I wasn't sure, but I *was* sure I wanted to get back to my room.

A minute later, she was gone, and Neely came into the gallery. She walked right up to me and hooked her arm around mine like a best friend, even though we'd barely ever spoken to each other. Sure, she was dating my brother, but I'd never met the guy.

"Where are we going?" I asked as she dragged me into the hallway.

"You heard what *Celeste* said. Stay on your side of the building and near other students."

"Great, so back to my room, and you're my escort service."

Neely smiled and nodded to some of the passing students as we climbed the stairs to the second floor. She may have had a smile on her face, but there was no joy in her voice. "Looks like we get to be roomies tonight. Won't that be fun?"

"I'm brimming with excitement." I rolled my eyes. "Since you obviously heard what she said, Brent is under supervision, so I'm pretty sure I'll be fine on my own. And why would you say her name like that? She was just trying to find out what happened today. She seemed legitimately concerned."

"Concerned?" Neely unhooked her arm from mine, stopped walking, and began to sort of whisper-hiss at me. "No wonder you need a keeper. That woman knows Brent did this to Ryan, yet she lets Brent walk around free, free to do *what* he wants, *when* he wants, while Ryan—" Her voice cracked, and she turned and started walking again. "Are you coming? You should get to bed early. You *really* need the beauty sleep."

I sighed and followed her. "You don't have to do this."

"I don't like it any more than you do. But I also don't like that Madam Harris is so interested in your personal life. What if she was in on it? What if she's not doing anything because... I don't know... she and Brent are a thing, and she's protecting him?"

"That's ridiculous." Though I had to wonder if it might be possible. Madam Harris was pretty and looked very young. She'd also winced when I said Brent and I were dating. I shook my head, trying to clear it of the image.

"You are my best hope of getting Ryan back," Neely said, "and I'm not taking any chances." She hooked her arm through mine again. "Besides, I'm not about to disregard one of Dean's *requests*."

Without another word, she took me back to my room, and a short while later, I was changing into my pajamas and climbing into bed, with Neely on a mat on the floor.

The rhythmic patter of the shower woke me, and I stretched and yawned like a lazy cat waking from a nap. It was almost nine when

Neely emerged from the bathroom, steam in her wake and a towel twisted on her head like a turban.

After taking my turn in the shower, I slipped on a pair of comfy yoga pants and a soft, rose-colored sweater, something cute for lounging in but easy enough to take off. Neely sat on my desk chair with her legs tucked under her, looking the picture of poise. Her damp hair was intricately braided down her back as if it had been professionally styled while I was in the bathroom.

"So when is Dean coming?" I asked, trying not to sound too anxious.

She smirked. "Oh. Weren't you able to take care of that?"

My jaw dropped. "That is not what I meant. And it's none of your business."

She shrugged. "He'll be here around noon. Are you hungry?"

Noon sounded like an eternity. But there was nothing I could do about that. "Um, yeah, but I'd like to check on Travis."

"Okay." She hopped off the chair and floated past me. "We can grab something to eat and take it to his room." Then she opened my door and waited expectantly for me to lead the way.

When Travis opened the door, I took one look at him and said, "Your bruise looks like my palette after I'm done painting for the day."

"I think he looks like one of those hot MMA fighters," Eric said from somewhere inside the room.

Travis rolled his eyes.

"Well, you are very handsome, but... I'm just so sorry." I ruffled his hair a little then followed him in and sat down next to him at the head of his bed.

"I told you before," he said. "It's not your fault. And I'm okay."

I tried to smile, but I didn't want him to see how forced it was, so I just rested my head on his shoulder for a second before he started to nod off again.

"I'll let you get some rest," I said then hugged him and left with my personal warden.

Neely and I got back to my room just past eleven o'clock, less than an hour before Dean was due. I went to my studio while she stretched out on my floor in all sorts of positions I'd never be able to get into... or out of. I should have been doing some schoolwork, but painting was way better for calming my nerves. However, when I heard the knock on my door, I still jumped and dropped my paintbrush.

"I'll get it," Neely said.

I heard her gather her things and open the door to my suite. I stayed in my studio, trying to act nonchalant, but all the while, my heart hammered away, and my hands shook as I reached for the brush I'd dropped. Splatters of flint-gray paint peppered the floor and my bare feet. In the other room, the two of them exchanged a few words, and then the door closed.

I expected Dean to come into the studio but refused to let myself turn to look for him. I tugged at the hem of my sweater, trying desperately not to pick at the polish on my nails. There was no way, with the chemistry between us, he could stay away.

But after a minute, and then two, and three, when I could hear him in the room and he still hadn't said anything, I couldn't stand it any longer and went to my studio door.

Chapter Fourteen

DEAN LOUNGED IN MY COMPUTER chair. He wore a burgundy, waffle-weave shirt with faded jeans. His socked feet rested on my desk while he read a World War One history book.

"Ahem."

"Yes?" he said without looking up.

"Um, are you okay?"

"I'm fine."

Fine! He's fine! I put my hands on my hips. "Is that all you have to say?"

He flipped a page. "What would you like me to say?"

"I'd like you to put down the damn book and look at me."

He took his feet down then laid the book on the desk. But it seemed like it caused him great pain to raise his head and look me in the eyes. "Now what?"

"I don't know, Dean. You tell me. Less than twenty-four hours ago, you couldn't keep your hands off me. And now a book is more interesting than having a conversation with me?"

"My actions yesterday were inappropriate." I could see his expression start to waver, but then he regained control. "I made a mistake and got carried away. I apologize. I'm sorry if I've given you the wrong impression. You need to concentrate on painting, and I need to concentrate on keeping you safe."

"You are such a jackass." Tears threatened again, but I wasn't letting him get away with treating me like that. "You're lying." I stabbed my finger at his chest. "You. Are. A. Liar."

He grabbed my hand so fast I never even saw his arm moving. "It's better this way."

I leaned in and placed my other hand on his thigh. "That doesn't change how you feel. But if you *think* you really don't want me—"

"I want you more than I've ever wanted anything in my entire life." He gripped my wrist harder, but not so tightly that it hurt. "I want you more than I want Ryan back, and it kills me to say that. I'm ashamed because I would pick you over him. Keeping my distance from you will get him back *and* keep you safe." As if to emphasize his point, he dropped my arm and turned his back to me.

I started to grab the back of his chair and swing it around, but he scooted out of my reach before I had the chance.

"Please understand. I just can't, Libby."

I spun on my heel and went back to my studio. *After everything yesterday, he shows up and thinks he can treat me like that. He thinks he can ignore what's going on between us, and imply my hormones are more important to me than rescuing Ryan, or being safe. So what if Brent knows Dean and I are together? It doesn't change the fact that he wants to lock me up in some painting.*

I sat down on my stool with a huff. Maybe I was the one who was wrong. Maybe I'd made the mistake. Maybe Dean just thought he wanted me because it was convenient, and once it started getting difficult, he needed to distance himself. And distance was exactly what it felt like. He was only a few feet away, but it felt like miles.

The door painting sat on my easel, mocking me. There was something I was missing, something deeper than just the door being opened or closed. I stared at it for a long time before taking it down and replacing it with a blank canvas. I painted a simple background of grayish-brown then filled in highlights of charcoal and muddy yellow. A form began to appear, and before long, the actual image took shape: the corner of a stone building with a low-hanging shingled roof. A patch of bushes hugged the edge, blocking any view of what lay beyond the structure. I was about to change colors when I felt Dean watching me.

"This isn't a spectator sport, and I don't like you lurking. Either come in, or better yet, get out." I slammed my paintbrush down into the easel tray.

"I suppose I deserve that."

"Supposing has nothing to do with it. You damn well deserve it." I spun around on my stool and crossed my arms over the pounding in my chest.

"How do you do it?" he asked in a tone so sweet and soft I knew right then he understood how upset I was.

I took a deep breath and lowered my arms to my lap. "Do what?"

"How do you turn a plain canvas into a work of art?"

"Lots of people do."

He stepped into the room, almost close enough to touch. "No, not like you."

"I don't know. Isn't that what we're trying to figure out?"

"I don't mean bring them to life. I mean how do you know what brush stroke to use where, and which colors will work and which won't?"

"The same way you make the world's worst dancer feel like she's a prima ballerina." I looked at the floor. The memory of us dancing together, holding each other while the rest of the world fell away, was too painful.

"We danced the waltz."

"You know what I'm saying." I rubbed my thumb over my bubblegum-pink-polished nails; *not* picking at them was becoming its own distraction.

He shoved his hands deep into his pockets. "Dancing is easy... with the right partner."

"I thought I *was* the right partner." The words slipped from my mouth before I could stop them.

He shifted his weight from one foot to the other, but he didn't reply.

Why do I keep embarrassing myself? I didn't know what to say either. I was still upset, but he was trying to... I didn't know, to make an effort to be friendly, I guessed. Finally, I just stood and motioned for him to sit down on my stool.

"What, you want *me* to paint?" A look of pure horror crossed his face. "I don't want to ruin it."

"Sit," I said.

And he did, reluctantly.

I placed a brush in his hand, trying to ignore the heat of his skin when I covered his fingers with mine. "There are several colors on the palette in front of you. Which one do you like?"

He looked down at the paints. "Just pick one?"

"Yes, any one you want."

"The green?"

"The technical name is zinnober, because it's more shiny like chrome green."

"I like that. Zinnober."

The corners of my lips twitched up as he said the name of the color. It had never sounded so incredibly sexy. "Okay, dab a little on the brush, like this."

I had to press against his back in order to reach the palette around him. His shoulders tightened when I leaned in. His dryer-fresh scent made me want to nuzzle him and breathe him in for the rest of my life. I had to tamp down my annoyance at that and move on to the next step in painting. After demonstrating how to dab a small amount of paint on the brush, I raised our hands to the canvas. But before the brush touched it, my arm quivered. I let go, stepping back.

He lowered his hand and moved to put down the brush. "Sorry, I—"

"Just sit for a second, okay?" I took in a slow breath then moved slightly to his side.

With him sitting on my stool, we were the same height, and my body was very much aware of how close we were. Heat rolled off him, and sweat beaded at the base of my neck when I remembered how good his skin felt on mine.

I placed my hand back on his, forcing myself to stay focused on the painting. "Where do you think the green should go?"

He moved his arm toward the upper left of the canvas. And together, we painted, our bodies moving in sync like dancers.

At one point, I placed my free hand on his back between his shoulder blades, and his taut muscles relaxed against my palm. As if instinctively reacting to him, my own shoulders relaxed as well.

"It's ivy," he said in surprise after we'd worked for over an hour.

"Yeah, you just painted an ivy wall."

He turned his head to look at me for only the second time since he'd sat down. Our faces were so close they may as well have been touching.

"*We* painted an ivy wall," he said, as a joy so sincere and unguarded spread across his face that I couldn't believe I was looking at the same Dean James I'd been furious with only hours before.

"We did." My voice shook. I lowered our hands and felt his tremble under mine as I placed the paintbrush on the easel.

"Together. Partners." He wrapped his arms around my waist.

I didn't move away or resist. Then, as if I weighed nothing at all, he pulled me sideways onto his lap. Trying to keep my breathing even, I tentatively put my arms around his neck. He drew me closer, resting his forehead against mine.

"I'm sorry about earlier," he said. "Thank you for painting with me."

I bit the inside of my cheek, unable to speak.

"Are you still angry with me?" I could hear the plea in his voice.

"Only if you don't kiss me *right now.*"

I didn't have to say it twice. His lips pressed to mine, and any of my remaining anger melted away. I pulled my fingers through his hair, and he raised me up to straddle him on the stool. I rolled my hips against his, and he leaned me back to kiss his way down my jaw and neck.

I'd never painted with anyone like that before. I rarely even let people see my work before it was finished. But then I'd painted with *him*, and we were making out in my studio, and all I could think about was how amazing it felt. The whole experience was freeing and frightening at the same time.

I moved to adjust myself on his lap, but when I put my hand out, it brushed the painting. Except it wasn't wet paint between my fingers but waxy leaves, cool to the touch. I gasped and jerked to look at it, effectively ruining the make-out mood.

"I'm sorry," he said, sounding out of breath.

"Oh! No, it's not you. It's the painting."

A crease formed on his forehead. "The painting?"

I climbed off his lap and pointed. "The leaves, I touched the leaves. They're real."

We both stared at the picture. I couldn't believe I'd done that. I'd touched my paintings a hundred times before, but that was the first time I'd ever felt anything other than paint.

"Try again," he said.

"What?"

He gestured at the canvas. "Try to touch them again."

Timidly, I reached out to the vines we had painted together. My hand didn't stop at the canvas where I expected it to. Instead, it went through and was wrapped in an abundance of green ivy. I yanked it back, afraid I might lose it.

"Hmm. That was different," he said.

I giggled. Even though I thought I might not get my hand back, I had to admit it was thrilling to be able to do that. "It's definitely better than another wooden door, and we created it together." I smiled at him.

He nodded, but then an odd look came over his face, and he studied the painting as if sizing up an opponent.

"Is something...? I mean, did I do something wrong?" I asked him when he didn't say anything for a while.

He slowly shook his head, but didn't stop looking at our ivy wall. "Where's the last painting you did of the door?" he asked in a low voice.

I picked it up from where I'd set it on the floor and handed it to him. He held the edge of the door painting against the edge of ivy wall and, as if it were supposed to be that way, the two paintings melded together. The ivy stretched across both canvases and clung to the stone frame of the ancient-looking door.

I stared at him then back at the combined paintings. "How did you do that?"

"I didn't do anything," he said. "I just can't believe I didn't recognize this before."

"You know where this is?"

"Yes. It's where Ryan and I grew up."

Chapter Fifteen

I STOOD IN THE DOORWAY TO my studio and watched him pace the floor of my bedroom. He clenched his fists then sat on my bed and grabbed a pillow. By the look in his eyes, I thought he was going to rip it to shreds, but then he stuffed it behind his back. The new image of the door with the ivy had obviously struck a chord with him. My excitement at being able to *touch* the ivy had receded with his over-the-top reaction to having recognized the location.

He rubbed his eyes with the heels of his hands, then dragged his fingers through his hair and placed them behind his neck, looking at me as if waiting for me to say something. But I didn't. His change in mood frightened me. Even more than that, I was afraid I'd caused it, and I wasn't about to say something that would make things worse.

He took a deep breath. "This has nothing to do with you, Libby. But I'd like to tell you something." One of his hands came down, and he patted the space beside him. "Would you sit with me, please?"

I hesitated then crawled onto the bed next to him. He wrapped his hand around mine and weaved our fingers together. For a long time, we just sat there. The gentle motion of his thumb swirling over the back of my hand lulled me into a trance-like state. I laid my head on his shoulder and listened to him breathe.

"I lived in that house for a long time. That's why I'm surprised I didn't recognize the front door." His voice was barely above a whisper. "The old man who raised me was... well, not a good person, to say the least. He didn't have a problem with beating me on a regular basis or treating me like a slave. I can't tell you if he was my father or not. He never said, but I don't remember anything before that cottage. Ryan showed up when I was four; at least I think I was four. It wasn't like we celebrated our birthdays. The old man would say, 'You're this old now,' and that was that. Anyway, one morning, I woke up and found Ryan lying on the mat next to me. He was still in diapers and couldn't walk or talk. The old man made me take care of him, and I did."

He paused and turned my hand over in his, tracing the lines of my palm with his fingertips. His feather-light touch was so tender against my skin and so at odds with what he was telling me. "Women came in and out of the house regularly. Some of them stayed for a while, but mostly it was just a stopover for them." He curled my fingers into his again. "As long as I did what the old man said, he stayed away from Ryan. For a while anyway..."

My whole body constricted. I had a feeling his story was going to get much worse.

"As we grew up, the old man got bored of beating just me, especially since I was getting better at taking it. Most of the time, he'd just shove Ryan around; a couple of times, he gave him a black eye. If I tried to step in, it made things worse, so instead, I just took the blame for whatever the old man happened to be pissed about at the time. Then, the summer after Ryan turned thirteen, things changed. We were making omelets. Ryan cracked eggs into the pan while I cut up the peppers. One of the eggs didn't make it. Shell got into the pan, and raw egg dripped onto the stove. The old man said Ryan was being wasteful and needed to be taught a lesson." Dean's hand tightened around mine. "I can still smell Ryan's burning skin and hear the sizzle of flesh. But the worst was Ryan's screams as the old man pressed his hand to the hot burner."

Bile rose in my throat, and tears stung my eyes. I reached over and put my hand on Dean's arm. I wasn't sure if it was for my benefit or his, but I wanted to let him know I was there, listening to whatever he needed to tell me. I wished I could hug Ryan, too. And I finally understood why he always seemed sad in my paintings.

"The old man was strong and carried a gun on him at all times. I didn't even know what I was doing until it was done. All I kept thinking was I had to get us out of there or we would end up buried in the cellar before we ever had a chance to live. I stopped cutting the peppers and..."

He didn't need to elaborate. I knew what he'd done.

I also knew I was shaking. I couldn't help it. Though he hadn't actually said the words, he'd just told me he'd killed a man.

"I'm sorry," he said and tried to release my hand.

But I wouldn't let him. I couldn't let him. I gripped his hand tighter and looked up into his eyes. It was shocking to hear his confession, but I didn't blame him for doing what he needed to do. "It's going to take me a minute to process. Okay?"

He nodded then leaned against the wall. Slowly, I stopped trembling. It didn't take me long to know in my heart that I was more upset about what had happened to him than what he'd done.

"Tell me what you did... after," I said.

"I bandaged Ryan up, and we got out of the house. We took what we could carry and hid in the woods for a few days. Eventually someone found the body, and the police came, but no one would have even known we were there, at least no one who would have come forward and admitted they'd been there. After that, we drifted, stealing food from farms, fishing or catching wild animals. Sometimes we'd work odd jobs for cash to buy clean clothes, and if we were doing really well, I'd let Ryan buy some art supplies."

"You never went to the authorities? I mean, it was self-defense. They would have seen that from Ryan's hand."

"Yes, but we'd basically been taking care of ourselves our entire lives anyway. And there was no guarantee we'd be able to stay together if we turned ourselves in."

I knew he was right, but I couldn't help thinking that it still might have been better than living on the streets. Of course, living on the streets was probably better than living with that man. "How did you learn to read and write? How did Ryan learn to paint?" My thoughts went back to the other day when Dean had shown me Ryan's watercolor painting from when he was three.

"We didn't have formal schooling, but the old man was adamant that we learn enough to pass in society in case someone ever came snooping around. One of the regular women that came to the house brought the watercolors. Ryan loved them so much he wouldn't let me touch them."

"But I only saw him in the one and then not again until I was a teenager?"

"Let's just say the old man didn't like it that Ryan had gone missing that day, and he took it out on me." He pushed his hair back by his right temple, revealing a thin, jagged scar pointing down toward his ear. "Ryan didn't paint again until we escaped."

Once more, tears filled my eyes, and a single one fell before I could blink them away.

"Libby..." He turned to face me. "Really, I'm sorry. You don't have to listen—"

"Yes." I squeezed his hand. "I do. Tell me the rest."

Dean sighed then nodded. "After we got away and fell into a sort of routine, Ryan was able to carry his paints and brushes and a few small canvases in his backpack. He begged me once to let him buy a bigger canvas. I told him it was a waste of money since we couldn't lug it with us everywhere we went. But he said he just wanted to paint on it, not keep it. And since I pretty much could never say no to him, I let him get one. Actually, I traded a craft store owner some time unloading deliveries for it. And while I worked at the store, Ryan went to a beachside park and painted."

I sat up and looked straight at him, realizing what he was telling me.

"That was a few days after he'd seen your picture at an art gallery and the day he met Madam Harris," Dean said with the hint of a smile. "She happened to be walking the shoreline and saw him painting. He said when she saw what he was working on, she looked horrified, and at first, he thought she hated it. But then she asked him all sorts of questions about his parents and where he lived and where he learned to paint. Of course, he couldn't answer any of her questions, but she kept insisting, so he told her he'd run away from a terrible foster father and had been living on the streets for over a year, which was basically the truth."

"It was Saugatuck, wasn't it?" I said, practically bouncing. "That was the beach where Ryan was painting."

"Yes, Ryan told me Madam Harris went to see you but stumbled upon him instead."

"Do you still think she's hiding something?"

"There's definitely more to her story, and I'm sure she knows Ryan didn't leave the school for family reasons, since he doesn't even have a family."

"He has us," I whispered.

"Yes, you're right. He does," Dean said as I leaned back into him.

"Why do you think she's covering it up? Just because it would be bad for the school?"

"Well, that and how would you explain or prove it to anyone?"

"I guess that's true." My shoulders slumped. I liked Madam Harris, and I hated to think there was something sinister behind her actions. "Do you think that's why she seems a little overprotective of me—I mean, more than with anyone else—because she knows what Brent did to Ryan and doesn't want the same thing to happen to me?"

He swirled his thumb on my hand again. "I think that would be a safe bet."

"I still don't get why Brent would care so much. Ryan and I never did anything to him. We just paint well."

"I don't have an answer for that one. I wish I did."

He pulled me onto his lap, folding me into his arms. I loved how every part of me warmed where he touched me. I rested my head on his chest below his shoulder. I placed my hand over his heart, feeling its strong rhythm beneath my fingertips.

"I don't want you to be afraid of me," he said, kissing the top of my head, sending a warm pulse from there to my toes. "I won't *ever* hurt you." He covered my hand with his, hugging me tighter as his body gave the slightest tremble.

I repositioned myself to see his face and had to hold back a gasp at how terrified he looked. "Hey, you only scare me when you disappear without a trace. I feel like I lose you every time, and I've already lost so much. I lost Ryan before I even had the chance to know him. So please don't do that anymore."

I moved my hand from his chest to his cheek, drawing him into a kiss, his lips soft against mine. I couldn't imagine him *purposefully* hurting anyone he cared for, and a pit formed in my stomach at the thought of someone hurting *him*. I wanted him to know there was good in the world, people who cared for him and would never hurt *him* either, and that I was one of those people.

When I pulled back, his eyes had lightened, and I detected a hint of the heat and hunger I'd seen in them the day before. The look mixed with playfulness as he skimmed kisses from my ear to the base of my neck and back up the other side. The sinking feeling I'd had changed to a pleasant flutter as I wound my fingers into his hair.

After maneuvering us so my head rested on the pillow, he hovered over me. I pulled him closer, the weight of his body covering me like a warm blanket in winter. I wanted to wrap myself in that blanket, to get tangled and twisted and tied up in it, to be sheathed in the heat and comfort it provided.

He kissed me lightly then hesitated, searching my eyes. I pulled in a jagged breath at his expression, which was somewhere between reverence and apprehension.

"Are you okay?" I whispered.

"You're captivating." He gently brushed a strand of hair from my face. "But we don't have to do this if you don't want to."

"I do. I want to," I said with certainty. The day before, we'd been caught up in the moment, passion preceding any other thought. But for me, *nothing* could be more intimate than painting with him.

I ran my hands down the front of him then pulled his shirt up over his head, revealing his chiseled torso. Grinning, he rolled to his side, then helped me slip out of my sweater and yoga pants, my skin searing everywhere he touched. He shimmied out of his jeans then leaned over to kiss his way across my collarbone from one shoulder to the other, leaving a trail of pleasant goose bumps along the way.

He took my hand in his, entwining our fingers and raising my arm above my head. His weight settled over me, and our bodies aligned as he pressed his lips to mine.

The kiss wasn't soft or sweet. It was heart-wrenchingly desperate. As if *not* being with me would end whatever peace he'd found.

My pulse still hadn't slowed when I lay in his arms afterward, tracing the lines of his muscles. "How did you get here after you convinced Ryan to go with Madam Harris?" I asked in a low whisper then felt him shake with laughter. "Why are you laughing?"

"That's what you want to talk about after..." He motioned to us and the bed.

"I suppose that's not appropriate pillow talk, is it?" I buried my face in his chest.

He chuckled then put his finger under my chin and made me look at him. "I really wouldn't know. So it's perfect. Okay?"

My heart sputtered when I saw his smile. I nodded, and he kissed me before I laid my head back down.

"In answer to your question," he said, "I got a job on a cruise ship, teaching dance lessons."

"Seriously?"

"Yeah. One of the women that came to the cottage on a more regular basis was big into dance. I picked it up easily, but Ryan... not so much."

"Apparently, that runs in the family too," I said. "Did you have any ID to work on the ship? How could they hire you off the street like that?"

"Let's just say the old man was good for at least *one* thing. He made most of his money by forging documents, and he taught us how to help him. Birth certificates, social security cards, driver's licenses, and passports."

"Those pictures you gave me at Christmas, that's how you did it."

He chuckled. "That, a copy center, and some stuff I stole out of the cottage before we ran. They worked well enough to get us both out of the country, but Ryan wasn't quite fifteen at the time and looked too young to pass for an adult."

"Wait!" I propped myself up to look at him. "If you didn't know your birthdays, how did you know how old you really were or what dates to put on all those documents?"

"We didn't, not for sure. When it came time to leave the States, we picked our own. Ryan actually picked your birth date, November 17, 1995."

"So you *did* know it was my birthday when you came to visit me while I was sick." I poked him in the shoulder. "But that doesn't explain how Ryan knew."

"Yes, I knew." He pulled me back down. "And it's amazing the things you can find on the Internet."

"Okay, I get it." I rolled my eyes. I didn't like that so much of my personal information was out there for the world to see, but there wasn't much I could do about it. "What day did *you* pick?"

My head rose and fell with his chest as he took a deep breath. "July fourth. Independence Day. The same day Ryan and I were free from the old man. It seemed fitting."

"It is," I whispered, saving the thought in my memory bank that he would be twenty in July.

"As I was saying..." Dean adjusted on the bed and rubbed my arm. "Ryan told me Madam Harris had some government connections and was able to get herself appointed as his guardian once he was here. I came over about a month later and never went back. The older women on the ship loved to dance with a good-looking young guy, so I made some pretty nice tips, too."

"Nice tips, huh?" I raised my eyes to meet his.

He grinned then kissed my nose. "Just dancing lessons. I swear."

I don't think I've ever seen him smile so much. "Good." I snuggled against him again.

"Anyway, one of the ladies I gave lessons to was on the board for a theater in London. She got me a job and helped me find a small flat. Some of the other guys at the theater were into martial arts and acrobatics, so I hung out with them, learning as much as I could, which eventually helped me when I needed to convince Madam Harris to let me enroll here."

"And she has no idea you and Ryan know each other?"

"I don't think so. Our last names aren't the same."

"Why 'James'? I mean, if you could pick whatever names you wanted."

"The old man called us Dean James and Ryan Nolan. I guess it just stuck."

"The movie star and the baseball player."

"Mm hm." He ran his fingertips lightly up and down my bare arm, lulling me into a mild trance. I wanted him to keep talking. I wanted to know more about him, to know everything about him. Unfortunately, I couldn't help the rumbling in my stomach.

He laughed. "You have the loudest stomach of anyone I've ever met."

I smacked him, and he feigned an injured shoulder, which made me laugh, too.

"All right," he said, sitting us both up. "We really should get something to eat other than Andes mints." He pointed at the pile of empty wrappers on my desk.

I covered up with the sheet, but he tugged at it, causing me to move toward him again. He laid me back down, kissing me. I knew we had things we needed to do, but as our kiss deepened and his fingers wove into my hair, I couldn't bring myself to think about anything other than being with him in that moment.

Eventually, my stomach refused to be ignored, and we were forced to stop and get some food. When we were both dressed, I headed to the kitchen while he went to Travis's room. I grabbed whatever I could think of for us to eat then went straight to meet him there. But I was surprised to find Travis already had company besides Eric and Dean.

"I hope you brought enough." Neely smiled from her perch on Travis's desk chair.

"Neely. I'm… I didn't expect you," I said as Dean took the food from my hands and set it out on the desk.

"Well, I didn't want to disturb you two lovebirds." She glanced at Dean then back to me. "I figured when you were ready to leave the nest, you'd come here first... well, second after the kitchen. Obviously, I was right about that. And since Travis is mostly drugged up on pain meds, I knew I wouldn't be disturbing anything here."

"It's ibuprofen, not oxycodone, Neely," Eric grumbled.

"Don't mind him." Travis sat up in the bed with his legs over Eric's lap. "He's crabby because she's won about fifty rounds of Angry Birds on his iPad. We were actually thinking of watching a movie."

I smiled at Travis then gave him a kiss just above his bruise line.

He took my hand and whispered, "You look good. Were you safe?"

I nodded but felt my face flush, so I just started making myself a sandwich.

A few minutes later, my stomach was appreciatively quiet, and Neely was trying to convince us to watch *Saw 25* or some other awful slasher movie. We all agreed we had enough craziness in our lives at the moment and didn't need to watch a movie about it, so we settled on a comedy. She'd begrudgingly started uploading the movie when, to my surprise, Dean commented on our ivy painting.

"So we think we figured out where the door is," he said. "It's at the house Ryan and I grew up in. I haven't been there in a long time, so I didn't recognize it until Libby painted some ivy around it."

I didn't add anything to how we'd made the discovery or what had transpired afterward, but Travis gave me a look that told me I'd better tell him later.

"Is that door the only way to find him?" Neely asked as the movie started on Travis's laptop. "Did you figure out how to get it open?"

"No." Dean shook his head, pulling me closer to him on our spot on the floor.

"It's too bad there's not a back door," Eric said.

And all our eyes snapped in his direction.

"What? What'd I say?" he asked.

"Eric!" Dean jumped up off the floor. "You're brilliant, man." Then he pulled me to my feet as well. "Come on. You have work to do."

Chapter Sixteen

Once in my suite, Dean shut the door and went into my bathroom. I could hear him rummaging around, but I didn't go in to see what he was doing. The man was on a mission, and I didn't want to derail whatever train of thought he was on. He emerged from the bathroom with the two paintings we'd hidden in my closet a few weeks ago. Grabbing my hand again, he ushered me into my studio, where the combined ivy wall and door paintings still sat on the easel. He set the orchard painting to the right and the tree with the broken fence to the left.

"The cottage was covered on three sides by ivy," he said. "There was one bedroom, one bathroom, and a kitchen-living-room combo with a fireplace. There was a tiny window in the kitchen and one in the old man's bedroom, but the other two windows were bricked over. The only way in or out of that cottage was through the front door. At night, he kept it locked with a padlock, and if he left during the day, he put a bar across the door on the outside. We were prisoners."

He glanced at me, then back at the paintings. "We were only allowed outside when he needed us to clean or repair things out there. There was an old cellar entrance attached to the back of the cottage. At the time, Ryan wasn't strong enough to open it on his own. Also, the interior entrance to the cellar was through the old man's bedroom, and I never let Ryan go in there. Ever."

I took a hesitant step toward him then stopped when he looked back at me. Tears stung my eyes—something I still wasn't used to. In one swift movement, his arms were around me. He was shaking, but the rise and fall of his chest was even and steady. Kissing the top of my head, he loosened his hold then turned me around in his arms to face the paintings.

"We could hear waves and seagulls in the distance on the days we were outside. Ryan and I used to pretend we were at the beach playing rather than working. Beyond that fence"—he pointed at the fence painting—"are the woods we hid in until someone found the old man. Way in the back of the woods is a creek with a small waterfall. A few miles away from that is an apple orchard. We stole apples from it after only eating wild berries for several days."

I tilted my head to look at him. "I need to show you something." I took his hand, leading him out of the studio. At my desk, I turned on my laptop. Dean stood behind me, resting his hands on my shoulders. I leaned back into him, waiting for my computer to boot. I'd never shown anyone but my parents what he was about to see.

I clicked on the file that housed the pictures of the paintings that either Ryan had appeared in or had come to life at one time. The first image that came up on the screen was the creek painting, currently on display in the student gallery.

"Ryan was leaning against that tree just before it fell," I said, then flipped to the bridge painting. "I didn't paint the snow. It came down on its own. And this one, I watched it turn from day to night. That was the night I met you."

Except for wrapping his arms all the way around me, Dean was very still and very quiet. The next image was of the orchard. I twisted to face him, and he brushed my hair off my shoulder, trailing his hand down my arm. I loved it when he did that. I loved the way he looked at me. I loved that I wasn't afraid to tell him about my paintings.

He smiled. "I already saw Ryan in this one."

"I know, but the first time you saw it, when Ryan waved and I knocked it down..." I eased out of his arms and reached into one of my desk drawers, digging in the back to pull out the apple.

He gave me a quizzical look and took the apple from my hands. "It's an apple."

"Yes, a bright red, perfect-looking apple... that Ryan tossed right before he vanished. I didn't see it come out of the painting, and it might have fallen out when I knocked the painting down, but..."

"Libby, that was months ago." Dean looked down at it again. "This apple should be rotten by now."

"It's not real. I mean, it looks real and feels real, but it doesn't smell like an apple, and I'm not going to take a bite from it."

Dean examined the fruit for another moment then set it down on the desk behind us. He pulled me toward him again, cradling me in his arms as I nestled my head into his chest. "You've been painting your brother's life all along." He rubbed my back and arms, holding me close and kissing the top of my head. "Are there any more?"

We sat down on my bed with my laptop between us and went through every painting from the watercolor, to the crackling fireplace Ryan had slept near to stay warm, to the cornfield he'd poked his head through, and finally to the door we still couldn't get open. As we went through them, I could tell the progression of Ryan's life by the images. Some of them were darker than others, especially the ones that had to do with the cottage. The later ones, the ones Ryan had started showing up in after they'd escaped, were brighter—not quite *cheerful*, but hopeful. I wondered how many more I would have seen him in if he'd kept painting when he was younger.

"Do you remember when I told you my favorite one was a portrait of my parents?"

Dean smirked. "You mean when you lied."

I swatted his arm. "Okay, Mr. Know-It-All. My favorite one is actually this one." I clicked open the picture of the dock. An early morning mist hovered over the dark stillness of a small lake, where an old wooden dock jetted out into the water. At the end of the dock sat two rickety, graying Adirondack chairs. "He appeared in the chair on the left. He didn't look at me, but he patted the seat next to him like he was asking me to join him." I gulped back my tears. "I'd seen him a handful of times before that, but it was the first time I ever contemplated the fact that maybe he was a real person."

"Silver Lake."

"What?"

"It's Silver Lake. There was an abandoned cabin and that old dock. We found it the fall after we ran away and stayed there for the winter."

"Now I know every place he's been." I rested my head on Dean's shoulder. "But I still don't know how to get him back. And I don't understand how he can move from painting to painting and how an apple can come out of one, but he can't get himself out. Do you think I should paint the cellar door? Maybe we can get him out that way."

"Maybe." Dean set my laptop back on the desk. "It seems a little forced though. All your other paintings came to you without previous knowledge."

"But isn't that what you were thinking when Eric mentioned a back door?" I sat up on my knees.

"Yeah, it was, but something seems... off about it."

"It's still worth trying."

He put his hand on my arm then glanced at the clock. "You're right. It is worth trying, but it's getting late."

"And that's a problem why?"

"Brent and I have early practice tomorrow."

"No, absolutely not! If I'm not allowed near him, then neither are you. And how do you know he'll even be allowed to practice after what he did to Travis?" My heart dropped into my stomach then threatened to come—unpleasantly—back up. "I know in your performance you're not supposed to touch each other, but I saw your cheek—"

Dean took my hands in his. "I don't know for sure that he'll be there, but we have a scheduled practice, so *I* at least have to go. Besides, I've sparred with him plenty of times the past few weeks, and he hasn't so much as bruised me."

"Are you telling me you've been *practice* fighting with him this whole time? That while I was keeping my distance, you were hanging out with him?" I vaulted off the bed and away from him.

"Libby, please, we're not *friends*. We're sparring partners. So yes, we fight each other. And you didn't exactly keep your distance *yesterday*."

"That's different. I wasn't looking for a fight."

He stood and came toward me, but I stepped away before he could touch me. A pained look crossed his face, and I felt instantly bad about it.

"I won't come near you." He held his hands up in defeat. "If that's what you want."

"No. It's not what I want." I crossed my arms. "I want you to stay away from Brent."

"I told you. He's my sparring partner. I have to go near him."

"Find a *different* partner."

"It's not that simple. Brent and I are well matched. Another student wouldn't be as challenging for either one of us."

"Let me get this straight. You're going to go fight with him the day after he hit my best friend, and you've been *sparring* with him since he and I broke up when he knew it was because of you. And now you're telling me he's as good as you are?" My body shook, and my eyes stung. I was beyond angry. I was furious.

Dean sat down heavily in my desk chair and ran his hand over his head then leaned forward with his elbows on his knees. "I said we're well matched. I don't believe he's better than I am. And yes, I've been sparring with him this whole time because we are assigned that way and I didn't want to stir things up when he already felt hostile. I didn't want to give him a reason to come looking for either one of us. I figured if he knew where I was, then he'd leave you alone."

"I don't know what to say." I stared at my feet and bit my lip. Then I looked back at him. "Look what he's already done to Travis and Ryan... and Neely. I can't stand the thought of him hurting someone else. Especially someone I care about." My anger ebbed, but it left behind fear and doubt.

"I'm sorry," Dean said, putting up both his hands. "I didn't know it would upset you like this. I guess I didn't think you cared that much about what I did."

"All right!" I put my hands on my hips. "Let's get one thing straight *right now*. I care. I care that you and Travis and Eric and even Neely are putting yourselves in danger because of me. I care that Ryan is stuck in my paintings, and I have no idea how to get him out. I care that you are here with me now, in my room, in my studio, in my..." I looked at the bed. "I care that this whole time you've been protecting me, and I can't do the same for you. I didn't know that's what you were doing and now... now that I do, I care."

I shook harder, balling my hands into fists, not knowing what else to say or do. Dean hung his head then stretched out his long arms and wrapped his fingers around my wrists, tugging me onto his lap. I circled my arms around his neck, breathing him in as my body slowly stopped trembling.

"Better?" he asked.

"No."

He rubbed my shoulders and back. "What more can I do?"

I squeezed him tighter. "Don't go."

"Even without DNA, I can guarantee you and Ryan are related."

"I find it hard to believe you'd let Ryan sit on your lap."

"Not since he was four." He chuckled. "But he often has outbursts like that and asks for things I can't do."

"I know you have to go." I sighed. "But is it okay if I never *want* you to go?"

"It's more than okay." He nuzzled his face into the crook of my neck.

I pulled away so I could look in his eyes. They weren't pained anymore. They were content but not truly happy, and I was pretty sure they wouldn't be until Ryan was safe.

"Is this weird for you?" I asked.

His eyebrows knit together as he shook his head slightly. "Is *what* weird?"

"Um..." I wasn't sure how to put what I was saying into words, and then I wasn't sure I wanted to anymore. "I mean, we're Ryan's—"

"Libby." Dean sat up straighter, looking me right in the eye. "You are *Ryan's* sister, *not* mine. And I've never once thought of you that way, okay?"

I nodded in relief then hugged him again. "What time will you be done tomorrow?" I asked.

"It's Monday." He lowered one of his hands to rub my hip and thigh while his other hand held me close to him. "We practice from five a.m. to five p.m. I can be showered and back to you by six," he said into my ear, his breath warm against my skin.

I nodded as he kissed his way down my jaw to my lips. The soft yet firm pressure of his hand rubbing my leg successfully distracted me.

"You're right," I said. "It's late."

"Hmm..." He kept kissing me.

"We should probably...um..." It was no use. I couldn't get any more words out as the hand he had on my back worked its way under my shirt and pressed to my bare skin. Then, as if he were trying to prove the point that he didn't think of me as his sister, he scooped me up and placed me on the bed.

He smiled down at me. "You were saying?"

"You read my mind." I grinned. "I was thinking we should go to bed."

Chapter Seventeen

I HANDED TRAVIS A GLASS OF orange juice. "Your cheek looks much better today, more greenish-yellow—kind of like a Klimt or maybe a Kandinsky."

"Yeah, my face is a work of art, isn't it? Thanks for that. It doesn't hurt nearly as much, but that is *not* what we're going to discuss today."

"Oh, and what's that?" I took a bite of my toast.

"Don't act coy with me, you little vixen. You know exactly what I'm talking about."

"If I remember correctly, *you* were the one wearing Vixen at Christmas."

"Don't change the subject."

"Who, me?" I was actually about to spill my guts *and* thank him for coming to get me after I'd tossed and turned for several hours when Dean left, but just then Maggie Bates entered the kitchen.

"Oh, Travis." Maggie walked right up to him. "I heard about your little incident. Does that hurt very much?" The way she fawned over him made the eggs I'd just eaten threaten to revisit in a very unpleasant way.

"Not much." He shrugged then kicked my foot under the table.

"I'm surprised Brent did that." Her voice made the same annoying cooing sound the pigeons did outside my bedroom window at home. "I mean, he's always been such a nice guy."

I took my plate to the sink as she continued to talk as if I wasn't even in the room.

"I can't imagine what you could have done to provoke him like that. Do you think it's because you're... gay?"

I dropped my plate with a crash and spun around to confront her.

"No, it's okay, Libby." Travis got up from his seat, came over to the sink, and patted my hand. "I really am gay." He turned to face Maggie. "But I think Brent was just having a bad day, and I happened to be the one he took his frustration out on." He put his dish down in the sink and turned on the water as he mouthed to me, "*Go now.*"

Storming out of the kitchen, I headed to my room. In the hallway, I barely registered Neely coming from the opposite direction and struggling with three large canvases.

"They're dismantling the gallery," she said, even though I hadn't asked and wasn't in the mood to talk to her.

Reaching my door at the same time she did, I took two of the canvases from her, and she followed me into my studio, where we set the paintings against a wall.

She pointed at the painting on my easel. "That must be the ivy you could feel. So did you guys figure out something with the back door?"

"The cottage has a cellar door," I snapped, my patience wearing thin. "I'm going to try to paint it today."

Her head bobbed as she glanced around at the other paintings. "There's a couple missing."

"Missing! What's missing?" I scanned the room.

"Paintings. The beach, the waterfall, the pond..."

"How do you know that?" I asked, wondering if Dean had told her about them in the short time we'd been apart.

"I've seen them before." She crossed her arms. "Ryan painted them and some others, but the school confiscated all of them."

"Oh." I hadn't even thought of the possibility that Ryan and I had painted other images that were the same. "You said a pond. I haven't painted a pond."

She just shrugged.

"Libby, let me in." Travis knocked. "That girl is going to be dangerous if we don't steer clear of her," he said when I opened the door, and Neely came out of the studio. "Oh, hi, Neely. I didn't know you were here."

"I just brought Libby's paintings up from downstairs. Who were you talking about?"

"Maggie Bates," Travis and I said at the same time.

Something flashed in Neely's eyes, but it was gone before I could identify it. "No one takes anything she says seriously."

"Why do I get the feeling there's something more to that?" Travis asked, obviously having seen the same flash.

Neely sighed. "Maggie has liked Brent for a very long time, and he's... well, let's just say he uses her, and she lets him, even when..." She glanced at me.

"Are you saying she put out for him while we were dating?" I spoke louder than I'd intended. *While he was,* ick, *touching me all the time, he was playing grab-ass with her.*

"Among other things."

"*What* other things?"

"Wasn't it Maggie who spilled punch on you the day you met Brent?" She put her hands on her hips. "And how do you think he knew you were in the theater the other day?"

"And how do *you* know all this?" I pointed at her. "I can't imagine you're the person Maggie would confide in."

"Don't you dare judge me, Libby Tanner! I may have done some things I'm not proud of, but you have no idea what it was like for me when Ryan disappeared. Maggie's a gossip; that's all there is to it. She'll talk about anyone and anything if it gets her the attention she craves. And she was pretty proud of landing Brent and too stupid to recognize when she's being used."

I couldn't decide what bothered me more: that Maggie had been spying on me or that she'd been sleeping with Brent while he was supposed to be dating me. Or was it that Neely had known the whole time and not said anything? Hopefully, I'd soon be able to talk to my brother about his sad taste in women.

"Basically you're telling me it won't matter what I do," I said. "Brent will find out."

"I'm telling you that Brent is psychotic, and the sooner we get Ryan out and figure out how to stop Brent, the better it will be for all of us, including Maggie."

"Does Dean know about Maggie?" I asked.

"Dean's been a little preoccupied the last few months, in case you hadn't noticed."

"Fine." I understood her meaning perfectly but couldn't think of anything else to say.

"I should go," she said abruptly. "I have practice soon."

When the door clicked closed behind her, the floodgates to my emotions broke open. I hadn't realized how much I'd been holding in until Travis hugged me and I began to cry into his shoulder.

"I hate crying," I said between sobs. "I just wanted to paint."

I repeated that over and over until I finally calmed down enough to actually talk to him. I told him about the cottage and the ivy wall and the cellar. I didn't go into as much detail as Dean had, but Travis understood that it was a bad place.

"I want to show you something," I said, pulling him into my studio. At first, I wasn't sure it would work. But when I put my hand up to the ivy painting, it shimmered for a second, and I was able to reach in and pluck a leaf from one of the vines. I pulled my hand back out and handed the waxy foliage to Travis.

He rubbed the leaf between his fingers then handed it back to me and grinned. "I've seen some pretty amazing stuff, but that is freaking awesome."

"Thanks. I feel like I'm getting closer to helping Ryan, but it's still just a leaf."

"You can do this, Libs. I know you can."

"I hope you're right."

"I'm always—strike that—I *am* right about this. Want me to check on you later?"

I nodded, and he gave me another hug before leaving.

Alone in my studio, I sat in front of my easel, wanting to paint the cellar door, but Dean was right. All my other paintings had just come to me. Even the three other wooden doors I'd painted had appeared in my head before I'd put paint on the canvas, but I couldn't picture the cellar door. It was too forced.

Frustrated, I got up and walked around the room. I usually didn't listen to music while I worked, but I needed the noise. The

Favorites list on my iPod was an eclectic mix of songs spanning the past seventy years, including Frank Sinatra, the Beatles, and Train. It served its purpose as I straightened my supply shelves and tidied up a little. Then I noticed the rest of my room with its unmade bed and clothes all over the place. Nervous energy got the best of me, and I cleaned up in there as well.

Finally, I went back to my studio, determined to paint something, anything. I wanted it to be the cellar door, but it could have been dogs playing poker, as long as I was putting paint on the canvas. I thought I'd try to paint something happy, something that didn't remind me of everything going on in my life. Maybe a rose garden or a sunrise or even a still life... but my hand wouldn't let me paint any of those things.

It was just after five o'clock when I heard a knock. Exiting my studio, I stopped and pulled the door shut. The image I'd painted was too personal to share, even with Travis.

"*You're* not Travis," I blurted when I opened the door to my suite.

"No, I'm not. Nice of you to notice." Brent barreled into my room, blocking the doorway.

I backed up a couple of steps. "Maybe I need to put this into words you'll understand. How did you say it again? Ah, yes... bugger off!"

"Oh, Libby." He tsked. I tried to go around him to get out, but he caught my wrist and kicked the door shut with his foot. "I'm hurt you don't want to talk to me. After all, we were pretty *close* just a few weeks ago." He smirked.

"Apparently not as close as you and Maggie Bates." I struggled to yank my wrist from his grasp, desperate to get away from him.

He tightened his grip. "Oh, yes, well, a guy has needs, and you"—his expression turned into a disgusted grimace—"could *never* satisfy them."

"I thought you were more of a gentleman." I shook my head. "I guess it's just something else I was wrong about."

"Gentleman? I'm much more of a gentleman than you realize, but I won't be using *her* anymore."

"What are you talking about?"

"Oh, she's given me everything I need and become rather boring, so it's time to move on." He took a step closer, tugging on me. "I haven't decided what I'm going to do with you, yet. But Dean—"

"What have you done to him?" I shouted. "You've already had time to shower and dress, so where's Dean?"

"Calm down." He let go of my wrist. "I merely gave him a warning. He's not as *skilled* as he thinks he is. It was a warning to both of you, actually. And you can tell him when he gets here that his little charade isn't fooling me. I'm on to him. Oh... and Libby, I wouldn't bother looking for Ryan. It's for your own good."

"*My* good? You haven't done me or anyone else any good since I got here. You're all of a sudden going to start now?"

"Yes." Brent opened the door to my room. "I put Ryan in his place, and you're lucky you haven't joined him... yet." Then he was gone.

A moment later, Travis appeared in the doorway. "What the hell was Brent doing in your room?" His tone was part accusatory, part concern.

"I... I thought he was you," I said around the lump in my throat. "I opened the door, and before I could stop him, he blocked me in then grabbed me." I rubbed my wrist.

Travis stepped in and pulled me into a hug. "I'm sorry. It's just... I saw him come out of your room with a smirk on his face and—"

"He admitted to trapping Ryan," I said quickly, hoping to abolish any thoughts Travis might have about me willingly allowing Brent in my room.

"What's going on?" Dean asked. "Why is your door open?" He came in and shut it behind him.

I looked over Travis's shoulder, afraid of what I might see. Of course, I'd imagined the worst, but Dean appeared unharmed. He was showered and dressed in jeans and a long-sleeved, button-down shirt, not something he usually wore, but there was no black eye and no scrapes on his hands or face. He actually looked better than Travis did, even though Travis's bruise was starting to fade.

"Why are you looking at me like that?" Dean asked. "Hey, Travis." He walked around and gave me a quick kiss. His smile faded as he looked between Travis and me. "What's going on?"

"Brent was in Libby's room," Travis said before I could stop him. "Look at her wrist."

"Did he hurt you?" Rage flared in Dean's eyes. "Show me."

I stepped back, slipping my arm behind me. "No. I'm fine."

"Please." He held out his hand. "Let me see?"

Sighing, I raised my arm. "Really. It's fine."

He ran his fingers over the spot that had turned pink from Brent's grasp. "Why did you let him in your room?"

"I opened the door, thinking it was Travis. Before I could stop him, Brent was in my room, blocking me from getting out." I pulled my arm away and plunked down on my bed.

Travis shook his head and sat down at my desk. "I should have come back sooner."

Dean ran his hand through his damp hair, ruffling it in all different directions. The action was almost distracting enough to keep me from noticing him squeezing his eyes shut. "Sorry," he said, opening his eyes and leaning against the wall across from me. He started to cross his arms then stopped and hooked his thumbs in his pants pockets. "So you're okay?"

"Yes, I'm fine," I said with a groan. "He said he was just here to give me a warning to stop looking for Ryan, who he admitted to trapping."

"But he grabbed you," Dean said.

"It's not even—" I looked at Dean more closely. His breathing was shallow, and he held his right arm close to his side while his left arm hung loose. I scrambled off my bed and stood in front of him, but he kept his eyes averted. "Lift up your shirt," I said. But he didn't make a move. "Now."

He cringed. "I can't."

I reached for the hem of his shirt and gently pulled it up to see what he was hiding. I gasped.

"Holy shit," Travis said.

Chapter Eighteen

"DID YOU REALLY THINK YOU could hide this from me?" I screeched at Dean, though it was more from fright than anger.

On his right side, just below his ribcage, a large bruise was beginning to form, and a bulge protruded as though one of his lower ribs was out of place. He tried to move away, but my elbow was pinning his shoulder, and the motion was obviously painful to him.

"I wasn't trying to hide it, but I couldn't exactly walk around shirtless," he said.

"Man, that looks really bad," Travis said. "Did you go to the nurse yet?"

"I'm not going to the nurse. I've had worse." He looked down at me. "And what about your arm? You were just trying to hide it a second ago."

"It's a little pink. It's *not* a dislocated rib." Dropping his shirt, I sat on the edge of my bed. "You told me you were better than him," I said softly.

He came to sit next to me, though his movements were slow and careful. "I am."

"I don't mean to disagree, Dean," Travis said, "but you're the one with a rib sticking out."

"It'll be fine."

"Fine." I felt the unpleasant sting of tears in my eyes. *Why the hell do I keep crying?* "You told me you'd be fine before you left, and look what happened." I realized I sounded like a shrew, but I couldn't stop. "We can't turn him in or prove he's done anything malicious since he's your *sparring* partner. So what are we going to do now?"

Dean wrapped his hand around mine. "We just keep doing what we're doing and try to get Ryan back on our own."

"He'll get worse," I said. "He even has spies watching me."

"Is it still Maggie?" Dean asked.

"Neely didn't think you knew about her," Travis said, sitting down in my desk chair.

Dean glanced at Travis then shrugged and pulled his right arm close to his side again. "I saw him with her when..." He looked at me and squeezed my hand. "I figured if she was with him and you weren't, then..."

"I was safe," I finished for him.

"Well, that..." A sheepish smile crossed his face. "And you weren't *with* him."

"Oh." Understanding hit me, and I shook my head. "No, I was never... I mean, he never even kissed me."

"He didn't?" Dean and Travis asked at the same time.

"No." I shook my head again. "I thought he was just shy or nervous or something. I didn't care, though." I darted my eyes at Dean then back to my shoes. "I mean, I tried to like him, but I never could. And apparently, he was... um... getting it from Maggie. Anyway, we still haven't figured out what to do. I'm guessing we can't just ignore Brent's warning, and if Maggie's not spying for him, then I'm sure someone else is."

"The first thing we're doing is getting a chain lock for your door," Travis said. "You can also learn this important phrase. Say it with me, 'Who is it?'"

I rolled my eyes, but I couldn't help but smile at how protective he was over me. "Thanks, sweetie." Then I looked at Dean. "You can't practice with your rib like that."

"I can't let him think he got to me, that I'm any less of a threat." Dean released my hand and put his left arm around my shoulders and hugged me close to him, coercing me into understanding, which I did, but hated the idea of it.

"What will you do about it then?"

"We don't spar tomorrow, and I'll guard myself better on Wednesday."

"Great," I muttered.

"Well, now that that's settled." Travis got up and went to the door. "I'm late for dinner with Eric, and I want to check with maintenance about that chain lock. I'll see you two later." He waved and left.

I didn't think a lock would make that much of a difference if Brent really wanted to get into my room, but at least it would make Travis feel better. I turned to Dean. "You have to take some aspirin." I got up off the bed, but he clutched my hand before I could go very far.

"I'm sorry," he said.

"For what?"

"Earlier, when Travis said Brent was in here... I shouldn't have thought..."

"No, you shouldn't have. I'm not Neely. I know she did what she did because she was desperate, but I'm not like that."

"I know," he said softly. "This is just new to me. I've been so consumed with finding Ryan for so long that—"

I yanked my hand from his and stepped away. "I know you said you wanted me before, but if you're just doing... this"—I waved my hand at the bed—"to get Ryan back, then you might as well get out right now." I pointed at the door.

Hurt and confusion crossed his face. "God. No. Libby, that's not what I'm saying at all."

"Then what *are* you saying?"

He shook his head and put his face in his hands, muttering something I couldn't understand.

"Would you mind repeating that so I can hear you?"

He dropped his arms to look up at me. "You're really going to make me tell you this?"

"You'd better." I tapped my foot.

He sighed then made a low grumbling sound. "Do you remember the day I saw the orchard?"

"Of course I remember. What does that have to do with anything?"

"Well..." He rubbed his hands over his thighs. "The reason I was down there was because I couldn't sleep. I couldn't get you out of my head after we'd danced. And not because I thought you were Ryan's sister, but you were the first girl... well, I was never really in a position to *date* before." Then he smiled the most adorable shy smile I'd ever seen, making it impossible to stay mad at him. "When I saw the light on in that room and noticed it was you in there, it was like... I don't know, like you knew I wanted to see you again."

"Instead you saw Ryan."

"Yeah." He laughed and shook his head. "I was *not* expecting that."

"What did you mean by *first girl*?"

He looked up at me with his elbows on his knees, his bashful expression making my stomach flip. "Libby, you're my first."

"First what?" I asked, stepping closer to him, wedging myself between his legs.

He wrapped his arms around my waist, though I could tell it was difficult for him with his injury. "First *everything*."

"Oh! I am... I mean... I was?" I fumbled all my words as my heart swelled and my cheeks blazed with heat. "I didn't know. I thought..."

He grinned, pulling me down to kiss him. "Yes, you were. All right?"

I nodded, resting my arms around his neck. He lowered his hands to my hips, and I leaned into him, kissing him again as he pulled me onto the bed. We kissed some more, but then I heard him groan in agony rather than pleasure.

"I'm sorry." I tried to give him more space, but he held me tight, preventing me from moving farther away.

"You don't *ever* need to apologize for kissing me."

"I wasn't apol—"

He kissed me again. "Shh," he whispered against my lips then moved to get farther onto the bed. But it was too much for him, and he had to pause to catch his breath.

I scowled, and when he reached for me again, I stopped him. "I refuse to kiss you again until you take something for your rib."

He feigned a pout, and I had to admit it was pretty cute, though I'd never tell him that.

"Fine." He sat up, wincing.

"I have aspirin on the shelf in my studio. I'll get you some water." I went to the bathroom, but remembered too late about the painting I'd been working on earlier. Darting from the bathroom and into my studio, I was just in time to see his face go white.

"I wondered why you had the door closed," he said.

I stepped in front of him to take it down. "I didn't mean for anyone to see this."

He touched my arm to stop me. "Is it... you?"

Letting go of the canvas, I wrapped my arms around myself and bit my lip. The woman in the painting was lying lengthwise on a bed with her back to us. Her left arm was propped under her head, and her long dark hair splayed behind her across the white sheets. The only other trace of color was the scarlet blood that stained the bed and the shadow of a man holding something in the corner. I knew the woman. I'd seen her in my dreams many times.

"No," I finally said, then turned away from the image. "She's my mother."

"Libby." He took a hesitant step toward me, but I stepped back.

"It's okay." I rubbed my arms. "I don't even know why this came to me today. Sometimes I just get pictures in my head that I have to paint, like all the ones with Ryan." I dropped my arms to my sides and tried to smile. "You should take that aspirin now."

"What?" He squinted. "Oh, yeah."

After that, we grabbed something to eat then started a movie on my laptop. I probably should have been doing schoolwork, but that was the furthest thing from my mind. Then, less than a half hour later, Dean was asleep.

I left him resting on my bed with the movie playing quietly and went to my studio. The haunting image of the woman still sat on my easel, so I took it down and hid it behind another painting before placing a blank canvas in front of me. It was a little forced, but I used the ivy wall and door paintings as references for what the outside of the cottage looked like, and a few hours later, I had completed the image I wanted.

When I heard Dean rustling around on the bed in the room behind me, I went and crawled in next to him.

While he didn't open his eyes, a smile crept across his face. "You were painting, weren't you?" he asked.

"Yes," I whispered as he gently wrapped his arm around me and then groaned. "You need more aspirin."

"Not yet." He hugged me tighter to him. "Did you sleep at all?"

"No."

"Hmm... what did you paint?"

"The cellar door."

Chapter Nineteen

Dean's eyes flew open. "You really painted it?"

I nodded then kissed him. "Aspirin first, then you can see it."

He grumbled a little but let me get him some water and pain reliever before we went into my studio.

"Wow," he said, looking at the painting. He'd fallen asleep in his clothes, and when he ran his hand through his sleep-disheveled hair, it made it messy and cute and sexy all at the same time. He didn't wince at the motion, which must have meant his side was feeling better, or he was getting better at hiding the pain.

"Does that look right?"

"It's exactly right," he said, but he wore an odd expression.

"But?"

"Well, you painted the cellar door closed."

"Oh." I scrunched my nose. "I hadn't even thought of that. Maybe it doesn't matter. Brent won't know about this door, so it shouldn't be locked, and I should be able to lift it open." I reached for the painting.

Dean snatched my hand back. "What are you doing?"

"I plucked ivy out of the other one. I thought I'd just reach in and open it."

"That door is way too heavy for you to do that."

"Maybe if I had a little leverage..."

"Leverage? Libby, there is no way. You are not going in that painting." He stood firmly between me and the canvas.

"What if all I have to do is open that door, and Ryan and I can both step back through?"

"How do you know you'll even be able to get it open? How do you know you won't get trapped on the other side? How do you know Ryan will even be there?"

"I don't know." I threw my arms in the air. "But it's better than what we've got so far."

He shook his head. "That's not very convincing."

The stone wall went up in his eyes. I'd thought maybe I'd been able to tear it down for good, but just then I understood it was his defense mechanism. If he showed no emotion, he thought he stood less of a chance of getting hurt. But it wasn't about him. It was about getting Ryan back, and we were running out of options.

"Well, we have to try *something.* I deserve a chance to rescue my brother." I put my hands on my hips.

"This conversation is over, Libby." He grabbed the painting off the easel and pushed past me to leave the room. "You are not going into this painting."

"I'll just paint it again."

He stopped but didn't turn around. "You wouldn't."

"You have a terrible habit of not looking at me when I'm talking to you."

"We're not discussing this any further." His knuckles turned white from clenching the canvas.

"Look at me!"

Almost imperceptibly, he shook his head.

"Please," I said softer.

He turned around slowly but didn't raise his head.

I took a quick step forward and pressed my hands to either side of his face. "Look. At. Me."

"Do you have any idea what it will do to me if I lose you, too?" he whispered, finally looking up at me.

My heart constricted at the terror on his face, and tears sprang to my eyes. "You won't," I said, still holding his face.

"You can't promise that."

"I can. Please, let me be the strong one this time."

The corner of his mouth twitched up as he tried to hold back a smile. "You already are, Libby. You're my strength."

"Which doesn't make you weak."

"Being scared does."

"No." I rubbed my thumb over his cheek. "It makes you *human*."

The painting dropped from his grasp and hit the floor just as his arms clamped around me. He pulled me into a fierce kiss. I circled my arms around his neck and felt a few of my tears escape as he continued to crush me against him. With what felt like great effort on his part, he loosened his grip and rested his forehead against mine.

"You have twenty minutes." He scowled. "If you're not back to me by then... so help me, I will find Brent and—"

"Twenty minutes," I said then pressed my lips to his again. "I'll take my pouch of paints and brushes in case... I don't know." I shrugged. "In case I need to paint my way back to you."

His eyes closed, but I didn't need to see them to know how he felt. Reluctantly, he released his hold on me then watched me pick up the painting and put it back on the easel. His gaze followed me around my studio as I gathered my travel pouch and supplies then stood in front of the painting.

I put my left arm into the image. The painting shimmered, rippling like the surface of a dark pool. Dean held my other hand. Eventually, he'd have to let go, but he wasn't ready yet, and neither was I. I extended my reach so that my whole shoulder was in, and then I felt myself being pulled farther by an invisible force. My head was through, and I could hear Dean say my name, but I kept moving forward, determined.

Something tugged my hand from the other direction. I tugged back, trying to release it, but lost my balance and began to fall. I landed on a sandy patch of ground, but my head hurt. Rubbing the pain away, I heard a groan, and when I opened my eyes, I saw Dean sitting next to me, rubbing his head as well.

I gaped at him. "How did you do that?"

He chuckled, then stood up and brushed the sand from his pants. "I didn't do anything." He put out his hand to help me up off the ground. "You wouldn't let go of my hand, and you pulled me in with you."

"I did?"

"Yeah." He gave me a quick kiss. "I told you you were strong." He turned to look at our surroundings.

It was amazing. We'd ended up in the exact spot I'd painted. I thought it would look and feel like walking around in murky oil paint, but it was as real as anywhere else. The hard sandy ground under my feet, the trees a few yards away, the sound of water in the distance, all of it was real... and also not real. I heard the waves quietly lapping at the shore and the leaves rustling in the trees, but I couldn't feel the wind on my cheeks, and the air was void of any smell. I wished we could explore the area to see how far we could go, but we had to help Ryan.

Feeling a little disoriented, I looked over at Dean, who'd already started tugging on the cellar door. But it wouldn't budge. There was no visible lock, but something was holding the door shut. I watched as he threw his foot at it in a wild kick. But he couldn't break it open.

"It's my painting," I said. "Maybe I should try."

He stepped aside and let me pull and kick at it, but I was no more successful than he was.

"What now?" I asked before realizing he wasn't next to me anymore. "Where are you going?"

"The front door." He stalked away.

When I turned the corner, he was already punching and kicking the front door of the cottage. He slammed his fist into it again and again.

"Ryan? Can you hear me?" Dean yelled.

When there was no response, he began hitting the door again. When he yelled again, it was in agony. Without a second thought, I put myself between him and the door. His fist came to a halt just before connecting with my chin.

"What the hell are you doing? I could have killed you." Then he dropped his arm, but the movement was too much, and he gripped his side, his breathing heavy and labored.

"I should have stopped you sooner," I said, helping him to sit down on the stone stoop. "You could have punctured your lung."

"I'm fine." He closed his eyes.

"You are not fine." I rubbed his back. "And this obviously isn't working."

"My entire childhood," he said softly, "I just wanted out of this cage. Now, all I want is back in."

"It's not the same place," I said, resting my cheek on his shoulder. "This is just a painting. And apparently, it's the wrong one."

"The wrong painting?" He tried to turn and look at me but grimaced and settled back. His words came out one breath at a time, and each one made his face scrunch up. "What do you mean?"

"Well..." I sat up and glanced back at the closed door. "Ryan was able to go outside the cottage, like to the orchard and the creek, so this must be the wrong cottage."

"Libby, that's it." He jumped up then gripped his side again and bent over.

I sighed and stood. "We have to get you out of here. You're just making your rib worse. We should probably walk back around to the cellar door where we came in."

I didn't know exactly how we'd get out, but I figured we'd probably have to go out from the same place where we had come in. I put my arms around his torso, helping him to stand more erect. He eased his arm up over my shoulders for stability, and together we walked back around the cottage.

"What now?" He breathed out heavily, painfully.

I glanced around for some sort of door or exit sign. The only thing that looked out of place was a steady shimmer in the air like the sun dancing on the water, except there was no water on that side of the cottage. I reached out to touch it, and my hand went right through and disappeared.

"This must be it." I pulled him close to me and took a long step forward.

We landed back in my studio. We didn't fall on the floor at least, and I was able to help him to my bed. He protested when I raised his shirt to look at his side, but there wasn't much he could do about it since he could barely lift his arms.

"You really need to see the nurse."

"It's better," he said, trying to pull his shirt back down, but he couldn't without cringing.

"Liar. If it's not better in another day, you are going to the nurse."

He nodded, though I thought he was just agreeing to appease me.

"Hmm..." He looked over my shoulder. "It's a good thing you pulled me in with you."

"What do you mean?"

He pointed toward my desk. "Look what time it is."

I turned to look at my clock, and my jaw fell open. "It's been three hours!"

"Looks like it."

I stared back at him. "Dean, it only felt like ten minutes, maybe fifteen."

"Like I said"—Dean took my hand in his—"good thing you pulled me in with you."

"Yeah, good... I hate to think what might have happened to you."

"Me? It's Brent you should be worried about."

"No, I meant worried about what would happen to you if you killed him."

"I wouldn't do that," he snapped. "I never said I'd kill him. Not that it hasn't crossed my mind. But that wouldn't help me get you *or* Ryan back."

"Hey." I put my hand on his face to make him look at me again. "I'm sorry, and I know, okay?"

He nodded once then kissed me. "What do we do now?" he asked.

I dropped my hand back to my lap. "I don't know. What were you thinking when I said we were in the wrong painting?"

"I was thinking I never saw Ryan exit a different painting than the one he entered. They weren't like... passageways, I guess. He couldn't go in one place and come out another, or at least, I don't think he could."

I pulled my legs up onto the bed and hugged my knees. "So you're saying it has to be something Brent did to the original painting that's preventing Ryan from exiting."

"Well, there might be a way to find out."

"How? We can't just go ask Brent how and what he did."

"No, but I still have a key to Madam Harris's office."

"That's right!" Then I narrowed my eyes at him. "Where did you get that anyway?"

He looked at me with a mischievous expression. "Live on the streets long enough and you figure out how to become pretty good at pickpocketing. Remember when she changed the locks a couple months ago?" He winked. "Anyway, we know you can get in and out of the paintings now, so maybe it's just a matter of going into the right one."

"Except I don't know which painting *is* the right one."

"We'll try them both. It can't hurt now that we know I can go in with you."

"Okay, tonight then." I looked at the clock again—almost noon. "I should probably do some of my assignments, and I want to go see Travis."

"Yeah, and I'm late for rehearsal." His breathing was so irregular, that it frightened me to think what more exertion would do to him.

"You should be resting, not rehearsing."

"Not an option," he said as he stood. "I'll bring the key with me after practice." He paused then said, "I know it's just down the hall, but I'd like to walk you to Travis's room."

By the time we'd reached Travis's room, he was fuming. "Where the hell have you been? I've been worried sick."

"I can explain." I launched into a recap of our trip into the painting and pointed out how bad Dean's rib was.

"You should really see the nurse," Travis told Dean.

"Yeah, I probably should." Dean gave me a quick kiss. "I'll be back to see you later." He left.

Travis shook his head then turned to me. "You look good but tired."

"Thanks." I plopped down on the end of his bed and rubbed my eyes. "I think."

Travis gave me a wary look. "How long has it been since you've slept?"

"A while." I yawned. "But I'm really hungry, and I have an assignment I need to work on." I got up and started for the door.

He moved to block my path. "I don't think so."

"What are you doing?"

"You sit. I'll go get you something to eat, and you can use my computer."

"Fine." I rolled my eyes. I didn't feel like arguing with him, so I let him go.

After he got back and I ate the turkey sandwich he'd made, I tried to do my schoolwork. But my eyes refused to stay open. Travis was working in his studio, so I just curled up on his bed and drifted off to sleep.

"Good morning, sleepyhead. Or should I say good evening?" Dean's voice, my new favorite sound, drifted to my ears as I rubbed my eyes and rolled over. He was sitting on the edge of the bed next to me.

I looked around but didn't see Travis. "What time is it?"

"Almost nine." He put his arm over me, leaning down to kiss me. "Travis left earlier to meet up with Eric."

"You let me sleep that long?" I yawned, glancing down at my rumpled shirt and paint-splattered jeans.

"You needed it." He smiled.

"Did you rest at all? How is your side?"

"Yes, I rested, and my side is much better. I promise."

I examined his face and decided he was mostly telling the truth. "When do you want to go to Madam Harris's office?"

"After you eat."

"And get a shower," I said, then noticed his grin. "Alone." I rolled my eyes but smiled inwardly.

"I told Travis not to worry about us until morning," Dean said as we headed to Madam Harris's office. "That way we'll have plenty of time to check out both paintings before anyone gets suspicious about us being gone."

My hands were sweating, and I bit my lip as he slowed and checked around a corner before continuing. We were using the back way, but there was no telling where Brent might be, or any other student he'd coerced into watching us. Dean turned the next corner and came to an abrupt halt. Fearing the worst, I peered around him to see why he'd stopped.

"What do we do?" I whispered, seeing light glowing from Madam Harris's open office door.

He took my hand. "We're just out walking. If someone's in there, they won't have any reason to wonder what we're doing."

We strolled, hand in hand, toward the office. When we reached the doorway and started past it, I chanced a look into the open room, and my mouth dropped open.

Chapter Twenty

"Madam Harris!" I dropped Dean's hand and ran to where she lay on the floor in front of her huge desk. I knelt down beside her just as Dean reached my side. When she groaned and moved her arm, I saw a bloody L-shaped gash above her right eye.

"What happened?" I asked, helping her to a sitting position.

She put her hand to the cut. "I... I don't remember." She averted her eyes.

I noticed that her desk was in disarray, and a chair had toppled over. "Who did this?"

Her chin quivered. "I don't want anything to happen to you."

"Madam Harris, did Brent do this?" Dean asked through clenched teeth.

She looked at him then back to me. "You have to stay as far away from him as you can." Her voice was anxious, begging. "If I could expel him from the school, I would, but I just can't."

Dean fumed, hands fisted at his sides. "He attacked you."

"Dean, look." I pointed at the painting behind her desk. "The door... it's open."

"Don't! Please!" Madam Harris tugged my arm as I tried to stand. "It's too dangerous."

I looked down at her pleading eyes and wondered how she could have any idea what we were thinking. "You know where Ryan is, don't you?"

Her shoulders fell, and tears began to stream down her face as she nodded.

"How do we get him out?"

"I don't know," she said. "I'm not even sure which one he went into."

"Brent knows," Dean said.

"Yes, but he wouldn't tell me. He was going into one of the paintings, and I tried to stop him, but I must have blacked out, and I don't know which one he's in."

"If the door is open," I said, "why doesn't Ryan just come out?"

"I don't know," Dean said. "Maybe it has nothing to do with the door being open or closed, just like the cellar. Maybe it has to do with which painting."

I nodded then helped Madam Harris off the floor. She wobbled a bit, and I gripped her elbow. "We should get you to the nurse."

"No." She sat down in the chair that was still upright. "I'll be fine."

I stepped away from her. Something about that door being open gnawed at me. I had to get in there. I had to see if that painting was the right one. I took a step toward it, but Dean gripped my arm.

"You're not going in there without me," he said.

"Neither of you are going in there," Madam Harris said, sternness in her voice.

"Celeste, I have to find Ryan."

She sighed then looked at Dean. "You can go in with her?"

"Yes. She can pull me in."

Madam Harris gave him a warm, familiar smile. "I honestly don't know which painting Ryan went into, but the one behind my desk is the one he painted, and the one there"—she pointed at the opposite wall where the painting with the door still closed hung—"is the one you painted, Libby."

"But I painted mine with the door open," I said.

"I know. Both doors were, but the morning after Ryan disappeared, both doors were closed."

I looked at Dean. "I don't get it. We couldn't even get the door in the other painting to budge. How are these opening and closing?"

Dean looked from one painting to the other, clearly as confused as I was. "Maybe it's just Brent playing games with us. But I know Ryan said he wanted to see if he could go into *your* painting. That other door may be open, but I don't think that's where Ryan is."

"Let's go then." I gripped his arm and pulled him over to the painting.

We climbed onto the table beneath the canvas, and I gave one final look back to Madam Harris, who nodded then dabbed the cut on her head with a tissue. Reaching into the painting, I felt for the door handle. Once I had it in my grasp, I yanked on it. The next thing I knew, Dean and I were sitting in a heap on the front stoop of the cottage.

"Are you all right?" he asked, sitting up slowly.

"Yes." I looked over at him, noting his strained expression. "Your rib—"

"Is fine." He brushed a strand of hair from my face, warming my skin where he touched it. Then he stood and reached down to help me up, but I waved his hand away.

"The door is still closed," I said, getting to my feet and looking over his shoulder. "I was hoping it would be open this time. Maybe we should look around, see if anything is different."

Just as in the cellar painting, I could hear the waves on the shore and the leaves on the trees, but I felt no breeze on my cheeks. I tried to step down off the stoop, but I couldn't. Some sort of invisible wall prevented me from leaving the small front porch.

"Libby," Dean said with a hint of apprehension. "What's going on?"

I pushed against the immovable air. "I can't go anywhere."

"We weren't blocked from walking around before." He put his hands up as well and pushed at the air wall, but nothing happened. "Okay, we're going back," he said as his forehead creased and the muscles in his neck tightened. "We have to get out of here." He took my hand, but I pulled it out of his grasp.

"Ryan's here. I know he is. We just have to figure out where."

"Libby, we can't go anywhere. We can't get off the porch, and we can't even get the door open." Dean grasped the knob and jiggled it angrily.

With a click, the door moved inward.

"But it never opens." I was shocked and a little chagrined that we hadn't tried that first.

He shrugged. "I guess we shouldn't have assumed."

He pushed the door open farther, and there, pacing the living room floor, was Ryan.

My heart leapt into my throat, and I let out a tiny gasp. When Ryan looked up, his mouth fell open. I didn't know who was more surprised to see whom. None of us spoke for a long moment, and I wasn't even sure if Ryan noticed me standing there behind Dean. The only movement I made was the uncontrollable shaking of my hands. Hope bubbled up in me, but I tamped it down. *He's going to vanish, just like in my paintings.*

"Dean?" Ryan finally said. "How did you get in here?"

Dean stepped tentatively across the threshold and gestured at me. "Your sister."

My brother.

Ryan peered at me. He was a little taller than I was, but we had the same green eyes and dark brown hair. And when he smiled, there was no denying we were related. "Hi, sis," he said. "It's nice to finally meet you."

Something came over me. Maybe it was that we'd found him. Maybe it was finally seeing him in the flesh after all these years. Maybe it was knowing my mystery boy was my brother. Whatever it was crashed into me like a freight train, and my feet couldn't move me fast enough. I threw my arms around his neck, nearly knocking both of us to the ground.

"You're here. You're here, and I can feel you and talk to you, and I'm not imagining you, and you're not disappearing," I said in one big breath, doing my best to keep from crying. Though I wasn't doing a very good job of it, and my whole body was shaking like crazy. "I just can't believe you're real." I squeezed him harder.

He hugged me back. "I'm real," he said into my ear. "And so are you." His arms constricted around me for another brief moment before he loosened his hold, and I stepped back to look at him as tears spilled down my cheeks.

He shook his head and wiped his eyes then looked up at Dean. "I thought you didn't believe she was my sister."

"I was wrong." Dean shrugged then stepped around me and gave his brother a hug as well.

"Well, I'm glad to see both of you," Ryan said once Dean stepped back. "But I sort of wish you weren't here."

Dean and I both gaped at him.

"What are you talking about?" I asked.

But before he had a chance to answer, Brent came through the door. "Well isn't this a nice family reunion?"

Dean moved so that he was standing between Brent and Ryan and me.

Brent laughed. "It's too bad Celeste couldn't join us."

"I swear, if you hurt her..." Ryan took a step as if he might lunge at Brent, but Dean stopped him.

"Oh, nothing to worry about," Brent said dismissively. "She'll be fine. Well, at least until she learns that you've *all* managed to get yourselves stuck in my painting."

"*Your* painting?" I asked.

He leered at me. "Didn't Ryan tell you?"

"Brent, don't," Ryan said.

"Ryan?" I looked back at him. "What's going on?"

"She's going to find out eventually." Brent started to laugh, but it was short-lived as Dean slammed him into the wall.

"Ryan, get Libby out of here," Dean said as he grappled with Brent, moving him away from the doorway.

Ryan grabbed my arm, pulling me toward the door. "Time to go."

"No. We can't leave without Dean." I tried to pull away from Ryan. "We have to help him."

Dean landed a swift kick on Brent's shin, but Brent recovered fast, throwing a punch into Dean's right side. I screamed when Dean gripped his rib, as if his pain were my own.

"Ryan, get out!" Dean yelled, ducking a kick.

"I'm not leaving you," I cried.

"Sorry, sis." Ryan wrapped his arms around my waist and dragged me toward the door.

I fought against him the whole way, thinking there had to be something we could do to stop Brent. Ryan managed to force me out the door and slam it shut behind us. Then, before I could protest his next move, we were no longer in the painting.

We were back in Madam Harris's office.

"Ryan?" she said.

"Hi, Mom," Ryan replied.

Chapter Twenty-One

My head spun as everything clicked into place like hitting the correct numbers on a combination vault.

"I can't believe you're out." Madam Harris grasped Ryan in a fervent hug. "Are you okay? Did he hurt you?" Her words were rushed, and then everything slowed down.

Something silver glinted in her hand, and I heard myself gasp, but my thoughts were already on overload. I couldn't connect the message from my brain to my feet fast enough, and before I could stop her, she slashed the painting we'd just come out of. I screamed and lunged at her, but Ryan held me back.

She turned to look at me. "It's the only way to stop him. He'd keep coming after you, and I can't lose you again. I just can't!"

"But Dean is in there! We can't just leave him." I struggled free from Ryan's grasp and went for the painting. But it was too late. The diagonal gash across the canvas destroyed whatever portal had been there. I fell to my knees with my face in my hands. "Why? Why did you do that?"

A gentle hand touched my shoulder, but I flinched away. "Don't touch me. I don't care who you are; you had no right to do that!" Panic and grief consumed me as heavy sobs wracked my body.

"He'll be fine," Ryan said. "We'll get him out."

I lowered my hands to my lap and stared up through my tears at the ruined work of art, the gash across it like a slice through my heart. "How can you say that? She's destroyed it."

"She destroyed this painting, but that's not the only way to get to Dean. Besides, he's sort of stuck in time right now anyway." He rubbed the palm of his left hand against his pants then shoved it in his pocket.

With all the other things going on, I hadn't paid attention to how Ryan looked. He was wearing a dark gray T-shirt, blue jeans, and black shoes. His hair was combed and styled, and I could smell his aftershave. Aside from being a little rumpled from our fall, he looked as though he'd just gotten dressed, instead of having been missing for months.

"You mean"—my voice hitched—"time is standing still in there?" I looked at the desk clock. It read just past midnight, which meant we'd been in the painting for over two hours before Ryan and I came out.

He nodded. "Yes. A painting captures a single moment in time, like it's on a continuous loop. So when you're in the painting, it's like you're frozen in that repeating moment. I guess I thought you knew that. Haven't you ever gone into any of your paintings?"

"I didn't know I *could* until yesterday," I said sharply.

The memory of how time had passed while Dean and I were in the cellar painting was just one of the many thoughts weighing on me. I tried to compartmentalize them, categorize them so that I wouldn't explode from the excessive emotions threatening to send me into hysterics.

"So right now," I said, taking a deep, shuddering breath, "Dean and Brent aren't fighting, and Brent can't hurt him?"

Ryan grimaced then looked away.

"Ryan." I stood up. "Tell me Dean is okay in there."

"He's okay, but it's still Brent's painting. Brent still has control over it." Ryan looked over at Madam Harris—a.k.a. Celeste, a.k.a. my mother? There was a butterfly bandage on her head, and she'd changed her clothes. "Mom, what did Brent do to you?" he asked, going over to her.

Side by side, there was no denying the similarities. Though styled differently, Celeste's short dark hair was the exact shade as Ryan's, and her green eyes matched both of ours. Ryan was taller and had a slightly different shaped nose and chin, but otherwise the resemblance was clear.

Do I look that much like her? How did I never notice that before?

"It's nothing," she said then looked at me. "I know this is all very confusing to you, and I'm sure you have lots of questions."

Anger burst through all the barriers I'd built up, like a caged animal clawing its way to freedom. "I've been here for months, and you never thought *once* to tell me who you were? Or that I had a brother!"

"Libby, I—"

I held up my hand. "Stop!"

Tears filled her eyes, and I had to look away. The whole scene was like being in one of the paintings—real... but not. I hadn't realized how much I wanted to know my biological family, how much I wanted to know where my talent had come from. But this was no way to find out.

"I was trying to protect you," she whispered and sank down into one of the chairs in front of her desk.

I turned and looked between her and Ryan, and then back at the slashed painting. "I... I'd just like to concentrate on finding Dean right now. Okay?"

"I understand," she said.

"Ryan, what did you mean by this being Brent's painting? I painted that."

"Yeah, you did," Ryan said. "But Brent has the same ability as us, and he painted over it."

"Wait." I looked intently at Madam Harris. "Did you know this?"

"All of the students at this school are gifted." Her lips twisted to the side. "Some students, including you, Ryan, Brent, Travis, Dean, and a few others, have talents that are extraordinary. I'm very good at seeing hidden talents in people, and I can see that in you, too. You tend to see people for who they are, not who they pretend to be. You just have to start trusting your instincts. It's how I knew who you and Ryan were. But Brent, he kept his talent hidden very well... from all of us."

"Neely did say Brent was a good actor," I said under my breath.

Ryan glanced at me when I mentioned her, but I didn't think it was the time to bring up *that* subject.

"But I still don't get why Brent would even care. If his talent is the same as ours, why does it matter so much to him?" I asked Ryan.

He looked at Madam Harris then back to me, but didn't say anything.

I stomped my foot. "What?"

"I'm so sorry, Libby," Madam Harris said. "If I'd known you and Brent were dating, I would have put a stop to it immediately. I've been so distracted and worried about Ryan. I tried to keep an eye on Brent, but I *never* expected him to..." Tears filled her eyes again, and she grabbed a tissue from a box on her desk.

I shook my head and looked back at Ryan. "What is she talking about?"

"Um... well..." He cleared his throat. "Brent is sort of our... um... half-brother."

All the blood rushed from my head. The room spun, and bile filled the back of my throat. "I need to sit down," I said, trying to keep myself from vomiting right there on the floor.

Ryan pulled one of the other chairs over for me, and I put my head between my knees, forcing my stomach to calm. *Breathe, Libby, in and out... in and out.*

"That's what he meant earlier when he said it was like a family reunion," I said, looking at the floor. "So he's her son, too."

"No," they said in unison.

"You had the same father," Madam Harris said. "I don't know how he found out about you and Ryan, but Brent is *not* my son."

I nodded slowly, keeping my head—and the contents of my stomach—down. "We *had* the same father?"

"He passed away quite some time ago," she said.

Ryan came over and knelt down in front of me. "I tried to tell you. Do you remember... in the garden?"

I raised my head then regretted it and put it back between my knees. "You said something about a key and a pond."

"Well, at least you understood part of it."

"I *don't* understand though."

Ryan sighed then stood back up again. "I don't know how Brent found out either. But he showed up in your painting right after I went into it. He said, 'Looks like I won the sibling rivalry game. Too bad our father's not around to see it.' Then he left, and I couldn't get out. He came back in one other time to gloat about getting you to like him. That's when I tried to talk to you."

"So he knew we were..." My stomach did a huge flip, and I covered my mouth with my hand, hoping to keep down whatever it was that threatened to come up. *Thank the stars he never kissed me, or I'd surely be vomiting right now.*

"Do you want some water or something?" Ryan asked, putting his hand on my shoulder.

"No, I think I'll be okay," I said. "How did he trap you?"

"Think of it like a house with only one door," Ryan said, leaning against Madam Harris's desk. "You can move from room to room, but if you want to leave, you have to go out the same door you went in. It's how I could get into your paintings, but not out of them. It just never occurred to me that that's what I'd always done until *after* Brent changed your painting."

"Changed it?" I asked, keeping my head down, figuring that was the best thing for me to do at the moment.

"A single brush stroke can change a painting, so once I was in your painting, he painted over it, and I was trapped."

"Then how are you out now?"

"Because you stepped in, and once that happened, it reopened the portal that allows you to go in and out. It wasn't changed after you and Dean came in, and I came out with you."

I raised my eyes a little to look at him. "Just like I was able to pull Dean in, I was able to pull you out." He nodded. "Is that how we'll get Dean out? We'll pull him through with us, through another painting?"

"Yes, but we have to find a way back to Brent's painting first."

"Can't we just go into one of his other ones like you went into mine?"

He grimaced. "Not exactly."

"Ryan, please..." I sat up fully then.

He sighed and rubbed his hand on his pants again. My breath hitched. That was what I had seen Dean do that made me originally think he was my mystery boy. But the truth was—biological or not—Ryan and Dean were brothers with the same nervous habit.

"Libby," he said, "it was extremely difficult for me to find your paintings, and even when I did, I couldn't stay in them for very long. I would lose my hold on them, and eventually, they just melded and became part of Brent's painting."

I understood exactly what he was saying. That was why I had only seen him for brief moments, why I never saw him twice, and probably why we couldn't find him in the cellar painting. "We have to get him out, Ryan."

"Is that Brent's only painting?" he asked Celeste, pointing at the door with the gash in it.

She nodded. "It's the only one I know of."

"Then we should get to the pond right away," he said.

"What pond?" I asked.

"The pond our father painted." He looked at Celeste as if needing reassurance on something, then back to me. "Remember, I tried to tell you about it?"

"It's the only painting all three of you have in common," Madam Harris said. "I don't know any other way."

"Let's go then." I stood up, still woozy but rejuvenated by the prospect of finding Dean.

"You should get some rest, Mom," Ryan said. "This might take a while."

"You know I can't do that." Her eyes glistened again as she stood up then wrapped her arms around him in a motherly hug. She stepped back and nodded at me, obviously knowing I wasn't going to hug her. All I wanted to do at that point was get out of her office and get to Dean.

Ryan headed out the door and down the deserted hallway. I had no idea what time it was, but from the quiet of the school, I figured it must be night or perhaps early morning.

"How long have I...?" Ryan's voice trailed off. "I'll find out soon enough," he said more to himself than to me. He came to a stop in front of the pond painting Dean had pointed out weeks ago, the one that didn't have a gold nameplate.

"This is it?" I asked, surprised.

"Yeah, I couldn't get to this one from inside, and I can't promise this will work, but..."

He reached out, and I gripped his fingers. We both raised our other hands to the painting. When we touched it, I felt that same pulling feeling as when entering the other paintings. Ryan gripped my hand harder until I found myself lying on soggy ground. I put my hand down to push myself up, and it sank into the mud.

"Sorry about that." Ryan helped me to stand.

Something in me snapped. "*Sorry*!" I curled my fingers around a cold lump of mud and chucked it at him. "I've known you for all of twenty minutes, in which time you pull me away from helping my boyfriend, I find out Madam Harris is my mother, Brent is my brother, and I'm now in my dead father's painting. You should be sorry about calling a woman who abandoned us *Mom*. But no, you're sorry about the mud!"

"Are you done?" He wiped the brown, gloppy mess off his face and neck. "You're right. It sucks. But Celeste didn't abandon us, so don't be angry at her. I call her *Mom* because that's what she is to me. And I really don't like hearing you refer to Dean as your *boyfriend*. It weirds me out."

"Would you prefer I call him my lov—"

"All right!" Ryan covered his ears. "I don't want to know."

"Can we just go now?"

"Yes." He dropped his hands. "Let's do that."

I followed him along the muddy shore, stealing glances at the rippling pond and lush green of the surrounding trees. The irony wasn't lost on me that I was using the painting of a man who'd abandoned me so many years ago so that I could save the guy who had risked his life to save mine. I took in a shuddering breath as the ground became firmer and the trees so thick I had to stay behind Ryan rather than walk beside him.

After a few minutes, he said, "I've seen you throw a temper tantrum before."

"When?"

"When we were fifteen, your mom wouldn't let you skip a field trip to stay home and paint."

I remembered that day. My mom and I had a huge fight about how I needed to be more involved in my school activities and not spend all my time painting. What she didn't know was that I'd just broken up with my first real boyfriend, and all I wanted to do was to see my mystery boy... Ryan... my brother. "The waterfall."

"Yeah, I wandered through right in the heat of the argument. I was kind of mad at you after that for a while."

"Mad at me? What did I do?" I stumbled on a tree stump, and he spun to catch my arm before I fell to the ground. "Thanks."

"You're welcome. I was mad at you because I thought your mom was right. You were missing out on so much by spending all your time painting."

"I was trying to..." I didn't want to say it. I was too embarrassed to tell him.

"You were trying to what? Avoid all social interaction with others?"

"No, I was looking for you," I blurted.

He stopped, and I ran right into the back of him.

"Why'd you stop?"

He turned to face me. "What do you mean you were looking for me?"

"I mean I painted because of you." I let out a heavy sigh. "Ever since I was little, I remembered you. And in every painting or drawing or doodle, I always wondered if you'd show up again. I know it sounds weird, but I always thought the more I painted, the more likely I was to see you, and I... well, I missed you when you were gone."

"It doesn't sound weird at all," he whispered. "I missed you too. I guess it's that twin bond thing." He rubbed his right bicep with his opposite hand. "When I figured out who you were, I wanted to meet you, but Dean and I had lived on the streets so long I was too embarrassed to even think about introducing myself." He started walking again.

I didn't know where we were headed, but Ryan seemed to know exactly where he was going. "Dean told me you saw my picture at a gallery."

"Yeah." He eased between two tight trees. "I met Celeste that day, but she didn't tell me she thought I was her son until about a year later, after I'd gotten to know her better."

"What did you mean when you said she didn't abandon us?"

"Um... we were taken from her. But I really think she should be the one to tell you what happened. Just give her a chance, okay?"

"Yeah, I'll try. For you. I am glad she found you, even if it did cause you to get stuck in a painting."

"It's better than living on the streets."

"Or in that awful cottage."

Ryan looked over his shoulder at me. "Dean told you about that?" He clenched and unclenched his left hand.

"I won't ever tell anyone," I said quickly. "I swear, Ryan. Dean did what he had to do to protect you, both of you."

"It's not that." He lowered his gaze to his feet. "Dean *never* talks about it, even with me." He was quiet for a second, then said, "I just... I wish we'd gotten out sooner."

"Me too." Talking about Dean was easier than talking about any of the other stuff, or at least I thought it was until another thought hit me. "Did Dean...? I mean, I'm sure he would have told me, but does he know about Brent being..." I couldn't even say it. The words made my insides twist.

"No," Ryan said, "unless Brent told him while I was trapped, but I doubt it. I didn't even know Dean was at the school until I saw him through your orchard painting. Thanks for that, by the way."

"You're welcome, I guess, but I have no idea how it happened."

He glanced back at me. "What do you mean?"

"Well, for one thing, we've been in here about five minutes, and if I didn't know that it was a painting, I would think it was a real forest." I waved my hand at the leafy trees and fern-covered ground. "So how you managed to see Dean and me through that orchard, clearly enough to wave, is simply amazing to me. And the apple, how did you do that?"

Ryan laughed. "I didn't know if that would work. I just threw it and crossed my fingers."

"Oh, it worked. And I still have the apple."

I tried to watch where I was walking. The trees had thinned some, but I still couldn't walk beside Ryan. When we reached a stream with a fallen log over it, I suddenly recognized where we were.

"This is the stream I painted," I said, in awe of the scene around me. I'd been so focused on everything else that I'd barely taken the time to appreciate the fact that I was actually inside a painting.

Ryan grinned. "Pretty amazing, isn't it? The waterfall isn't much farther up this way."

"It's incredible." I held my breath for a second to listen. "Why don't I hear any birds?"

He'd already crossed the log and was standing on the other side of the stream. "I didn't paint any birds. Did you?"

"Oh. No, I guess I didn't."

I crossed the log, and we continued to follow the edge of the stream as it got wider. The sound of rushing water grew louder. We soon stood on the upper bank of a narrow waterfall. The low-lying area was only about ten feet below us, but we had to climb on slippery rocks to get there. Ryan went first, but my pulse still raced as I moved my hands and feet from one slippery stone to the next.

When I finally reached the bottom, I let out the breath I'd been holding the entire way. "I can't believe I did that without falling. Are we close yet?" I brushed some of the moss and debris off my knees.

He pointed east. "The stream runs off that way and turns into a river, but the cottage is in this direction." He waved toward the northwest.

The trees thinned even more as we walked away from the river, and the ground became sandier. I remembered the ground being sandy in the other paintings. I also remembered Dean straining his rib trying to get into that cottage. "Why *that* door?"

"What was that?" Ryan asked.

"Oh, um, I was just wondering why you painted that door. Why paint something that was the source of such pain?"

"I don't know." He shuffled his feet. "Control, I guess. Control over something that controlled *me* for so long."

"Dean didn't recognize it at first, not until we painted the ivy wall."

"We?" Ryan glanced back, eyebrows raised.

My cheeks instantly warmed. The memory of what had happened after Dean and I painted together was clear in my mind.

He groaned. "Right, I really don't need to know that stuff, sis."

I smiled. "I like it when you call me that."

"Yeah?"

"Yeah."

There was enough room for me to walk beside him, and soon I saw a familiar fence, and in the distance, a small, ivy-covered cottage.

"There it is," Ryan said. "Are you ready for this?"

A lump formed in my throat, so I just nodded as we headed toward the cottage and, hopefully, toward Dean. I could see the cellar door as we got closer. My body screamed at me to run for that door, but I kept telling myself I had to let Ryan lead the way. I had to trust him, and he was taking it one excruciatingly slow step at a time.

"How will we know if it's the right one?" I asked.

"We won't. Not until we get there."

"How do you know if you've moved from one painting to another? It doesn't feel like we've changed paintings at all."

"Everything sort of becomes part of the same one you entered, so while we've probably passed through other paintings, they've melded into this one."

I stopped walking. "You mean we've come all this way, and even if that's Brent's painted cottage ahead of us, it might change as we get closer? Dean could be there, but we could lose him just by walking up to it?"

Ryan stopped as well and faced me. "I tried to tell you before we came in here. This isn't an exact science. I don't know what will happen when we reach the cottage. But I do know we've already been in here a while, so whatever *does* happen, we need to figure it out and get back as soon as possible."

I followed him to the edge of the tree line, praying the whole time that we'd be able to get Dean out. A few dozen feet later, Ryan stopped abruptly and took a step back, almost as if he'd bounced off of something.

"What is it?" I asked.

He stepped forward again and put out his hand, pushing it forward in several places. "Put your hand up here. I never noticed this before."

I moved to stand next to him and reached where he was touching. I expected my hand to keep going, but it met resistance. I pressed harder then tried with both hands and my shoulder.

"It's not fair," I screamed, beating at the invisible wall.

"Libby." Ryan grabbed me around the waist. "We'll figure it out."

"No! Dean and I felt something like this before. We couldn't step off the porch right before we found you in the cottage."

He rubbed his head. "I don't get it. I could walk around everywhere when I was here before." He paced a few steps away then turned back.

"Yes, you could walk around before, but you were already *in* that painting." I pointed at the invisible wall and the cottage just out of reach on the other side of it.

He nodded. "It must have to do with the fact that it was originally your painting, then Brent painted over it, changing it."

"Then Madam Harris destroyed it," I grumbled.

"You don't have to be so formal with her. You said you'd try." He shoved his hands in his pockets.

I glared at him.

"I'm just saying—"

"I know what you're saying." I threw my hands in the air. "But I have a mother, who I miss very much, back in the States."

He looked away. "Yeah, you're right."

A twinge of guilt twisted inside me, and I put my hand on his arm. "I'm sorry. I didn't mean it that way. I just meant that it's different for me. But I will try, okay?"

"Sure."

"So what do we do now?" I asked, dropping my hand and eager to change the subject. "And why could you and I get off the porch before, but we can't get back now?"

"Wait! That's it." He grabbed my hand. "We went through together."

"I don't understand."

"I was in the painting before it was changed, and you came in after." He looked at me expectantly.

I could feel my whole face brighten as I looked into his excited eyes. "So the only way in or out is *together*."

At once, he pulled me forward. I stumbled then regained my balance a few paces ahead of where we'd stood, as if the invisible wall hadn't been there at all. We looked at each other.

Then we both ran.

Chapter Twenty-Two

When we rounded the corner to the front of the cottage, the first thing my eyes fell on was Dean sitting on the porch steps. I didn't think he even realized we were there until I knelt in front of him and wrapped my arms around his neck.

"I can't believe we found you." I hugged and kissed him, but it took me a second to register that he wasn't reciprocating my enthusiasm. I stepped back and looked at him. "What's wrong?"

He smiled faintly. "It's nothing." He tried to push himself to stand but had trouble. "Could you help me out?" he asked Ryan.

I looked between Dean and Ryan, and then… "Oh, my God, your shoulder!" His left shoulder was slumped lower than his right, and that arm hung limp at his side.

"I need you to turn around for a minute," he said firmly.

"What?" I shook my head. "Why?"

"I need Ryan to put it back in place. Please turn around?"

"You really don't want to see this, sis." Ryan came up behind me. "And you might want to cover your ears."

"You've done this before," I said, and the two of them shared a glance. "How often?" I asked, horrified by the thought that it was often enough for Ryan to know how to fix it.

Ryan twirled his finger in a turn-around gesture. "Just trust me, okay?"

I hesitated at first, then turned away from them and covered my ears. My knees trembled, but I forced myself to stay standing when I heard a muffled, agonizing yell. I dropped my hands and spun back around.

"There, good as new." Ryan patted Dean's arm, and Dean grimaced. "Oh, sorry, maybe not *quite* as good as new."

Dean rolled his eyes then put his arms lightly around me. "Thank you for coming back," he said, kissing me.

"You didn't think I would?" I buried my face in his chest, causing him to take in a sharp breath. "Oh, I'm sorry. Your rib. I forgot."

He smiled, but I could tell it was forced. "It's better." He kissed me again. "Tender. But I think Brent actually put it back in place for me."

"Ahem!" Ryan interrupted. "As much as I'd like to see my brother and sister make out, we should probably get going."

"He's right." Dean stepped out of my arms but took my hand. "We need to go."

"Where's Brent?" I asked, scanning the yard.

Dean squeezed my hand. "He vanished shortly after you two did."

"Madam Harris slashed the painting," I said. "So he couldn't have gone far."

"If she slashed the painting, how did you get back here?"

"Come on," Ryan said. "We'll show you."

The three of us walked back toward the pond. Ryan took my other hand, and we pushed back through the barrier surrounding the cottage. Dean and Ryan both took one last look at the place that held so many awful memories. Dean had asked me not to destroy any of my paintings, but I had already decided to burn every last one that had anything to do with that cottage.

When we reached the waterfall, I almost fell once while climbing back up, but Dean already had my hand and caught me before I even had a chance to think about hitting the rocks below. A short time later, we were standing near the pond again.

"Where do we get out?" I asked.

"Out? Now why would you want to leave?" All three of us whipped around to see Brent standing a few feet away... with Neely. Brent held a small knife to her throat.

"Ryan, I'm sorry," Neely cried. "I didn't know what else to do. I'm so, so sorry."

"Neely, it's... just don't move, okay?" Ryan said.

"Oh, she's not going anywhere." Brent snaked his other arm around her waist. "Are you?"

She flinched, and a tiny bead of blood bloomed on her neck at the tip of the blade.

"Get your hands off her," Ryan growled.

Neely sobbed, tears streaming down her cheeks. "I just wanted you back. I thought he'd let you out..." Her words were caught on another sob, and I could sense Ryan tense beside me.

Dean squeezed my hand. "Brent, Neely has nothing to do with this," Dean said, sounding far more calm than I knew he felt.

"No, but you really didn't think I'd come into Libby's painting without collateral, did you? Or should I say *my* painting?" He shifted his eyes to me. "Of course, I didn't need to go to all the trouble of painting the doors closed, but it was more dramatic when your dear mum realized what I'd done."

"What do you want from us, Brent?" I asked. "You can't get out without us."

"Out! Why would I want out? I have my brother, my sister, my friend, and my lover all right here. What more could a guy want? Wait. That's right. I don't have any of those things. We may share the same father, but I don't consider you my siblings," he said, looking at Ryan and me. "And you"—he lifted his chin toward Dean—"you pretended to be my friend all those months, but it was nothing more than an act, just like Neely here." He pressed his lips to her ear. "At least you were a good time."

Ryan took a step forward, but I put my arm out to stop him. Dean's fingers crushed mine with the hold he had on them. And if he didn't know that Brent was my brother before, he did now. That wasn't exactly the way I wanted him to find out.

"What is it you *do* want then?" I asked Brent.

"I want the life I was supposed to have. I want the life your whore of a mother stole from me." His hand tightened on the knife handle, and Neely whimpered as more blood trailed down her neck.

"She didn't steal anything from you!" Ryan shouted. "Our father was the thief."

"Ryan—" Dean started.

"No. He thinks we did some horrid thing to him by being born, but he has no idea what my life was like. He has no idea what happened to me. He has no idea that I was sold off to a psychopath who forced me to watch him beat you, then tried to burn my hand off." Ryan held out his left hand. The scarring on his palm and fingers made it look like wrinkled wax on his skin, except that it *was* his skin.

"We've been in this painting a long time," I finally said, trying to sound calm. "I think it's time we all got out of here." I pointed at Brent. "I don't know what happened between... our parents." My voice cracked a little then. "I... I don't know what happened to you either, but none of this is our fault, and it certainly isn't Neely's."

The air in front of me shimmered—the painting's exit. Brent and Neely went fuzzy for a second. When their images became clear again, Brent's expression had changed. The bitterness was still there, but I thought there might have been regret in his eyes.

Neely suddenly twisted and hooked one of her legs around his. She reached up and pushed the knife away as Brent's feet went out from under him and he fell to the ground. Clasping her hand to her neck, Neely lunged toward us.

Ryan caught her with one hand then grabbed my arm. "We're getting out of here now," he said, tugging on me.

I pulled my arm from him. "Ryan, we can't do that."

"Why not?"

"Because then we're no better than *he* is." I pointed at Brent, who'd rolled up onto his knees.

"She's right, Ry." Dean squeezed my fingers. "We can't just leave him in here."

"Fine," Ryan said, keeping one arm wrapped around Neely. "But I'm not helping him out."

Dean nodded and looked back at Brent. "Stand up, man," he said.

"I'm not doing a damn thing you say." Brent shook his head. "There's nothing left for me out there anyway. Just leave me."

"See? He doesn't even want to go," Ryan said.

"Brent," Dean said firmly, "Libby thinks you should be let out of this painting. And while I'd be happy to let you stay in here and rot, I'm going to do what she wants, whether you like it or not."

Dean clutched my hand and took a few steps forward. The space in front of us shimmered again, and I realized what he was doing. He reached down and grabbed a fistful of Brent's shirt. I shot my free hand back and clutched Ryan's arm, then I saw the shimmer one more time before feeling the pull that meant we were leaving the painting. The next thing I knew, I was lying on the school's marble floor in front of the pond painting with Dean's arms wrapped around me.

"There they are!" Madam Harris said.

Then someone else grunted before Eric yelled, "Now, Travis!"

Dean pulled me up off the school's marble floor, where I had landed in front of the pond painting, and wrapped his arms around me. There was more commotion behind me, and I spun around. Madam Harris was sitting on the floor with Ryan, pressing her cardigan to Neely's bloody neck. Travis and Eric stood to one side, looking at something.

"What's going on?" I asked.

Travis and Eric stepped back, and I saw Brent encased in the stone arms from one of Travis's sculptures. The huge statue had six arms wrapped around his body and one hand covering his mouth.

Travis looked at me and shrugged. "I knew you'd come back eventually, so we waited."

The sound of Travis's voice broke down every ounce of strength I had left. By the time I reached his arms, I was crying full-blown, body-quaking, fat tears. Travis held me there a good long time while I soaked his shirt.

When I finally calmed down, I took a small step back and checked on Brent. He was unconscious, hanging limply in the sculpture's arms. I looked back at Travis and tried not to shake when I asked him to let Brent go.

Chapter Twenty-Three

"NOT BEFORE WE CALL THE police," Dean said.

"And how are we going to explain this?" I gestured at Brent, entrapped in the stone arms.

"We can hold him until the police get here," Eric said. "Then Travis can let him go before any of them see. We'll just tell them that Brent assaulted Neely, and Dean stepped in to help, which is basically the truth."

We all gaped at him.

"You really are a genius, Eric," Dean said.

"I agree." Madam Harris stood from her spot next to Neely. "But we need to do this quickly, and I don't think Eric and Travis should be here when the police arrive. The fewer people involved the better. We should also move Brent into my office so none of the other students see him."

Eric helped Travis and Dean move Brent to Madam Harris's office, then Eric left a minute later. Travis grumbled about releasing Brent from the statue but did it anyway. Travis helped Dean put Brent in a chair before he took off as well. By the time the police arrived, Brent was awake, but groggy. The four officers took each of us aside, questioning us about what had happened.

I was glad we'd worked out our stories beforehand. "Dean and I were out... um... walking, and we heard someone shouting. When we came down the hall, Brent had a knife to Neely's neck, and Ryan was trying to get him to calm down."

"Do you know how the disagreement started?" the broad-shouldered officer asked me.

"Well, I know that Brent was jealous of Ryan and Neely..." I dragged my words out to make it sound as though an innocent high school crush had gone too far.

"So once the two of you arrived, what happened then?"

"Brent got distracted, and Neely tried to get away from him. Dean grabbed Brent, but Brent elbowed Dean in the face. Dean tried to hold Brent and calm him down, but Brent kept fighting back, and they both lost their footing. I think Brent hit his head on the wall or the floor when they fell."

"And when did Madam Harris arrive?"

"Shortly after we did."

"Very well, but we may need you to make a formal statement later," the officer said, then he turned his attention back to the others.

They'd already handcuffed Brent. He hadn't said a word to anyone, and I wasn't sure he was even fully aware of what was going on.

"The ambulance outside will take the young lady to the hospital," the officer said. "Madam Harris, I think it would be best if you accompanied her." Then he looked at Dean. "You probably should get checked out as well, and we'll need to take a few pictures."

I watched as Brent was loaded into the backseat of the police car, and Madam Harris climbed into the ambulance with Neely. Other students had gathered and were watching and whispering about what might have happened. I heard someone ask what Ryan was doing there, but I didn't have time to process that thought as one of the school's drivers pulled up and Dean, Ryan, and I got in and followed the ambulance to the hospital.

Dean wrapped his arm around my shoulders, and I rested my head against his chest. Ryan sat across from us, staring out the window in silence.

"Why didn't you tell me about Madam Harris and Brent?" Dean asked Ryan.

Ryan didn't take his eyes off the window. "Oh, hi, Ryan, so nice of you to join us in the real world after being stuck in a painting for God knows how long. Why don't we talk about your family tree now?"

"I'm not in the mood for your sarcasm."

Ryan snapped his head in our direction. "And I'm not in the mood for one of your lectures."

Dean pointed a finger at him. "If you'd listened to me in the first place, you wouldn't have gotten into this mess."

"Dean." I sat up and looked at him.

"You know," Ryan said, "I'd think you'd be thanking me right now. If it weren't for me, you two might never have met, and it looks like you're pretty cozy."

"Thank you?" Dean dropped his arm from my shoulders and leaned forward. "Fine. Thank you for not listening to me. Thank you for jeopardizing the lives of all the people you care about. And most of all, thank you for scaring the shit out of me when I thought I'd never see you again. I really appreciate that."

Ryan rubbed his hand on his leg. "I didn't tell you about Celeste because you didn't like me talking about Libby, and I didn't want you to think that just because I'd found my family I didn't want you as my brother. I think Celeste knows who you are, though. She's never come right out and said anything, but she asked once or twice who I talked to on the phone. As for Brent, he didn't say anything until after I was in the painting. I don't even know if I believe him." Ryan glanced at me. "But how else would he be able to go in and out of our artwork like he did?"

Dean sat back and put his arm around me again. He held me tight and kissed the top of my head as we reached the emergency entrance. Ryan got out of the car and rushed inside to find Neely. Dean and I got out as well, but I hesitated before going into the building.

"What is it?" Dean asked.

"I... I think I should go to the police station."

"Why?" Then he sighed heavily. "I'll come with you. I don't want you going alone."

"You need to have your rib and shoulder looked at."

"They can look at them *after* I go to the police station with you."

My chest constricted. "Dean, I'm not... I mean, he's—"

"He's what? A psycho who could have gotten you and Ryan killed? Not to mention what he did to Neely!"

"I'm sorry. I know. But he's behind bars now, and there are some things I need to talk to him about."

"Things?" Dean shouted then looked away from me.

"Don't do that." I reached up to touch his cheek. I half-expected him to pull away, but he didn't.

He looked into my eyes. "A brother should protect you, take care of you. He's done nothing but lie and manipulate. How do you know he won't do that now?"

"I don't, but I have to try. I'll tell you everything. I promise. I just don't know everything yet."

He wrapped his arms around me, crushing me against him. "Please, *please* be safe." Then he took my face in his hands and kissed me. "Don't be gone too long. I'll worry about you the whole time."

He walked me back to the car and held the door open for me. When I climbed inside, the driver turned and gave me a questioning look, but he didn't argue when I told him to take me to the police station. I waved at Dean and watched him go through the emergency room entrance before the driver pulled out of the hospital parking lot.

Once at the police station, after much finagling and a little sweet-talking to the guards about being a sister in distress, they finally let me in to talk to Brent.

"Hi," I said timidly once the officer had left.

"Why are you here?" He was alone in a holding cell, sitting on a hard bench with his head against the wall. "Come to make sure I would corroborate your story?"

"I actually came to check on you."

"Me?" He snorted. "I'm great."

"I'm serious. They should have taken you to the hospital, too. You could have a concussion."

He pushed himself off the bench, walked over, and put his hands on the bars. "Don't patronize me, Libby. You came for answers."

"Yes, partly," I said, inching back a bit. "But is there anyone else who should know you're here?"

"No." He let go with one hand and ran it through his hair. "I don't have anyone to tell. Our father died when my mother killed him—and herself—seventeen years ago, and my grandmother raised me, but she died shortly before I enrolled at Aldridge."

Seventeen years ago? That meant our father must have died right around the time Ryan and I were born. "I didn't know," I said. "I'm sorry."

He dropped his other hand, went to the back of the cell, and put his hands on the wall as if someone were about to frisk him. "You want to know what the worst part is? The worst part is I thought he loved you more. I thought that was why my mum did what she did, because he was leaving us for *you*. I guess I should have believed my grandmother when she told me what an awful person he was. Whenever I got in trouble, she told me I was acting exactly like my rotten father."

"Brent—"

"It's fine, Libby." He spun around and faced me again. "I suppose I *am* just like him... since I'm in here." He waved his hand to encompass the cell. "Sins of the father and all."

"Is that really what you think? You think you have some genetic predisposition to be a terrible person?"

He gave a curt laugh. "One of us had to get the bad genes." He sat down on the bench and rubbed his eyes with the heels of his hands.

I chuckled. I couldn't help it when I remembered what Travis had said about his sister. "Siblings can be a real pain in the ass sometimes," I said, repeating his words. "I'm sure they want to get rid of each other now and then. You took that to the extreme, but that doesn't mean it's in your nature to be a bad person. You could still do good things in life."

"Yes, I could do some bloody brilliant things behind bars."

"I didn't come here to listen to your pity party."

"Well, don't let me keep you then." He leaned back against the wall and closed his eyes.

"The least you could do is tell me the truth. Tell me how you knew who we were."

"The truth?" He jumped up off the bench, startling me. "Here's the truth. I enrolled at Aldridge because my grandmother recognized Madam Harris's picture in the *London Times*. The article said how young and gifted she was and how lucky the school was to have a former student as their new leader. My grandmother said, and I quote, 'That's the slut that killed my little girl.'"

"Celeste didn't *kill* anyone," I said, though it felt odd defending the woman who'd lied to me for so long.

"That's not how my grandmother saw it. Because when it comes right down to it, my father's affair with your *mother* drove *my* mother to take her own life... and his."

"So you enrolled just to get revenge against her then decided kidnapping her son would be better?"

"I *enrolled* because this is one of the best performing arts schools in Europe. I wasn't lying when I said I was pushed into acting. My grandmother made me take acting and dancing lessons from the time I was two. I hated it. I wanted to paint, but she'd never let me. And if she caught me drawing, she'd..." He shook his head. "When I got here and found out about Ryan, trapping him was like a perk, compensation for having to act rather than paint." He sat back down and was quiet for a second.

He seemed to be showing signs of regret, but in the back of my mind, I kept hearing Neely's words. *He's a good actor.*

And Dean's... *He's done nothing but lie and manipulate.*

"So what about Ryan?" I asked. "How did you know?"

Brent looked at his feet. "Coincidence really. I enrolled under my grandmother's name. Ryan had already been here for a while. It was easy to tell he was one of Madam Harris's favorite students. It wasn't the janitor I overheard her talking to about your painting. It was Ryan. The two of them were saying how great it would be for all of you to meet one day. It was clear they'd already figured out who you were; at least, Ryan was sure you were his sister." The corner of his mouth twitched, and he looked over at me. "And believe me, it was bloody awful trying to figure out how to kiss you—knowing you were my sister—without *really* kissing you. I may have retched if I'd had to do *that*."

My stomach rolled at the memory. *At least he feels weird about it too.* "I'm sure we're in agreement that we dodged a bullet and avoided decades of therapy. So now what?" I leaned against the wall behind me.

"Now I get to sit here for a bit, while the rest of you live happily ever after. But don't worry about me. Madam Harris and I have an understanding."

"And what's that supposed to mean?"

"Let's just say, she keeps my secrets, and I keep hers. You didn't really think I was without a contingency plan, did you? Now run along and leave me be."

"You're still our brother."

He stood up again. "I don't want to be your brother, Libby. Don't you get it?"

"You never gave us a chance!" I fisted my hands at my sides. "You assumed all sorts of things then blamed us... for what? Finding each other?" I'd raised my voice and knew it would draw the guard's attention.

"You're right." He rushed forward, startling me when he grabbed the bars again. "I assumed you were both raised by loving parents and also had a mother who loved you enough to want to reconnect with you. While I was abandoned by my mother and raised by a woman who hated the very sight of me. Is that what you want? To flaunt your happy ending at me?"

"No, it's—"

A guard appeared in the hall. "Miss, I'll give you five more minutes, but you'll have to be going then." I nodded, and he left.

"I'm not worth your time, Libby. And I don't want it. I wasn't even worth my own parents' time."

"I'm not *them*," I said.

He sighed and sat back down. "You're fighting a losing battle."

"You just told me you don't like to act. At our picnic, you said you prefer to be yourself. I wish that's the person I'd met, because I don't think it's who you are now."

Whether he was going to respond or not, I would never know. The guard came back to escort me out, and I left Brent sitting there, alone, trapped in a cell.

The sun started to come up as the driver took me back to the hospital. The rays glistened on the snow, and I closed my eyes to feel the warmth through the car window.

"It's going to be a beautiful day," the driver said.

"Too bad it's a weekday. No one will get to enjoy it."

"It's Saturday, miss."

Saturday? Four days! We'd been in that painting four days. My heart began to race. I couldn't breathe. I rolled down my window a bit to let in the cool air. It helped, but not enough. I needed something... something comforting, something stable.

"Do you have a phone?" I asked.

The driver handed me a cell phone. I didn't know what time it was at home or if they'd even be there, but I had to try.

Dad answered, "Hello?" his voice groggy with sleep.

Hot tears filled my eyes, threatening to spill over. "Hi, Dad."

"Libby?" Then I heard my mom say something in the background. "Hang on. Your mom's getting the other phone."

"Okay," I said, my tears falling freely.

"Hi, sweetie," Mom said. "Is everything all right?"

I pressed my fist to my mouth to hold back a sob while I pulled myself together. "Yeah, I just miss you guys."

"We miss you too," Dad said, his voice tinged with concern. "I can't wait to see all the great paintings you've been working on."

"I'll send you some pictures, okay?"

"Are you sure there isn't something else wrong?" Mom asked.

"I'm sure." I was lying, but I needed that, a normal moment in the middle of my messed-up life. I knew I would have to tell them at some point, but not yet. "I love you. I'll call back in a few days at a more reasonable time."

"You can call us any time, sweetheart, day or night," Mom said. "I love you, too."

"I'll watch for the pictures," Dad said. "Love you."

I said good-bye and hung up then handed the phone back to the driver. He glanced at me in the rearview mirror but didn't say anything. We pulled into the hospital parking lot, and I thanked the driver before getting out and going inside the emergency room entrance.

Dean got up as soon as I entered and wrapped his arms around me. "I'm glad you're back."

"Where are the others?" I asked, sitting down with him.

"They're discharging Neely now. A police detective came to take pictures of our injuries and asked a few more questions, but he told us we could return to school as long as we didn't go anywhere until the investigation was complete."

"And what about your rib and shoulder?"

"They're fine. They gave me something for the pain, but I probably won't even need it."

I nodded, leaning into him over the armrest of the chair. "Do you want to know—"

"Later," he said as Ryan walked into the waiting room with Neely and Madam Harris.

On the way back to the school, I nodded off on Dean's shoulder. When we arrived, Madam Harris instructed us all to get some rest, then asked Ryan and me if we would join her for dinner that evening. I agreed, but I was a long way from feeling part of a happy little family. She was still the headmistress of my school, and I had trouble seeing her as anything more.

"You should probably go see Travis first," Dean said while practically dragging me up the steps.

I nodded absently. "I can't believe you're even standing right now."

He smiled. "One of the many things I learned growing up. I don't require much sleep."

"Well, I do, and I haven't slept in four days. Sort of." I yawned and leaned against him, using him for support.

Students stared at us and whispered amongst themselves, but I didn't care. All I cared about was seeing Travis then sleeping for several hours, maybe days.

We reached Travis's door, and he swung it open before Dean had a chance to lower his hand from knocking. "What took so long? What did the police say? Are they pressing charges?"

"Um..." I yawned again then tried to form words but was unsuccessful.

"Let me take her to her room, and I'll come back in a few minutes," Dean told Travis.

We went to my room, where I fell onto the bed. I vaguely felt Dean kiss me before he left, then everything faded away as I fell fast asleep.

Chapter Twenty-Four

"Libby, it's time to get up. We have to meet Mom for dinner."

I opened my eyes, expecting to see Dean, but it was Ryan standing over me.

He scowled. "You don't need to look so disappointed."

"Sorry," I said hoarsely. Then I looked around to see if Dean was there.

"He came to get me about an hour ago so he could sleep," Ryan said, answering my unasked question.

I sat up and stretched my arms. "Do I have time to take a shower?"

He nodded and sat down in my desk chair, but something in his expression worried me.

I pulled my legs up and hugged them to my chest. "I know we don't really *know* each other, but I've seen your face enough times to know that something is bothering you."

The look on his face worsened. "Why me? I was sold, kidnapped, and..." His voice cracked, and his eyes filled with tears. "What did I do wrong?"

"Oh." I jumped off my bed and flung my arms around him. "You didn't do anything wrong."

He hugged me back. "Will it get better? I mean, now that we've found each other."

"Yes," I said firmly. I couldn't tell the future, but anything had to be better than his past. "It will get better. I promise." I moved back to sit on the side of my bed.

He rubbed his eyes. "Did they know?"

"Did who know what?"

"Did your parents know? I mean, you knew you were adopted, but..."

"Oh. Um..." I pulled my legs back up and sat pretzel-style as I picked at my nails. "Not for sure. No." I shook my head. "They were turned down by a lot of adoption agencies because my dad got caught with marijuana in college. His roommate had hidden it in their dorm room, and there was no way to prove whose it was so... anyway, they finally found an agency willing to work with them, and they adopted me when I was about a year old. When I was two, maybe three, they happened to see a news special about kids being sold on the black market, and the adoption agency my parents used was listed as being involved. They kept thinking the police would come around asking questions, but whoever they got me from either didn't keep very good records or they destroyed them because no one ever came. I always knew I was adopted. But the other stuff, they told me that when I was older, old enough to understand, I guess."

"So they had no idea?" Ryan asked softly.

I bit my lip, knowing what he was really asking. "Ryan, if they'd known about you, I know for certain they would have adopted both of us."

He nodded, rubbing his hand on his leg. "Okay. I'll wait here while you get ready."

"Can I ask you a question?"

"Sure."

"Did someone tell you how long you were missing?"

He nodded.

"How long did it *feel* like? I mean, we were in the pond painting for four days, and it felt like maybe an hour."

"Less than a day. I wandered around, which is how I found my way to your other paintings, but I knew all along that time outside was passing faster."

"I'm sorry I couldn't get you out sooner. For so long, I wanted to know you in real life."

"Well, I'm here now, and we have a dinner to get to."

"Okay." I climbed off my bed. "I'll just be a few."

When we got to Madam Harris's office, she had a small table set with dinner for the three of us. I noticed that both of our paintings no longer hung on her walls, and the space felt cold and uninviting even with the meal waiting for us.

"I hope you both like roast," she said.

"I'll eat anything." Ryan smiled, taking a seat at the table. "I'm starved."

Celeste gestured for me to sit in the seat across from him. We passed the dishes between the three of us, filling our plates.

"I didn't know," Celeste said. "I didn't know your father had a wife and son until after he was gone. I was a good ten years younger than he was and a student here at the time. I thought he loved me. I got pregnant just after graduation. When he found out, he set me up in an apartment and had a doctor come check on me once a week. You were born in that apartment. The doctor who delivered you said he was giving me something to ease the pain. When I woke up, I was in the hospital. I remembered giving birth to two babies but nothing after that. I asked the nurses what had happened, but all they could tell me was that I'd been left in the emergency room.

"The police came and questioned me. I told them to contact your father, but he was already dead. He'd been killed by his wife, then she'd killed herself, leaving behind a six-month-old son. They looked for the two of you and the doctor, but you'd all disappeared. For years, I hounded the police, but eventually, it became a cold case, and they gave up."

I started to say something, but she held up her hand. "No, please let me finish. I wanted to find you. I wanted you both so much. I don't know why, but I thought being in the art world might bring me closer to you. So I worked my way through school by restoring paintings for museums, and eventually, I got a teaching position here at the academy. A few years later, I became the headmistress. The next summer, I read an article about a young girl whose paintings were selling for unheard-of amounts." She nodded at me. "When I saw your picture, it was like looking at an old photograph of me."

"That's when you came to the States," I said. "You came to see me."

"Yes." She twisted a napkin in her hand. "But I lost my nerve. I talked with your parents briefly and saw how much they loved you. I couldn't bring myself to say anything. I didn't want to intrude on your life. Instead, I went for a walk along the beach that afternoon. That's when I met Ryan." She smiled at him. "You were painting the exact same scene as the one and only painting I have of your father's."

Ryan nodded then said to me, "The pond. The image came to me after I saw your picture at the art gallery. I couldn't get it out of my head."

I wiped my eyes with the back of my hand. I didn't know what to say.

Celeste sighed. "I couldn't believe the two of you were so close and didn't even know it. I didn't know who Brent was until Ryan went missing. Brent bragged about it to me after he'd locked Ryan away. He said he wanted me to suffer the same way he did. He had no idea I'd been suffering since the day you were born. If I'd known you two were..." She shook her head and looked at me. "I had no idea he knew who you were, too. I wanted to get to know you, but I kept my distance because I was afraid Brent would get suspicious. I only allowed him to stay at the school because I thought he'd eventually let Ryan out."

I interrupted to ask, "Why didn't you call the police?"

She let out a grim laugh. "And what would I have said? One of my students trapped another in a painting? I think they'd have put me away somewhere."

I conceded that she was right. I hadn't told anyone about my paintings for almost the same reason.

"That's also why I've been away so much," she continued. "When Brent enrolled here, I had no idea who he was, since he'd taken his maternal grandmother's last name. The academy took temporary custody of him since his grandmother had passed away, and he had no other known relatives. I didn't think to look too deep into his records until after he'd kidnapped Ryan. It didn't do me much good, though. It only told me what I already knew from your father's death. I was working on trying to find another distant relative of your father's, hoping they might know how to get Ryan out, when Brent..." She put her hand to the bandage on her head. "Anyway, that problem is being dealt with."

"Um... about that," I said, my hands shaking. They both looked at me, and I had to take a deep breath before finishing. "He said he had some sort of... backup plan."

"What kind of backup plan?" Ryan said. "Painting the inside of a padded room?"

"I'm pretty sure that's not what he meant." I looked at Celeste. "He said you two have an *understanding*."

"If you call blackmail an understanding, then yes," she said.

"Mom, you can't be serious!" Ryan slammed his hand on the table. "He's the one who sliced my girlfriend's neck open."

"I know, but Brent knows too much about the two of you."

"And I think he has suspicions about Dean, too," I interjected.

Ryan flinched at that. We both knew Dean had a lot to lose if anyone found out what he'd done.

"Blackmail or not," I said, "I think we need to help Brent."

"Help him with what?" Ryan gripped his fork so tightly, his knuckles turned white. "Picking out stripes or a straitjacket? He's crazy, Libby. He deserves to be locked up."

"I know you feel that way, but he's still our brother. He needs help, and we're the only family he has."

"He's not *my* brother." Ryan jumped up, causing his chair to fall over. "Dean is the only brother I've ever known, and if you think I'm going to act all nicey-nice with Brent, then you're not my sister either. And what the hell do you think Dean would do if he found out Brent was allowed back here?"

I recoiled from the venom in his voice. I had known he would be upset, but I hadn't expected such a strong reaction. "You of all people should know that desperate circumstances call for desperate measures."

"Okay." Celeste held up her hand. "I couldn't allow Brent back here even if I wanted to. He assaulted another student with a deadly weapon. But Libby's right. He does need help."

Ryan picked up his chair and sat back down at the table. "I'm not helping him."

"I don't expect you to, but I want you to respect your sister's wishes."

I could see the hurt and pain in his eyes. "He has no one, Ryan."

He sighed. "Fine. But you get to explain it to Dean."

"He'll understand." *I think.*

When we finished dinner, Ryan said he needed to get some air, and Celeste told him his room was just the way he left it.

"Libby?" she said before I stepped out of her office. "I'm sorry. You have no idea how much I wanted to tell you. I hope..."

"We'll just... see what happens," I said with a shrug.

"Will you tell your parents?"

I looked at my hands and resisted the urge to pick my nails. I didn't know how to answer that question. What was done was done, and I couldn't change that. My parents deserved to know, but I didn't want to hurt them or Celeste. I knew I'd never consider her my *mom*, at least not the same way Ryan did. I had a mom. When I glanced back at her, tears filled her eyes, and my own grief overwhelmed me. I took a few tentative steps toward her. Celeste pulled me into an awkward hug, shaking with sobs.

"Can we talk about it, together, later?" I asked when she'd calmed down and let go of me.

She wiped away the last of her tears with a tissue. "I'd like that."

I nodded and said good night then went to find Travis. I didn't have to look far.

"I thought you'd never finish eating," he said, meeting me in the main hall. He hooked his arm through mine. "So I want the whole story."

"Once upon a time," I said, and he laughed. It was nice to hear. It felt normal, like before any of the kidnapping stuff.

When we got settled in my room, I told my best friend the whole story, from the day I was born to the moment we were sitting there together. Some of it he already knew, but I repeated it all anyway. Then I realized there was so much I still *didn't* know.

"Wow. Huh. Madam Harris is your birth mother, and Brent is your half brother."

I nodded. "Yeah. It's a little creepy."

"At least I know my family's not the only one with issues." He nudged me, and I smiled. "But if you were sold off as an infant, where was Ryan before he ended up at that cottage with Dean? And how did Dean end up there?"

I shrugged. "My parents didn't find out my adoption was illegal until I was two, about the same age Dean said Ryan showed up at the cottage. That might have something to do with it. And Dean… I don't know. I don't know if he does, either. What did he tell you after I fell asleep?"

"Not much, except…"

"Except what?"

"Let's just say that boy's got it bad for you. I mean *real* bad," Travis said.

I smiled, knowing I was blushing.

"And apparently you feel the same way." He chuckled and squeezed my shoulder. "I'm glad you're okay. Those four days were probably the worst of my life."

"You guys didn't stay out there the whole time, did you? And how did you know that's where Ryan and I were?"

He rubbed the back of his neck. "When you didn't come back the next morning, I knew something was up. And then Eric said he hadn't seen Neely or Brent for a few days. We confronted Madam Harris, and she decided it was better to let us help. She said we'd see you in the painting when it was time, so we took shifts to keep watch for you."

I shook my head. The whole concept still seemed so strange. "Thank you." I kissed him on the cheek.

"Be careful." Travis wagged a finger at me. "Lover boy might get jealous."

"Dean wouldn't dare lay a hand on you."

"Ha! I could take him. But I was actually talking about Eric, who's probably waiting for me."

"You'd better go find him then."

Travis got off the bed and went to the door. "Remember when you said all you wanted to do was paint? It was a lot easier keeping track of your social schedule when that's all you did." Then he winked and left the room.

I left a few minutes later and wandered downstairs. It was late, but I knew I couldn't sleep again until I saw Dean. The halls were already quiet, and I found myself stopping in front of my father's painting. My fingers itched to touch the heavy pattern of the brush strokes, but I held my hand back.

"You're not thinking of going in there again, are you?" Dean wrapped his arms around my waist from behind.

He always knows where to find me. "No." I leaned into him, and he rested his head against mine. "I was actually thinking about Brent." Dean's arms tensed. "I was just thinking that, of the three of us—Brent, Ryan, and me—I had the best childhood. And while we were all orphaned, Brent's mother made that choice. Ours didn't. I guess I can see why he'd be angry."

"That's not an excuse for what he did." Dean breathed out heavily but relaxed a little.

"No, it's not. But maybe if he'd been the one to grow up with parents who loved him, none of this would have happened."

"You would trade your childhood for his?"

"No, I just wish he'd had a better one. I wish you *all* had."

"And that is why I love you."

I tensed and turned to stare at him.

He chuckled and nuzzled his face into my neck. "Like you didn't know already."

"You've just never said it out loud."

"Now I have," he whispered, tightening his grip around me and kissing my ear.

"I love you, too."

"I know." He pressed his lips to mine, fitting them perfectly together.

I turned to lean into his chest again and could almost feel the beat of his strong heart against my back. "Are you going to tell me what your talent is? Other than protecting the people you love."

"What are you talking about?" He nuzzled my neck again, lower, kissing the base of it near my nape.

I let out a moan. "Are you trying to distract me? Because you're doing a damn good job of it."

"I wasn't trying to, but I can," he said playfully. He kissed me just below my ear, and I bumped him with my hip. "Now *that's* distracting."

"Dean, I'm serious. I want to know. Madam Harris said you had a special talent, like my painting and Travis's sculpting."

"I guess you could call it a talent." He stopped his assault on my neck.

"It's something like supersonic speed, isn't it?" I teased, though I half thought that might be what it was.

He laughed. "No."

"Then tell me already."

"I can see the future," he said, "but only in seconds and only in actions, not words or thoughts."

"Huh. That actually makes a lot of sense." I remembered the time I'd almost slapped him and he'd grabbed my hand before it connected with his cheek, and how he'd stopped pounding on the cottage door when I stepped in front of it the first time we'd gone into a painting.

"You surprise me sometimes though," he said.

"I do?" My lips spread into a grin as I turned to look at him again.

"Don't you remember? When you kissed me for the first time, in the sauna, I did *not* see that coming."

"Oh. Yeah," I said, feeling my cheeks warm from the memory.

"It's also what makes me a better fighter than Brent, and a better dancer."

"Well, he must have surprised you too." My smile fell, and I faced forward. "He did manage to dislocate your rib and shoulder."

"He got lucky."

"Fine, he got lucky. But if you're also a better dancer, why didn't you perform the tango with Neely that night?"

He rubbed my arms and kissed my head. "Dancing isn't about the music or even the steps." He paused for a moment as if to collect his thoughts. "It's about the person you're dancing with. Brent and Neely, they've always danced the tango."

"Do you think Ryan will forgive her?"

"Ryan has a big heart like you. They'll work things out."

"Yeah. I guess." I pressed my cheek to his. "But I do wish I could dance as well as she can."

He gripped my hand, spun me out, then back, and dipped me before pulling me into his arms, facing him. The whole move happened in the blink of an eye. "I told you," he said, then kissed me. "Dancing is about your partner."

When I looked at his face, I couldn't see even the slightest trace of the stone wall. What I did see was joy, his happiness and love reflecting back at me. "So I'm a good partner for you?" I whispered.

"No, you're the *best* partner for me. You're the only one I'll ever want, whether it's dancing or painting or this..." He pressed his lips to mine.

I wrapped my arms around him, certain I could paint the world as long as he was in it.

Acknowledgments

To you, the reader, thank you for sharing your time with me and the characters in this story. I hope you enjoyed it!

This novel would not be what it is today without the help, love and support of the following people:

To the fabulous team at Red Adept Publishing, especially my editors, Michelle R. and Lynn M. Thank you so much for your dedication and belief in this story and for helping me truly bring Libby's art to life.

To Chanda S. for encouraging me to send my manuscript to Red Adept Publishing. You are made of awesomeness!

To the folks at Streetlight Graphics for all your hard work on my gorgeous cover!

To some of my early readers, Kathy N. (Nana), Laurie and Genna C., and Kim and Dana from our writer's group at Blue Phoenix Books. Your input and encouragement are immensely appreciated.

To Mandy Hubbard and my classmates from LitReactor. You are an amazing group of writers, and I hope to see all of your stories in print one day. (P.S. Thank you, Kristina, for loving Brent. Every bad boy/anti-hero needs a fan.)

To Rachel B. for loving Dean and Libby and for your honest "teen" input. You rock!

To Joani, Lizzie, Syd and Val, the Mean Girls/Twitter Angels. Your messages and tweets were often the only thing pushing me through the wee hours of the morning to finish my writing and editing. *Big Hugs*

And to all my other pals out there on Facebook and Twitter. I wish I could thank you all personally, but that would make this section longer than the book, so just know I appreciate each and every one of you!

To all my coworkers at my day job, especially Angie, Jamaican, Jess, Staci, and Tracey, for listening to me endlessly talk about writing and publishing, and for making me laugh every day and being an amazing group of people. Working with friends makes the time so much more enjoyable!

To Ron and Sue for raising the incredible man I'm married to. Your constant love and support is appreciated more than you could ever know. And to the entire Kolar clan, I'm so blessed to have all of you in my life.

To my brothers, Mike and Tim, and their beautiful families. I love you!

To Dad and Carol. You may not know this, but the idea for my very first novel came to me while at your house on the lake. Though that story will probably never see the light of day, it did lead to this one, and for that, I am grateful.

To Mom, my first and biggest fan, for everything you've done and continue to do for me on a regular basis. For the hours you spent reading and re-reading this book, for the weeks you spent taking care of me after my surgeries and while I was writing, and for the years you spent raising us, thank you so very, *very* much.

To Meghan D. and Becky H. for showing me how much fun being lost in the pages of a book can be and for loving me unconditionally. You two are the definition of BFF!

To Erica Lucke Dean, my critique/writing partner—where do I even start? Thank you for being my sounding board, my punching bag (not literately, of course), my comic relief, and my friend. Thank you for loving these characters as much as I do and being excited about where their story takes them. Thank you for making me add more kissing scenes. (Dean and Libby, thank you, too!) Most of all, here's to our stories yet to come. May they be more richly rewarding with every new chapter.

To my beautiful daughter. Thank you for reminding me that there is a world outside my books and for making it worth living. Mommy loves you with all her heart!

And to my husband. Thank you for our marriage and our life together. Thank you for loving me when I'm not lovable. Thank you for being patient with me when I fall behind on the daily tasks of life. Thank you for giving me space when I need it and for bringing me back to reality when I need that too. Thank you for all the big and little things you do for me day in and day out. Thank you for being the best father our daughter could ever have and the most wonderful man a wife could ever ask for. Forever yours, Laura.

About Laura M. Kolar

Laura M. Kolar lives with her husband and daughter in a one-stop-light town in northern-lower Michigan. Though she didn't discover her love of books until she turned thirty, as a self-declared hopeless romantic, she has spent the past few years reading and writing stories with mostly happy endings.

If she's not at her day-job or with her family, you will find her sipping a cup of chai latte while sitting in her favorite rocking chair, hunched over her laptop writing or spending entirely too much time on Twitter.

29333337R00139

Made in the USA
Charleston, SC
09 May 2014